*A romantic rescue during
the French Revolution . . .*

Lili de Beautemps put her foot on the first step leading up to the guillotine platform. "Look at her, in silk," someone spat. "Soon that silk will be drenched with blood."

All at once Lili's heart burned white-hot with anger. Recovering her dignity, she rose to her feet, holding her chin high. They might murder her as they had her father and brothers, but they would never crush her spirit.

As Lili walked slowly across the platform toward the guillotine, the laughter died away and the crowd fell silent. One of the men who had been restraining her now pulled her hands behind her back. Lili felt a wave of nausea and terror as she stared at the bloodstained blade.

The executioner grasped her arm and began to force her to kneel at the block. Then a new sound permeated Lili's consciousness, thundering above the voices of the mob. The pounding of hooves.

She looked up just as a horseman burst from the forest, riding at full gallop straight toward her. Then he jumped from the horse's back. Before anyone could stop him, he'd scooped Lili up in his arms and leaped back onto his horse. "Go!" he roared.

THE FOWLERS OF SWEET VALLEY

Written by
Kate William

Created by
FRANCINE PASCAL

BANTAM BOOKS
NEW YORK · TORONTO · LONDON · SYDNEY · AUCKLAND

RL 6, age 12 and up

THE FOWLERS OF SWEET VALLEY
A Bantam Book / December 1996

Sweet Valley High® is a registered trademark of Francine Pascal.
Conceived by Francine Pascal.
Produced by Daniel Weiss Associates, Inc.
33 West 17th Street
New York, NY 10011.
Cover art by Bruce Emmett.

ISBN: 0-553-57003-X

Published simultaneously in the United States and Canada

Bantam Books are published by Bantam Books, a division of Bantam
Doubleday Dell Publishing Group, Inc. Its trademark, consisting of the
words "Bantam Books" and the portrayal of a rooster, is Registered in U.S.
Patent and Trademark Office and in other countries. Marca Registrada.
Bantam Books, 1540 Broadway, New York, New York 10036.

PRINTED IN THE UNITED STATES OF AMERICA

OPM   0 9 8 7 6 5 4 3 2 1

To Anita Elliott Kaller

The Fowlers of Sweet Valley
Family Tree

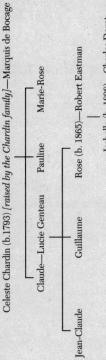

Lili de Beautemps (b. 1773)—[falsely married] Count Matthieu de Bizac

Celeste Chardin (b.1793) [raised by the Chardin family]—Marquis de Bocage

Claude—Lucie Genteau   Pauline   Marie-Rose

Jean-Claude   Guillaume

Rose (b. 1865)—Robert Eastman

Isabelle (b. 1898)—Charles Doret

Alan—Emily Barr   Paul

Grace (b. 1952)—George Fowler   Robert

Lila

1789. The Loire Valley, France.

Lili de Beautemps stood in front of a mirror in her bedroom, her maidservant Marie Oiseleur standing right behind her. Lili held her breath as Marie pulled hard on Lili's corset strings. "Tighter," Lili commanded, studying her reflection in the full-length glass. Her waist was small, but she wanted it smaller. She wanted to have the best figure at the ball that night.

Marie grimaced. "That's as tight as I can make it," she told her mistress, grunting as she gave the strings of the corset one final tug. She tied a quick knot, her fingers nimble and experienced.

Sixteen-year-old Lili cocked her head, pretending to be dissatisfied. She didn't want Marie to get lazy just because the girl had the privilege of being

1

her closest confidante as well as her maid. "Tighter," Lili repeated firmly.

Marie sighed. Loosening the knot, she began again and pulled with all her strength. At last Lili nodded, a smile adorning her face. "That will do, Marie," she said cheerfully.

Next Marie carried a silk brocade ball gown to Lili, who remained posed in front of the mirror. As she helped Lili into the elaborate, lilac-colored dress Marie beamed approvingly. "It's exquisite."

"Exactly the shade of my eyes, wouldn't you say?" Lili fluttered her lashes, enjoying the way the silk made her big, lavender-blue eyes look positively purple.

When she was buttoned into the gown with its fitted, low-cut bodice, tight sleeves that ended in a cascade of lace at the elbows, and full skirt, she sat down carefully at her dressing table so Marie could begin work on her hair. Soon the long, dark curls were piled high on Lili's head, decorated with artificial flowers and colored feathers and powdered lightly. Marie placed a hand on the lid of Lili's jewelry box. "The diamonds?" she asked.

Lili nodded. *"Bien sûr."*

Marie opened the box. With reverence she lifted out an ornate diamond necklace. She placed it around her mistress's neck and fastened the gold clasp. Lili put a hand to her throat, touching the teardrop-shaped gems. "My first ball, Marie," she said softly. "If only *Maman* were here to see me."

2

The necklace, and the rest of Lili's jewels, had once belonged to her mother, who died when Lili was a little girl. Lili barely remembered her—she knew only that Françoise de Beautemps had been beautiful and affectionate. *When she hugged me, she smelled like a whole garden of roses,* Lili recalled with a wistful sigh.

She gave herself a mental shake. Looking once more into the mirror, she lifted her chin and turned her face slightly. Marie knew what to do without being told—she reached for the pot of rouge.

"I'm very lucky, you know," Lili announced, "even though I lost my mother."

"Don't talk—I'll make a mess of this," Marie cautioned, carefully dabbing a fingertip of rouge onto Lili's pale cheek.

Lili paid no attention. "I'm mistress of Winterthorn, one of the great châteaux of France," she continued gaily. "I'm glad I'm Papa's only daughter. He dotes on me, and so do my brothers."

"You *are* lucky," Marie agreed, "to be born to a life such as this."

"I suppose you wish *you'd* been born a de Beautemps rather than an Oiseleur," Lili teased.

"I'm proud of my family," Marie declared.

Lili found it hard to believe that Marie would rather be a servant than a noblewoman. She stole a glance at her friend, who was really quite pretty with her raven black hair and porcelain complexion.

3

We're alike in so many ways, Lili thought, *and yet so different!* The two girls had been playmates as children, and they still joked and laughed together. When Lili had good news to share or when she needed a shoulder to cry on, she turned to Marie. But of course it wasn't a friendship between equals. Lili's father and brothers were aristocrats, while Marie's family worked on the estate as they had for generations. Lili had been born to a noble station in life, Marie to a humble one.

Lili didn't dwell for long on the social differences between herself and her maid. She was more concerned with her appearance. At last her dress, hair, makeup, and jewelry were complete. "Perfection," Marie announced.

Lili couldn't help but agree. "And it's time," she exclaimed, grabbing her painted fan. She heard horses outside—the carriage was waiting. "Do you know, they say even the prince might make an appearance!"

"He'll have eyes for no one but you," Marie predicted.

Swept away by excitement, Lili dashed out into the hall, wobbling a bit in her high-heeled silk slippers. At the top of the staircase she recollected herself and slowed to a more stately pace. Her gown rustled as she made her way downstairs. A handsome middle-aged man in an elegant velvet waistcoat, matching knee breeches, and a powdered wig was waiting for her. "Look at you, Lili,"

4

the Viscount de Beautemps exclaimed. "Why, just this morning you were a child. What an exquisite young woman you have become." As he bent to kiss her hand Lili glimpsed a tear in his eye. "The very image of your beloved mother."

Lili embraced her father. Then she pulled on his hand. "*Merci*, Papa. Now come. I don't want to miss a single dance!"

The strains of Mozart filled the ballroom and drawing rooms of Bellegarde, the Fontaine family's château. Lili stood by a window, fanning herself, a triumphant smile on her rosy lips.

"So you danced with the prince," sniffed Clothilde Fontaine, a girl Lili's age. "I think he's rather plain, and much too plump."

"Yet he dances very well," Lili said pointedly. She enjoyed rubbing it in—the prince hadn't asked gawky Clothilde to dance!

Just then Lili's aunt Josephine appeared at her elbow. "My dear, I would like to introduce you to Maxim Saint-Germain," said Josephine, "second son of the marquis and marquise Saint-Germain."

The young man bowed at the waist. Lili gave him a quick inspection as she curtsied. *Only a second son,* she mused. *Well, if the property is large, that might mean wealth enough. And he's not bad looking.*

"I was hoping you would join me for this min- uet," Maxim said, his admiration apparent.

Lili was only too happy to return to the dance floor, leaving behind a miffed Clothilde. "With pleasure," she replied.

As she danced with Maxim, Lili was pleasurably aware that all eyes in the room were on her. She fancied she knew what people were saying. *"See that breathtaking girl, the viscount's only daughter. What beauty and spirit she has! And how wonderful for her to be singled out at her debutante ball by the prince himself, who only danced with two other women before leaving!"*

Lili moved gracefully around the room in Maxim's arms. She glimpsed her father among the onlookers, his face glowing with pride, and Aunt Josephine with a row of potential suitors for Lili lined up at her side.

"You're a delightful partner," Maxim was saying. "Might I engage you for another minuet later this evening?"

Lili shifted her attention back to Maxim. No, he wasn't bad looking. Of course, she didn't intend to settle for a second son, but for the time being she was perfectly satisfied with the prospect of wrapping this boy and all the others at the ball around her little finger.

She flashed Maxim her most brilliant smile. "You might."

"So it was as I expected," Marie remarked as she helped Lili out of her gown late that night. "You were the belle of the ball."

Lili pirouetted around the bedroom in just her chemise. "*Oui*. Papa told me on the drive home that simply *everyone* was talking about me. And the prince . . ."

She gave Marie a detailed account of every word that had passed between them. Marie put a hand to her forehead, pretending to swoon. "Must I call you Queen Lili soon?" she teased.

Lili gave her friend a playful slap on the arm. "Yes, and you must treat me with far more respect."

Half an hour later Lili was ready for bed. Alone in her room, she extinguished all but one candle. She knelt at the windowsill, gazing out at the starry night. "I've never felt less like sleeping," she announced to the crescent moon. "In fact, I still feel like dancing!" Springing to her feet, she darted across her room to the door, slipping her emerald green silk dressing gown over her white nightdress as she went.

Winterthorn was quiet and dark. Lili padded barefoot along a parapet walk, then took the turret staircase down to the ground floor. Outside, she whirled in a delirious circle. *What a night!* she thought. And it was only the beginning. There would be dozens more parties and balls, hundreds of handsome suitors. It was true that someday she'd have to choose one for her husband and settle down. But until then what fun she'd have!

She skipped down a path between the tall,

neatly clipped hedges in one of Winterthorn's manicured gardens. She held out her arms, embracing an invisible dance partner. "Yes," she murmured to the imaginary prince. "And your mother, Queen Marie Antoinette. Is her health good?"

Lili spun around, her eyes closed dreamily. Then she backed into something solid. It didn't feel at all like the prickly hedge. *"Mon Dieu,"* grunted a masculine voice. "What on earth—"

Lili clapped a hand to her mouth, stifling a scream. When she saw who she'd bumped into, her knees buckled with relief. "Oh, Georges," she gasped. "Thank heavens it's only you!"

Marie's older brother, Georges Oiseleur, was gaping at her with astonishment. Lili folded her arms across her chest, embarrassed at being discovered *déshabillé*, with her hair down and flying every which way. Not that Georges hadn't seen her half dressed before. They'd all romped together as children: Georges and Marie and Lili and her two brothers. Of course, now that they were grown up, it wasn't proper for them to associate in such a manner. Still, Lili felt almost as comfortable with Georges as she did with his sister.

"Georges." She shook a finger at him, her eyes on the bulging canvas sack he gripped in one hand. "Have you been poaching rabbits on my father's land again? I declare, I'll tell him!"

His white teeth gleamed in a grin. "And shall I

8

tell him how enchanting you look in your green silk nightgown?"

They both burst out laughing. Lili collapsed on a wrought-iron bench. Georges bowed to her. "I might as well dress these while they're fresh," he said. "Good night."

"No, stay," Lili called. "I want to tell you about my evening at Bellegarde."

Georges turned back. "Is that a request or an order?"

"Does it matter?" She smiled coyly. "You'll obey either way, won't you?"

He grinned again. "Yes, Mistress Lili."

He lowered himself to the bench, keeping a distance between them. Lili launched into a detailed description of the ball. "The gowns, Georges," she began, her voice high-pitched with excitement. "And the jewels! Mine were the plainest there. Clothilde Fontaine had so many rubies around her neck, she could barely hold up her head." Lili dimpled mischievously. "So it was fortunate, really, that she sat out so many dances. The music was enchanting." Lili hummed a few bars of her favorite Mozart minuet. "We drank champagne from solid gold goblets. I didn't eat a bite because I was too busy dancing, but there was a table about a mile long heaped high with food. A whole roast pig, and dozens of roast geese, and beef and pies and pastries and cheese and fruit and—"

Lili stopped prattling abruptly. Georges's brow was furrowed with disapproval. "Why are you looking at me that way?" she demanded, pouting.

Georges lowered his eyes. "That some people should have so much while others go cold and hungry," he muttered.

She shrugged. "But it's always been that way."

"That doesn't mean it's right. Lili, I've been reading a lot lately," he said earnestly. "The new philosophers all believe that men have natural rights, given by God and not by the king. Each and every man possesses these rights equally."

Lili stared at Georges, stirred by his intensity. How had she never noticed how handsome he was, with that thick black hair, the strong chin, the blazing eyes? She was glad the night hid her blush. "Natural rights," she scoffed. "You know, Georges, you are talking treason."

"Treason to some, freedom to others," he countered. "The bourgeoisie, the third estate, has called a meeting of the Estates General. You have heard that, surely? They are going to demand the abolition of the monarchy and the creation of a new government in which the people are sovereign—"

"I don't believe any of it," Lili said dismissively.

"Well, you should," Georges told her. "It was a hard winter and the peasants are restless for change."

"Oh, Georges." Lili laughed. "When did you get so intellectual? It is utterly boring."

"But Voltaire writes that—"

She reached out, touching her index finger to his lips. "Not another word," she commanded. "Don't spoil my night! And besides, you know better, Georges." She jumped lightly to her feet. "The old order will never fall. How can it when it's *my* turn to shine?" Before he could respond, she darted back indoors, her silk gown fluttering behind her.

Upstairs in her quiet bedroom she collapsed on the bed, her hand pressed to her pounding heart. *What an escapade!* she thought, giggling. *Sneaking out in my nightdress and bumping into Georges!*

Georges . . . her heart was still galloping. Lili rose and crossed to the mirror. Her long dark hair was in a wild tangle and her face was flushed. "All because of silly old Georges?" she whispered disbelievingly.

It was true. No other man, not even the prince, had ever made her feel like this. *And he wants me,* she thought, hugging herself. She didn't have much romantic experience, but she'd recognized the light in Georges's eyes.

Lili's lips curved in a smug, scornful smile. It wasn't so surprising that Georges should desire her. She was so far above him! It was natural for a person to want what he could never have. "Of course *he* means nothing to *me,*" Lili told herself. Flirting was one thing. But she was a noblewoman. She could never care for a commoner like Georges Oiseleur.

The June day was sultry, with a warm haze hanging over the river valley. Lili and one of her many new suitors, Maxim Saint-Germain, cantered their horses briefly, then slowed to a walk.

As Maxim bragged about his prospects of inheriting a large portion of his family's estate, Lili listened politely. But her thoughts were wandering. *Papa thinks I should marry Laurent Villesavin*, Lili mused, using her riding crop to flick a fly from Swift's withers. *Or the Fontaines's eldest son, or the Duc de Montpensier.* She recalled a recent conversation with her father. "Of course, Lili," he'd said genially, "if you prefer Maxim, I'm sure his parents would make a generous settlement in order to secure an alliance with us."

"I don't prefer *any* of them," Lili had told her father, and he'd laughed and pinched her cheek, thinking she was just being coy. But it had been the truth. Lili eyed Maxim as he chattered on. For a month she'd been besieged by suitors. They were all well bred, well dressed, and well mannered. Some were young, some old, some smart, some handsome. All were wealthy. *But all the money in the world can't make a man interesting,* thought Lili.

"So I am thinking, when the land is mine, I might try grape growing and wine making," Maxim was saying. "Just as a hobby, you know."

Lili couldn't help it—her mouth stretched wide in a yawn. Maxim frowned. "I am sorry if you find this topic dull," he said stiffly.

Lili shook her head impatiently. "No, you see, I am just so *hot.*" She indicated her close-fitting, dark blue riding habit with its long sleeves and high neck. "Come. Let's canter again—I crave a breeze."

Before Maxim could reply, she touched Swift with her crop. At the same instant the sound of a gunshot broke the summer stillness. Swift reared with a startled neigh, then broke into a panicked gallop.

Lili clutched the reins. "Swift, whoa!" she cried. She tossed a frightened look over her shoulder, but Maxim just stood frozen in the path, staring helplessly after her.

I must stay calm and get the horse under control, Lili thought, but as she tried to get a better grip on the tangled reins she dropped them altogether. Clinging to the horse's heaving neck, she struggled to keep from slipping from the sidesaddle. Just as she thought she couldn't hang on any longer, she glimpsed someone galloping across the field in her direction. *Maxim?* she wondered, dazed. No—this man was astride a roan horse, not a chestnut, and his hair was black, not fair. He was dressed in the plain, dark clothes of a working man.

Georges whipped his horse, which was frothing at the mouth from the exertion. In seconds he and Lili were galloping side by side. As Georges leaned over to grasp the loose reins that flapped from Swift's bridle, Lili squeezed her eyes shut, waiting for her horse to swerve and fling her from the saddle. Instead, miraculously, she felt Swift's pace slow. "Whoa, there," Georges bellowed, his voice deep and commanding. "Steady, boy."

Breathing hard and glistening with sweat, Swift slowed to a canter and then to a trot. When Lili tried to sit up straighter, spots danced before her eyes. "Georges," she murmured as she toppled from the saddle in a half faint.

He had already jumped from the back of his own horse and was there to catch her as she fell. "I'm sorry. I'll be all r-right in a m-minute," Lili stammered, resting her cheek against Georges's chest.

She was standing on her own feet, but his arm was still wrapped firmly around her shoulders. "Just relax," Georges advised. "Catch your breath."

"I was scared," she whispered.

"You're safe now," he assured her.

At the sound of hoofbeats Lili looked up, brushing the hair off her forehead. Maxim trotted up, reined in his horse, and dismounted crisply. "Out of the way," he snapped at Georges, shoving him aside and putting his own arm around Lili. Georges stepped back, silent. "You've caused enough trouble with your rifle." Maxim pointed to the gun and brace of quail hanging from Georges's saddle. "Firing off shots and scaring horses. Be gone, I tell you."

Georges didn't acknowledge Maxim with a look, word, or bow. Not meeting Lili's eyes, he turned and mounted his roan horse. "Hmpf," Maxim snorted as Georges trotted off. "What an insolent lout! Handling you in that overly familiar way—I should have taught him a lesson in manners."

"He's a trusted family retainer," Lili said weakly.

"And ready and willing to take advantage of that trust, I daresay."

Maxim helped Lili up onto the front of his own saddle, then swung a leg up behind her. Leading Swift, they started slowly back toward Winterthorn. "Are you all right?" Maxim asked, his arm still circling her waist.

"I'm quite fine," Lili replied.

She cringed at the forced contact with Maxim. *I can't wait to get home and be rid of him!* she thought. His nearness disgusted her. Whereas when Georges had his arms around her . . . Lili tingled, remembering his strong embrace. She was glad her face was turned away from Maxim. She wouldn't want him to imagine that she was blushing because of him.

Late in the day, having refreshed herself with a cool bath, Lili sat in the garden with her sketchbook. She drew the birdbath and some rosebushes, then pushed her art supplies aside. After cleaning her fingers with a handkerchief dipped in lemon water, she strolled toward the stables.

She found Georges shoveling dirty hay out of a stall. When he saw her, he straightened up, raising one brawny arm to wipe his dripping forehead. "I won't keep you from your work," she said quickly. "I only wanted to thank you for saving my life today."

Georges leaned on the pitchfork and fixed her with a steady gaze. "It was what any man would have done," he said, shrugging.

"Oh." Lili stared at him. He continued to stand, and after a few moments she recollected herself, realizing that he was waiting for her to leave before resuming his labor. "Well, thank you again. Good day." She hurried out, peeking back once. Georges had gone back to cleaning the stalls as if saving Lili de Beautemps's life was all in a day's work.

She considered his words as she walked back to the château. *What any man would have done* . . .

Suddenly she laughed out loud. *Why, the bold scamp!* she thought, Georges's implication becoming clear. If Georges had played a man's part by going after the runaway horse, then Maxim was less than a man for hesitating.

So in addition to being vain and boring, Maxim is a coward, Lili reflected. She stopped in her tracks, her forehead wrinkled in confusion. "But Maxim is noble and Georges is common," she mumbled to herself. "By definition Maxim is far superior!"

She returned to her sketch pad, but instead of drawing she sat looking blankly at the garden, her thoughts in a turmoil. A horse had run away, an insignificant event, but all at once the old standards by which she used to judge people no longer made sense. Lili wasn't accustomed to entertaining deep thoughts—hadn't she teased Georges about his philosophy? But now she had some new questions of her own to ponder. What was manliness? What was nobility? Did a lofty aristocratic title mean anything if a man's deeds didn't live up to it?

"You know what they're celebrating today in America?" asked twenty-two-year-old Henri de Beautemps, the heir to Winterthorn, as he dipped a silver spoon into his soup. "Their declaration of independence from England thirteen years ago this July Fourth."

The family was seated at dinner. "Hang America," remarked Lili's other brother, Philippe,

17

who was twenty and an officer in the king's guard. "If we'd known when we helped them win their little war that our own people would start clamoring for reform, we might not have gotten involved."

Lili's father patted his lips with a linen napkin. "France is in a sorry state indeed," he agreed. "All over the countryside peasants are rioting against their lords. And fat King Louis is utterly powerless."

As Marie Oiseleur's younger sister Nanette served the main course—roast beef with a rich wine gravy and a terrine of fresh summer vegetables—Lili listened to her father and brothers with ill-concealed boredom. For weeks now talk in the French countryside was of nothing but politics. *Everyone says we're on the brink of a revolution,* Lili thought, delicately chewing a bite of beef. *I wish we would get on with it, then, so Papa doesn't keep putting off our trip to Paris to purchase new gowns!* "Here is the thing, Papa," Henri was saying earnestly to his father. "I believe we can avert catastrophe in our own village if we confront the situation head-on. Beat them to the punch, so to speak."

"You mean give in to every unreasonable demand the peasantry makes?" scoffed Philippe.

"Not all their demands are unreasonable," Henri countered. "They want bread on the table and a roof over their heads. They want progress, Papa. If we bring about gradual change, there will be no need for revolution."

"Well, son, as I see it—" the viscount began.

Lili pushed back her chair. "I'll be working on my needlework in the parlor," she announced tartly. "Join me after your wine if you're in the mood to talk of something more amusing!"

The men chuckled as they rose to bow her out of the room. Lili flounced off, wishing that she had a sister. *Someone to talk to about suitors and gowns. Someone to take my side against all these serious men!*

"There is a small party tomorrow night at Fond du Lac," Lili chattered as Marie helped her prepare for bed later that evening. "I was thinking that you might do my hair with some of those cunning little birds. Do you know? Nothing garish, of course. But they would look so sweet with my flowered gown."

Marie buttoned Lili's nightdress in silence.

"I turned down three offers of marriage this week, Marie," Lili went on, changing topics in hopes of engaging her friend's interest. "From Maxim and *both* Tremont brothers. Isn't it too amusing? I am expecting an offer from Laurent Villesavin any day now. Papa wants me to accept him, and of course he is immensely wealthy, but I simply don't know if I can wake up every morning and have to look at those droopy eyes and that long nose!"

Lili burst into peals of laughter at the thought.

Marie, busily brushing Lili's hair, did not join in her merriment. "Marie, you are as gloomy as the grave tonight," Lili chided. "At this rate I might as well be alone, so finish my hair and be gone."

To Lili's surprise, Marie dropped the hairbrush and burst into tears. "Marie!" Lili exclaimed, astonished. "What on earth is the matter?"

"Oh, mistress, if I tell you . . . !" Marie wailed.

"Tell me what?"

"I can't." Marie shook her head. "They'll punish me."

"You must," Lili insisted. "No one shall punish you, I promise."

Marie dabbed at her tears with the corner of her apron. "The servants have been holding secret meetings," she said at last.

Lili's eyebrows arched. "Secret meetings? Whatever for?"

"The townspeople are plotting to take up arms against your family, and they want your servants to gain them access to Winterthorn." Marie clasped Lili's hand, her eyes imploring. "Pack up your gowns and run away, Mistress Lili," she begged. "I don't want them to hurt you!"

Lili laughed heartily. "Oh, Marie, let me guess. Georges has been scaring you with stories from his philosophy books."

"It's not Georges; it's—"

Lili cut her off. "Marie, you mustn't listen to your brother. He'll put ridiculous ideas in your

20

head. Now get to bed and be in a more cheerful mood in the morning." Marie opened her mouth, but Lili gestured sharply. "I said good night."

Lili smiled to herself as she extinguished the candles and slid between her crisply ironed sheets. *Silly Marie. What an impressionable goose!*

The summer night was mild, so she left the curtains of the four-poster bed drawn back to allow a breeze from the open window. Snuggling under the covers, Lili closed her eyes. But sleep didn't come. She found herself listening to the quiet night noises of the château with a new feeling of foreboding. Of course, Marie's tale was pure nonsense . . . or was it? The night seemed peaceful. Was this a sign of real security, or did it mask a lurking evil?

There can't be anything bad going on, Lili told herself. There had always been noble families in France. Her father was a generous, thoughtful landlord whose tenants were far better off than most.

She wanted to believe this, but the seed of doubt had been planted. There was unrest throughout the countryside . . . why not here? She had to consider the possibility that her sense of safety was completely misplaced. At that very moment there might be people plotting to destroy her family's property, her inheritance . . . and maybe even her life.

3

By the light of morning Marie's tale seemed out-
landish. All the next day Lili went about her usual ac-
tivities with a carefree spirit, laughing at the memory
of how she'd shivered under the bedclothes, suddenly afraid of her own shadow. When she bumped
into Georges in the garden, she couldn't resist baiting
him. "You should watch what you say around Marie,"
Lili teased, her tone playful. "You mean something in
jest, but she takes it literally." She laughed. "Or are
our trusted servants really conspiring against us?"

She expected Georges to laugh with her.
Instead his face darkened. "You foolish, frivolous
girl," he said hoarsely. He gripped her arms with
strong fingers, giving her a shake that rattled her
teeth. "When are you going to see that the danger
is real? Marie should have held her tongue, but she
was only trying to help you."

"Let me go!" Lili cried, wrenching herself free from

Georges's grasp. "How dare you speak to me like this!"

"Because you asked for the truth, though clearly you weren't prepared to hear it." Georges dropped his arms to his sides. "Because I'm concerned about you too," he admitted. "Pack your bags, Lili, while there's still time."

"That's just what Marie said to do." Lili shook her head. "Really, the two of you. You are positively hysterical."

"My feet have never been planted more firmly on the ground." Georges resumed his work. "But if you won't heed me . . ."

Lili placed her hands on her hips. "Georges Oiseleur, you know our people love us. They would never hurt us!"

"Perhaps they love you," he replied, his mouth twisting in a cruel smile, "the way the French people love their queen."

Lili felt as if she'd been slapped. Marie Antoinette, who had once been popular with her subjects, was now universally hated and seen as a great reason for the monarchy's decline. "You don't understand, do you, Georges?" Lili snapped. "That's why you're angry. You're a peasant—you don't know what it means to be noble, to have traditions and responsibilities. Do you really think you could do better than to live and work at Winterthorn?"

"I could work for myself," he muttered.

"You're working for no one right now," she pointed out tartly, gesturing at his idle hands. "See to it that you do a thorough job." She spun on her heel and flounced off, her skirts swishing vigorously. She knew Georges was watching, his rake still lying on the ground. *Let him stew,* she thought. *I got the last word!*

Yes, she'd gotten the last word. Lili pursed her lips. Why, then, did it taste so bitter?

"Are you sure you want to go with me?" Henri asked Lili as he prepared to hand her into the carriage. "It looks like rain."

"I haven't been out in the longest time," Lili answered. "I will gossip with Mimi and her mother while you do business with the men."

"As you wish," her brother consented. "To Fond du Lac, Hubert," he said to the driver, Hubert Oiseleur, Georges and Marie's uncle. "And step lively. Let's beat the storm."

Hubert nodded wordlessly, gathering up the reins. When Lili and Henri were comfortably settled, the horses started off at a brisk trot. Soon they had reached the boundary of the estate. As the road entered the village Lili, who had been looking idly out the window, sat up and pointed. "*Attendez,* Henri," she said. "That crowd of men, just standing around in the middle of the day! Shouldn't they be in the fields? Will you say something to them?"

Henri sat forward, his eyes narrowed. As the carriage drew abreast of the men a few of them stepped into the road, brazenly blocking the way. Rude eyes stared in at her. Lili shrank back in her seat.

It was customary for the men of the village to doff their hats and stand respectfully when members of the de Beautemps family passed by. Instead of paying the usual deference, these men muttered insolent remarks. Some seemed angry; others flashed gap-toothed grins. "Henri, what do they want?" Lili whispered, her eyes round with fright.

"I don't know," her brother replied. But he remained collected. "Drive on, Hubert," Henri commanded, his voice ringing out with cool authority.

Hubert shook the reins and clucked. The horses plunged forward and the men scattered. They left the village and followed a road winding along the Loire. Lili no longer felt like paying a social call, but neither did she want to order her brother to turn around and drive her home. She didn't want to run that gauntlet again. "Henri," she asked once again, "what did it mean?"

Once again he answered, "I don't know."

Lili huddled in the corner of the carriage, her stomach in knots. For some reason Georges's voice echoed in her head. "You foolish, frivolous girl," he'd said to her just the other day. "When are you going to see that the danger is real?" *Was he right?* Lili wondered. After centuries of peaceful coexistence had the common people come to hate her privileged family?

Lili was in a deep sleep when a loud noise woke her abruptly. She sat up in bed, staring wildly into the blackness. For a moment she thought a nightmare had disturbed her. Then she heard more noises coming from a distant part of the château. The crash of breaking china and crystal. The sound of screaming.

"Marie!" Lili shrieked. "Where are you? What is happening?" She grabbed the velvet cord by her bed, the one that rang a bell in the servants' quarters, and tugged it desperately. "Marie, come to me this instant!"

There was no response.

Lili leaped from the bed and ran to the window. Her room was filled with an eerie, flickering light. Looking outside, she saw a crowd of shadowy forms moving toward the château, many bearing torches. *"Mon Dieu,"* Lili gasped, her heart in her throat. "They *are* coming for us. Just as Marie warned!"

There was no time to waste. Darting across the room, Lili struggled to drag a heavy oak armoire in front of her door. Before she could get it in place, though, the door was kicked open. A man with a scarf tied across his face barreled in, followed by half a dozen more men right behind him. Lili backed up, pulling her silk dressing gown more snugly around her body. "Out of my room!" she commanded, her voice shrill with terror.

The men laughed harshly. One of them flung Lili facedown on the bed, tying her hands behind her back. Another hauled her back onto her feet and kicked her toward the door. Before she could protest further, a rag was stuffed into her mouth.

The men dragged her down the hall, down the

staircase, then down more stairs into the château's dank, dark cellar. Along the way Lili saw ripped tapestries and defiled carpets, paintings with the canvases slashed, and mounds of broken china. Everywhere strangers were looting the cupboards and drawers. *What are they going to do to me?* she wondered, terrified.

Deep beneath the living quarters of Winterthorn was the ancient dungeon where the de Beautempses had once imprisoned their enemies. Now Lili, Henri, Philippe, and their father huddled there together on the cold earth floor.

Water dripped down the stone walls. A single candle lit the gloomy space. Lili's hands had been unbound and the gag removed. They had been alone in the dungeon for hours . . . or was it only minutes? "Will they come back for us?" she asked her father, sobbing. "Or will they leave us here to rot?"

The viscount exchanged a glance with his sons. All three men were bruised and battered from struggling with their captors. "I know not, my child," he answered gruffly.

They weren't in suspense for much longer. Soon the stone door scraped open. Eight brawny men entered, two for each prisoner, and hauled Lili and her family to their feet. Their captors had scarves tied across their faces. But as Lili focused on the man who'd broken down her bedroom door, she thought she recognized him. Hubert Oiseleur, Marie's uncle!

The de Beautempses were dragged upstairs to the great entrance hall of the château and out the tall double doors. Lili expected it to be morning, but when they emerged, the sky was still black. No sooner were they clear of the building than a group of men with torches ran inside. As she was propelled forward Lili twisted her neck to look back over her shoulder. The heavy brocade curtains that framed each ground-floor window were already ablaze.

The men led them quickly across the lawns and into the fields. Lili stumbled through the tall grass, her delicate silk slippers soon in tatters. *Perhaps they're taking us to the woods to set us free,* she thought hopefully. *They have our land and possessions. That's what they want, isn't it?*

Then Lili lifted her head. When she saw where she and her family were being led, her heart skipped a beat. At the edge of a field bordered by trees rose a crude platform surrounded by people. Even from a distance Lili could tell what stood on top of the platform. The blade of a guillotine caught the light of countless torches and glittered cruelly.

Lili flung herself toward her father, but rough hands constrained her. They were lined up now at the base of the platform: Philippe, Henri, the viscount, and Lili. "They can't mean to kill us, Papa," Lili cried, searching the crowd for a kind face, for Marie or Georges or another of their loyal servants.

But Philippe was being hauled up the wooden steps. They forced him to kneel and place his head on a block of wood. The blade was raised. Lili buried her face in her hands. "No!" she screamed. "Spare him!"

The mob was merciless. "For your crimes, de Beautemps!" they roared. "We want bread and property and votes, and all you've given us are taxes and hard labor and poverty!" The roar reached a crescendo as Lili heard the heavy blade drop. The crowd cheered. *My brother,* Lili thought, feeling the blow to the core of her being. *He's dead. They've beheaded him.*

She could not watch as her other brother and then her beloved father were led, each in turn, to the place of execution. She kept her hands pressed to her eyes, whispering prayers into fingers wet with tears. "Please, preserve their souls." She struggled to hold her body erect as her knees and spine threatened to crumble. "And please, help me to be brave."

The shouts reached a fever pitch. Lili knew without looking that the mob was cheering the death of her father. *Of all my family, only I remain alive,* she realized.

She didn't have time to grieve. Coarse, cruel hands grasped her arms and dragged her forward. Lili stumbled to the base of the platform, hovering on the brink of consciousness.

It was her turn to die.

4

Lili put her foot on the first step leading up to the platform. "Look at her, in silk," someone spat. "Soon that silk will be drenched with blood."

She froze, unable to move. Rough arms grabbed her around the waist and hurled her up onto the platform. She fell to her hands and knees and the mob crowed with jeering laughter.

All at once Lili's heart burned white-hot with anger. Recovering her dignity, she rose to her feet, holding her chin high. She would not cower. They might murder her as they had her father and brothers, but they would never crush her spirit. *No matter what these people say,* Lili thought, *no matter what they believe me to be guilty of, I know they are wrong and I am innocent.*

As Lili walked slowly across the platform toward the guillotine, the laughter died away and the crowd fell silent. One of the men who had been restraining her now pulled her hands behind her back and looped a rope loosely around her wrists. Mercifully the three corpses had been removed, but Lili felt a wave of nausea and terror as she stared at the bloodstained blade.

The executioner, his face masked by a piece of black cloth, motioned Lili to kneel before the wooden block. She paused for a moment, her lips moving in a prayer. Suddenly her fear drained away and a strange calm filled her soul. *My last moment on this green earth,* she thought with unbearable sadness. *My last breath of air.*

"But she is just a girl," a voice called out.

The crowd grumbled impatiently. "She is one of them," someone snarled. "To your knees, woman. Do not think we will pity and pardon you!"

Lili summoned all her courage. The executioner grasped her arm and began to force her to kneel at the block. Then a new sound permeated Lili's consciousness, thundering above the voices of the mob. The pounding of hooves.

She looked up just as a horseman burst from the forest, riding at full gallop straight toward her. People dove out of the way, screaming. The rider, his features hidden by a hood, did not rein in until he was abreast of the platform. Then he jumped from the horse's back. Before anyone could stop him, he'd scooped Lili up in his arms and leaped back onto his horse, flinging her like a rag doll across the saddle in front of him. "Go," he roared, kicking his horse hard in the ribs.

Whinnying frantically, the horse lunged forward, breaking free of the hands that sought to restrain it. Galloping hard, they reached the edge of the field within seconds and disappeared into the black woods.

The rider urged his horse at full speed through the tangled undergrowth. Branches whipped Lili's face and arms. "Who are you?" she cried out. Though she'd been saved from the guillotine, she was still overcome with terror. This might be death in another guise—perhaps the masked man planned to ravage her before killing her. "Where are you taking me?"

Her rescuer remained silent and the horse forged on.

Finally, after what seemed an eternity, he pulled on the reins. The horse slowed to a trot and then a walk, his rib cage heaving. Lili sat up and looked around her. The forest was dark and silent. She could no longer hear the shouts of the mob that had ransacked her home and murdered her family. She could no longer see the light of the fire burning the château. Instead of blood and gunpowder the scent of moss and earth filled her nostrils.

Lili twisted to look up at the horseman. Dark eyes glittered through the holes cut in the hood. *Do I know those eyes?* she wondered. Their expression seemed somehow familiar. "Who are you?" she repeated, her voice trembling.

Lili held her breath as he touched the burlap cloth that covered his face. Free of the hood, he shook out his black hair. His eyes locked on hers, and though he didn't smile, there was immeasurable kindness and something else . . . love? . . . in his gaze.

The horseman was Georges.

They rode through the night, reaching Paris just before dawn. There was so much Lili wanted to know, so many questions she wanted to ask, but her heart was too full to speak. Georges too, was pensive and quiet, though his arm, firm and warm around her waist, spoke volumes.

"Georges, look," said Lili, pointing. "The city. Is it a battle?"

Ahead of them the pale lavender sky of early dawn flickered with gunfire. The muffled booms of cannons reached their ears. "The old prison, the Bastille," said Georges, gesturing to a massive stone edifice. "They're storming it to set the prisoners free!"

Lili was still puzzled. "*Who*, Georges?"

"The people," he said simply. "I told you it would come, didn't I? It's here at last. In the city, in the countryside. The Revolution."

"I understand . . . sort of." Lili's eyes brimmed with tears. "But why do they have to kill to get what they want?"

"They've been downtrodden for hundreds of years. They're hungry for vengeance." Georges touched her cheek gently. "I'm sorry I couldn't save your father and brothers too, Lili. Not all of us desired bloodshed, but my voice was one against many."

They rode another half a mile. Then Georges stopped the horse at a crossroads on the outskirts of the city. "Where are we?" asked Lili.

He dismounted, helping her down from the horse's back. "Within walking distance of a Paris neighborhood where I know the people to be hardworking and kind. You'll find shelter there."

Lili gaped at him. "You mean, by myself?"

Georges turned his face away from her beseeching gaze. "I must return to the village. If it's discovered that I was the one who liberated you, it will be my neck on that chopping block. I can't do anything more for you, Lili."

"But Georges!" She clung to his arm. "You can't leave me when I . . . when I . . ." She stopped, blushing in confusion. She'd been about to say, "When I love you." *Can it be?* she thought, dazed. *I love Georges Oiseleur?* Then she saw it, as clear as the dawn that was breaking over Paris. Of course she loved Georges, and always had. It had been impossible before for her to acknowledge her feelings, even to herself—impossible because of their different stations in life. But now that the world had been turned upside down . . .

"Because I . . . need you," she finished lamely.

"I bet you'll surprise yourself, Lili de Beautemps," he said gruffly as he wrapped his wool cloak around her shoulders. "You'll find for

34

the first time in your life that you can be self-sufficient. You don't need anyone."

He put his hand on the pommel of the saddle, preparing to mount. Lili made one last appeal. "Georges, please."

He turned back to her and their eyes locked. For a long moment they stared deep into each other's souls, and Lili saw that he loved her too. "Georges," she whispered.

He pulled her into his arms, crushing her body against his. Lili lifted her face and their mouths met. The kiss was deep and searing, warming her down to her toes. Then he pushed her away from him again. She saw his jaw tighten with determination as he swung his leg over his horse. Before she could call after him, he had set off at a canter. He didn't look back.

Lili watched until Georges disappeared in the blinding light of the rising sun. She wanted to run after him and beg him once more not to abandon her. She wanted to crawl back into the woods and curl up in a ball and die. Instead she squared her slender shoulders, drew the heavy cloak close around her body, and faced the city before her.

Her heart pounded with a mixture of terror and hope. Paris—all of France—was in turmoil. She was alone, without family, friends, or possessions.

But she was alive.

5

1792. Paris.

Lili de Beautemps strolled in the Jardin des Tuilleries on a Sunday afternoon in May. The spring sunshine felt delicious after a long cold winter when she often hadn't been able to afford sufficient coal for a fire. *I made it, though, didn't I?* Lili thought, pausing to admire a statue. She couldn't help being proud of herself. Almost three years had passed since the horrible night when she lost her home and family. They'd been years of hardship and loneliness, but at last she was making ends meet as a seamstress.

She thought of her current residence, a cramped but lovingly tended garret in the Marais, an elegant Parisian neighborhood. She liked to imagine that someday she'd have enough money to live in one of the lovely, airy apartments on her building's lower floors. In the meantime she did what she could with what she had, brightening her room with fresh flowers, hanging her sketches on the walls, sewing pretty pillows and curtains from scraps of fine cloth left over from her dressmaking. She tried not to dwell on memories of Winterthorn: the long galleries and countless rooms or the acres of gardens and miles of riding trails.

Lili plucked a fragrant white narcissus blossom and tucked it under her shawl. Then she sat down on a bench with a view of a poplar-lined path. It was good to rest. Many nights she went to bed with fingers cramped and aching from too much sewing. Because she couldn't afford to hire a carriage, she went on foot to her customers' homes, all over the big city, often carrying heavy bolts of fabric wrapped in brown paper and tied with string.

Just then Lili spotted a friend who worked as a governess for a wealthy family in her neighborhood. "Babette!" she called, waving a gloved hand.

The girl hurried toward her, a cheerful smile wreathing her round face. "You have the afternoon off too, I see," said Babette. "Freedom is precious, isn't it?"

"I can't get enough of it." Lili patted the bench beside her. "I want to hear about this new beau of yours."

Babette blushed a rosy pink. "I can't talk about him now because I'm on my way to meet him. Will you come to supper later?"

Lili laughed. "I'll be there."

She smiled to herself as Babette bustled off. It was truly strange and funny. Three years ago she'd have looked down her nose at Babette. *Because she's not an aristocrat,* Lili mused, *but now neither am I!*

As she sat lost in thought Lili didn't notice the occasional passerby turning to take a second look at her. Her beauty was still fresh and her figure striking. Combined with a new maturity and quiet grace, she presented a picture as radiant as the spring day. Most of the time she felt at peace, happy to be alive and grateful to have work and friends. Friends who were not noble by the old definition, perhaps, but who were industrious, honest, and kind. She'd learned the hard way about equality and now cheerfully performed many a task once considered beneath her if it meant putting bread on the table.

To preserve her serenity, she tried not to think about her life before the Revolution. But sometimes she found herself searching for a certain face in the crowd. *What would Georges think if he could see me now?* Lili wondered. *Would he be proud of me? Would he still love me?* It was pointless to speculate, of course. When she'd finally recognized Georges's true nobility, it was too late. Years had passed—what were the odds of finding him now? She hadn't the heart to venture back to the countryside and face the desolate ruins of her former home—land that was no longer hers, the unmarked graves of her murdered family.

The sun was sinking behind the trees. Lili realized she was hungry. It was almost time for supper. She would share Babette's simple meal and tease her friend about finally meeting Monsieur Right.

Lili walked briskly homeward, feeling very complete in her solitude. She was delighted that her friend had found a beau, for she knew Babette wanted very much to marry so she could resign her governess position. Lili herself didn't expect the same good fortune. Her heart still belonged to Georges. Since they were only likely to be reunited in her dreams, she accepted that she would spend the rest of her life alone.

Lili traced the neckline of the dove gray gown with her index finger, then examined the details on the sleeves. Straightening, she gave the headless mannequin an approving pat. "This is just what the younger Mademoiselle Verlaine would like," she murmured, making a mental note of the pattern. "I can re-create it in that shell pink muslin. It will be a perfect dress for a summer afternoon."

She had stopped in the elegant dress shop on her way home from the Verlaines's. The shop was one of Lili's favorites. Madame Christophe displayed the latest fashions, and she didn't mind Lili studying the patterns so she could copy them for her own customers. She'd had the shop to herself for half an hour and was making a final examination of the decorative braid work on a riding habit when the door swung open. Lili glanced at the new arrival, then looked away quickly, trying to keep her face hidden from view. But the woman had recognized her. "Lili de Beautemps!" she exclaimed. "Can it be?"

In all her years in Paris it was the first time Lili had encountered an acquaintance from before the Revolution. She curtsied to the older woman, feigning delighted surprise. "Why, Countess! What an unexpected pleasure."

The woman shook her finger playfully. "Don't 'Countess' me, my dear. I am good, plain Madame Fouchette now, just as you are good, plain Mademoiselle de Beautemps." She smiled archly. "Or have you married?"

Lili blushed uncomfortably. "No."

"Let me take a look at you." Madame Fouchette stepped back and surveyed Lili critically from the top of her head to the hem of her gown. "A quieter way about you, but as stylish as ever, my dear," she said with approval.

Lili gulped. It was true that her clothing, while simple, was of quite good quality. She'd become skilled at making over the cast-off dresses of her well-to-do clients. *She is clearly still wealthy herself*, Lili thought. *I can't let her guess the truth about my circumstances.*

Madame Fouchette chattered on. "I'm so glad to see you, Lili. We'd heard that your entire family perished."

"I . . . I was spared," Lili mumbled.

"That awful time. We fled to Italy ourselves."

She clucked her tongue. "But since then Monsieur Fouchette has made quite a success in trade. We've nearly the quality of life we enjoyed before the Revolution. And you live where now? With whom?"

Lili gave her address, not mentioning that she rented the attic space. "My . . . my aunt and uncle took me into their home," she lied, praying Madame Fouchette wouldn't press for details. "They're elderly. We don't go out in society much."

"Well, we'll see what we can do about that," promised Madame Fouchette. "A lovely girl like you, still in the bloom of youth, shouldn't be hidden away from the world. Now, what did I come in here for? Oh, yes." She gestured to Madame Christophe. "Some gloves, please. Half a dozen pair."

Lili's nerves were frazzled. Madame Fouchette completed her purchase, and Lili accompanied her to the door. Outside, the mist had turned to rain. Madame Fouchette indicated her carriage, waiting in the road. "May I offer you a ride home, my dear?"

"Oh, no. That's not necessary," Lili said quickly. "My aunt's carriage will be around for me shortly."

Madame Fouchette gave Lili's hand a light squeeze. "I'll see you again soon."

The driver handed Madame Fouchette into her seat. The horses trotted off, their hooves squelching in the mud. Lili gazed at the rain. She didn't relish a long walk home in the worn-out shoes she'd been careful to keep hidden under her dress hem. Sighing deeply, she pulled her shawl over her

41

hair and tied it snugly under her chin. Then she set out into the rain.

A week later Lili took a break from her day's sewing to walk to the butcher's. When she returned, she found a letter on the table in her building's foyer. The envelope was of a heavy, cream-colored stock and her own name was written on it in bold black script. Intrigued, she ran upstairs with it.

In her room she slit open the envelope and quickly read the enclosed card. "An invitation to a party!" she exclaimed. Madame Fouchette and her husband were hosting a soiree the evening after next. There would be dinner, conversation, music. "Music," breathed Lili, her eyes starry. "Oh, and dancing!"

She whirled about the garret, her heart singing. A party. A party! It had been three whole years since she'd been invited to one, unless you counted the occasional modest gathering with Babette and her other new friends. Lili felt like a girl again, bursting with excitement. *I wonder how many people they'll invite? How will I dress my hair? And what shall I . . .*

As quickly as it had lifted, her mood collapsed. Lili sank on the edge of her bed, her chin dropping into her hands. "What shall I wear?" she finished with a defeated sigh.

Of course she couldn't go. What had she been thinking? *I fooled Madame Fouchette in the dress shop,* Lili remembered glumly, *but at a party?* She pulled aside the curtain that served as a closet in

42

one corner of her room and examined her neat but meager wardrobe. There was not a single dress remotely appropriate for a formal occasion.

Lili's eyes brimmed with tears of regret. She was about to let the curtain fall again when a glimmer of emerald green arrested her. She pushed her other clothes aside. It was the silk dressing gown she'd been wearing the night Georges rescued her from the executioner, the only remnant of her old life. After that journey the gown had been splattered with blood, earth, and tears, but she'd carefully cleaned and preserved it.

Lili fingered the material, a speculative look in her eyes. The silk was still bright and smooth. And the new fashions required less fabric than the gowns of old. . . . Slowly a smile returned to her face. She had an idea.

Lili stood at the gate in front of the Fouchettes's elegant Paris town house, her heart hammering. *I can't do it,* she thought, her feet frozen to the flagstone path. *I can't go in there. I've forgotten how to speak, how to act. They'll see at once that I'm a fraud!*

But another part of her mind urged her forward—the thought of fine food and wine, music and dancing. *What's the worst thing that could happen?* Lili wondered, laughing at her trepidation. *They'll throw me out onto the street! I've lived on the street before, and eaten scraps and dressed in rags. If they scorn me, I can handle it.*

She walked on, her carriage regal. At the top of the steps leading up to the house, a footman awaited the arriving guests. "Allow me, madame," he offered, taking her arm and escorting her through the door.

Inside, the splendor took her breath away. She'd forgotten about crystal chandeliers and gilt wall sconces glittering with candles, about brocade curtains and Persian carpets and furniture polished until you could see your reflection. Lili paused, enraptured. An aproned maid appeared at her side. "May I take your wrap, madame?"

Lili hesitated. She hadn't wanted to give up her shawl so soon. "Of course," she said weakly, swallowing her fear. *Let them see me. Let them judge!*

With a graceful motion she slipped the shawl from her shoulders. She stepped forward to greet Madame and Monsieur Fouchette, who were in the hallway receiving their guests. "Lili!" exclaimed Madame Fouchette, her eyes lighting up. "My dear, you are stunning. That gown—it is the most exquisite I have ever seen. I must know the name of your dressmaker!"

Lili's knees nearly crumpled with relief. At home, in front of her own little mirror, she'd studied herself from every possible angle and felt *almost* certain the dress was perfect. It took all her skill to transform the fabric of the old dressing gown into a simple, elegant evening dress, high waisted with a draping skirt, with enough material left over to cover a pair of old dancing slippers.

Until the dress had passed public muster, however, she hadn't been able to relax. Now she smiled at her host and hostess. *It's going to be all right,* she realized. *I'm going to carry it off!*

Madame Fouchette led Lili into the salon and presented her to some of the other guests. Instantly Lili found herself the center of an animated group, carrying on a lively discussion about art and literature. "Now, Mademoiselle de Beautemps," one man said in a genial manner, giving her a courtly bow, "you cannot mean to say that you believe the reading of novels to be as advantageous to the moral sensibility as the study of history and the classics."

Lili laughed. "I did not at all mean to imply that novel reading can be considered *study,*" she responded. "But as vehicles to improving our understanding of human nature, why, yes. I do feel we can learn much from them."

The hours flew by like minutes. Lili wasn't alone for an instant—she was constantly attended by one or more handsome, intelligent men. Members of the new Parisian aristocracy, they hadn't all been born to wealth, but they were well educated and charming. They brought her glasses of champagne and begged the favor of a dance as if their lives depended on her consent. They listened with admiring interest to her conversation. Basking in the attention, Lili bloomed like a flower long deprived of water and sunlight.

She knew, though, that the glorious transformation made possible by the green silk gown was just for one evening. It was nearly midnight—time for her to slip away. *I can't rejoin this glittering circle,* she thought with regret as she edged toward the door. *I'm a working-class woman now.*

As she was about to leave, Lili cast one last glance into the large drawing room, where chairs had been moved aside for dancing. Just then, in the far corner of the room, a man stepped forward. Lili's heart skipped a beat and then began to race madly. *Georges!* she thought. When the man's eyes met hers, she saw immediately that she'd been mistaken. It wasn't Georges, of course, though the resemblance was striking. The black hair, the piercing gaze, the strong chin and broad shoulders . . .

Lili realized she was staring and dropped her gaze, blushing profusely. When she looked up again, the man was standing before her. He bowed slightly, then held out a hand. "May I have this dance?"

It wasn't Georges, but Lili's heart was pounding as of old. She nodded, her eyes shining. "Yes."

The music stopped and her partner released her. Lili stepped from his arms reluctantly. They'd danced so beautifully together, as if their bodies had been made for each other. Bending, he kissed her hand, his lips lingering for a long, warm moment. Then he melted into the sea of party guests.

Slightly breathless, Lili dropped into a chair near the wall, fanning herself. A girl in a pale blue gown spoke to her with envious amazement. "Four dances with the count, you lucky thing!" she said to Lili.

"The count?" Lili repeated.

"Don't you know who that was?"

Lili shook her head, embarrassed to admit her ignorance.

"Count Matthieu de Bizac," the girl told her. "The most powerful man in Paris!"

The girl in blue strolled off, leaving Lili alone to contemplate her encounter with the count. She'd heard the name, although she couldn't recall in what context. Was he in the government? In business? *Not that it matters,* she told herself as she collected her shawl and ducked out the door. She hurried away from the Fouchettes's house, the shawl pulled close to her face so no one leaving the party by carriage would recognize her. *I'll never see him again.*

As she walked quickly home, however, her feet were still dancing. She and the count didn't move in the same circles, but she could dream. "Matthieu de Bizac," she whispered.

6

The next morning, as Lili was leaving with a bundle of sewing in her arms, she noticed an elegant coach parked on the street in front of her building. This wasn't unusual, as the other occupants were people of wealth and social status. *"Pardonnez-moi,"* the footman called out to her. "I'm looking for a Mademoiselle de Beautemps. Is this the right address?"

Lili stared. "Why, yes. But . . ."

The footman approached with a large bouquet of flowers. Bowing low, he presented them along with a note, saying courteously, "For you, then."

The coach clattered off. Unable to restrain herself, Lili tore open the note. The name inside, written in a bold black script, made her heart pound. "The count," she breathed. Thank goodness the footman hadn't discovered that she lived in the attic!

She went up to her garret with her arms full of clothing and flowers, then sat down to read the note. Like dancing with the count the night before, it left her giddy. "'My dear mademoiselle,'" she read aloud. "'Forgive me for taking the liberty of requesting your name and address from Madame Fouchette. I'm sorry I did not obtain a proper introduction last evening. I will not rest until I have the pleasure of meeting with you again. Will you honor me with your company for a drive through the park this afternoon?'"

Lili tucked the note into her pocket. She buried her face in the fragrant bouquet, hiding a smile of surprised delight. "He wants to see me again," she marveled. "This very afternoon! But I can't. I shouldn't."

Quickly she crossed the room and sat down at her writing desk. With trembling fingers, she composed a note in reply to the count's invitation.

The next few weeks were a whirlwind of activity. Lili was in the Count de Bizac's company nearly every other day. It took all her ingenuity, but she managed to convince Matthieu and his elegant friends that she was as rich and carefree as they were. She "borrowed" dresses that she was supposed to be altering for customers. She begged a loan of costume jewelry and other accessories from Madame Christophe's dress shop. She used up her own meager savings, as well as Babette's little nest egg, to hire a carriage and driver and therefore be in control of her own arrivals and departures. The deeper the deception grew, the more crucial it was that her new acquaintances not learn the truth.

One night the count hosted a dinner at his Paris residence. He seated Lili at his right hand, singling her out from all his other guests, and it was Lili alone with whom he conversed throughout the meal. "There are so many things I still don't know about you," he said to her in a low, caressing voice. "How is it that I didn't discover you until so very recently?"

Lili smiled. "Paris is a large city."

"But you are the most beautiful woman in this city. You stand out from the crowd like a priceless jewel."

She dropped her eyes, blushing. "I lead a quiet life."

"Tell me more about that life." He touched her hand lightly. "How do you spend your leisure hours?"

Lili didn't have any leisure time. When she wasn't with the count, she was home, bent over her sewing, working late into the night. "I've always enjoyed sketching," she said. "To be with paper and pastels in a country garden on a bright summer day is my idea of heaven."

His eyes gleamed. "What a bewitching picture you paint. *My* idea of heaven would be to see you in such a pose."

The gentle but intent flirtation continued throughout dinner. Later, during card games in the parlor, Lili and the count were separated, but at all times she was aware that his eyes were on her. She couldn't help responding to his attention. It brought back such memories of her old life, when flirting was her favorite pastime and she was always surrounded by admiring beaux. *Though he's not at all like the boys I knew in my youth,* she thought, darting a glance at his handsome profile. Only once in her life had she felt herself so strongly attracted to a man. . . .

"I can't believe you have the nerve to carry on such a masquerade," Babette said to Lili the next night. She shook her brown curls. "Pretending to be a fine lady!"

Lili bit her tongue to keep from saying that she didn't have to *pretend* to be a fine lady—she'd always been one. "It is too naughty of me, isn't it?" she agreed.

They were dining together in Babette's cozy flat. Babette poured Lili another cup of tea. "I almost think it's more than naughty," she said, her expression growing solemn. "Isn't it dangerous too?"

Lili blew lightly on her hot tea. "What do you mean?"

"You're spending all your money. And some of mine," Babette added. "All to make the count

51

believe you're someone you're not. Among your own friends you have a reputation as an honorable woman. *I* know your intentions are good. But what will other people think when they learn what you've been up to?"

"First of all," said Lili, "I'll pay you back as soon as I can. You have my word, Babette. As for what other people will think, since you're the only one I've confided in, why should I worry?"

"Of course I'll never tell," Babette promised. "Oh, but Lili." She searched her friend's face with earnest eyes. "This game you're playing must have an end. What are you after, really?"

Lili propped one elbow on the table and cupped her chin in her palm. "I want to be saved," she said after a moment's thoughtful silence. "I was saved once before . . ." She let the sentence trail off, not explaining. "I don't want to be poor anymore, Babette. I shouldn't *have* to be poor, with fingertips calloused from too much sewing." Sitting up straight, she pounded her fist on the table. "I deserve a comfortable home and a carriage of my own and fine things to eat and wear."

"Of course you do," Babette said soothingly. "We all do. But do you really think the count is the one to save you?"

"He's falling in love with me," Lili declared with certainty.

"And when he discovers that you've been misleading him?"

She waved a hand. "He never needs to know."

"I hope you're right." Babette smiled, her usual cheerfulness returning. "If anyone was born to be a countess, Lili, it's you."

Lili smiled back. "I think so too, Babette. And before the week is out, I wager you . . ." Her eyes sparkled. She knew how men acted when they were infatuated, and the count displayed all the classic signs. "Before the week is out," she repeated.

The Fouchettes were having another party, and the count offered himself as Lili's escort. From the start she sensed that the evening would be special. There were sparks between them. The count was more attentive than ever, touching her hand and gazing into her eyes frequently. Lili's whole body thrilled with expectation. *Something is going to happen tonight. I know it.*

As she made her way with ease and familiarity among the Fouchettes' guests, she wanted to laugh at how anxious and hesitant she'd been at the soiree a month earlier. Intoxicated by her return to the heady world of high society and with the devoted count at her side, Lili felt invincible. *It's not my destiny to be a seamstress forever,* she thought, recalling her conversation with Babette. *Wealth and privilege are my birthright.*

After dinner there would be dancing and cards. "Which do you prefer?" Lili asked the count.

He slid his hand up her bare arm to her shoulder. A shiver tickled her spine. "I prefer . . . to be alone with you," he murmured.

Lili allowed him to lead her outside to the garden behind the house. They sat side by side on a bench and he took her hand in his. "Lili," he said, his eyes serious. "I am in urgent need of certain information."

"Yes?"

"I need to know who I should ask for your hand."

Lili's heart flooded with emotion, but she managed to maintain a calm appearance. "Since the death of my father, I've been cared for by my elderly aunt and uncle," she said, repeating the story she'd told Madame Fouchette. "But I am of age and independent. I make my own decisions."

He pressed her hand. "Then you're free to accept my proposal on your own behalf if you so desire?"

She nodded.

"And do you desire?" He leaned closer to her. "Will you be my wife, Lili?"

Lili had been wishing for this moment, but now that it was here, it was even more wonderful than she'd dreamed. *He wants to marry me!* The future, which for years had seemed dark and uncertain, was now as rosy and bright as the dawn. Lili nodded again. "Yes," she said with quiet joy as the count bent his head to kiss her. "Yes."

When Matthieu suggested they be married in a quiet, private ceremony, Lili quickly agreed, since she hadn't the means to provide herself with an appropriately lavish wedding trousseau. "My aunt and uncle aren't well enough to attend me," she said. "Yes, let's avoid a fuss."

"I just don't want to waste another hour," Matthieu explained, taking her hand and turning it upward in order to press a long kiss on her palm. "I want you to be mine."

Their engagement was deliriously brief. Lili had only time to pack a few things and say good-bye to an astonished Babette. Then, for the last time, she walked down the stairs from her garret apartment. *In an hour I will be a married woman!* she thought as she rode in her hired carriage to the small chapel where Matthieu would be waiting for her.

All at once Lili felt a little bit scared and a little bit lonely. *If only Papa had lived to see this day*, she thought, a tear sparkling in her eye. She wished Babette were with her. Someone with whom to share these final moments, someone to throw rose petals as she stepped into her new life and identity. Babette had been a bit hurt that Lili didn't want to include her, although she'd claimed to understand her friend's reasons. *It would have been impossible*, Lili thought, *for Matthieu to meet Babette and realize that this is the sort of person with whom I've been consorting!*

"I have said good-bye to Babette forever," Lili murmured, another tear springing to her eye, "and to my other friends. We can't meet in the future. I'll be Countess de Bizac. Lili de Beautemps, the seamstress, must be dead and buried."

The coachman drew up the horses in front of the chapel and helped Lili down. Matthieu stepped forward to take her hand. "You're breathtaking," he said, his eyes glowing with admiration. "The bride of my dreams."

Lili had worried about what to wear until Madame Christophe offered her a cream-colored silk gown that she'd designed for a customer who decided it didn't suit her after all. Lili wore only the jewelry she'd had with her when she escaped from Winterthorn in 1789, and she'd dressed her hair simply in the current style.

Inside, the chapel was decorated with candles and flowers. The priest awaited them at the altar. Matthieu took her arm. "Are you ready?" he asked.

She took a deep breath, then nodded.

They stood together before the altar while the priest read a simple marriage service. As Matthieu slipped the gold ring on her finger, Lili found herself trembling. *How did I arrive at this moment?* she wondered dizzily. She looked into Matthieu's face. They were passionately in love and yet in so many ways still strangers. Their courtship had been a whirlwind, the decision to marry almost impetuous.

"I now pronounce you . . . ," the priest began.

A sharp pang of regret pierced Lili's heart, tempering her joy. She didn't want to acknowledge the feeling, but it forced itself to the front of her consciousness. *If only Georges Oiseleur were the one standing beside me.*

". . . man and wife," concluded the priest.

Matthieu pulled Lili toward him, taking her into his arms. "My wife," he whispered.

Lili closed her eyes as Matthieu brought his mouth to hers for a kiss. *Matthieu is the man I love,* she reminded herself, banishing all thoughts of Georges once and for all. Matthieu would give her everything she'd always wanted and more. The past was behind her now, both the good and the bad. She must never look back.

7

"I believe I could be happy spending the rest of my life in Italy," Lili declared. She smiled prettily at Matthieu. "What do you think, my love? Strolling among the antiquities, picnicking in the olive groves, basking in the golden Mediterranean sunlight . . . is there a single reason our honeymoon need ever come to an end?"

"The golden light does become you." He touched her cheek with the back of his hand. "Yes, Italy was created for lovers. But aren't you eager to begin setting up house back in Paris?"

They'd been in Italy for a month, enjoying the sights of Rome, Venice, Siena, and finally Florence. Lili had loved each romantic and picturesque city better than the last. Their hotels were always luxurious, and Matthieu had bought her trunks full of new clothes. Each day brought a gift of jewelry or art, a bouquet of flowers, a bottle of perfume, a box of chocolates. She had never felt so loved or so rich.

Only a few discordant notes marred the harmony of husband and wife. Matthieu, who'd been a courteous and devoted suitor, now revealed himself to be occasionally moody and distant. One moment he was tender, the next brusque and even cold. Often Lili had no idea what caused the transition. She'd decided it must be her own fault. When she was better at being a wife, Matthieu would have no reason ever to be anything but perfectly contented.

She didn't realize she'd spoken the thought out loud. "I wish we didn't have to go back."

Matthieu raised his eyebrows. "And why not, my darling?"

Lili turned toward the window, hiding a telltale blush. She wished they could start a new life in Italy. She didn't want to go back to Paris and run the risk of bumping into Babette or Madame Christophe or one of her old dressmaking clients. "As I said before, I just want our honeymoon to go on and on."

He gazed at her steadily. Lili felt her complexion grow even warmer. "Come, Lili," he said finally. "Won't you tell me what you really meant? Why is it that you're reluctant to return to your native city?"

She looked puzzled. "I *did* tell you."

He laughed indulgently. "Oh, Lili. Instead of waiting for you to make a confession, perhaps I should make one of my own and confess that I know what you've not yet confessed."

His words were cryptic, but Lili grasped his implication. The color drained from her face. "I—I don't understand you," she stammered.

"My darling wife." There was the faintest note of sarcasm in his voice. "You are a better actress than that. It was a perfect masquerade!"

The color returned to her complexion in a hot flood. Lili pressed a hand to her flaming cheek, speechless.

Matthieu chuckled at her discomfort. "It's all right, my darling. I don't think less of you because you only pretended to be a woman of means. In fact, I admire you for having the courage to aspire to a finer life."

Lili still couldn't untangle her tongue. "But how . . . ?"

"I wanted to know more about my future wife," he explained, "and as you may recall, you were not very forthcoming. So I did a little research and learned that there was no beneficent aunt and uncle." He took her hands and rubbed her fingertips, which were still slightly calloused. "My poor, hardworking angel."

"Oh, Matthieu." Lili snatched her hands away and burst into tears. "I'm so ashamed. You must hate me!"

"I love you, my pet." He hugged her to him. "If it bothered me, do you think I'd have married you?"

She gazed up at him, her face tear streaked. "Do you really still love me?" she asked in disbelief.

"I do," he said firmly.

Her heart swelled with gratitude. "How lucky I am!" she cried, pressing her face against his neck. "What can I ever do to be worthy of you?"

"First, you must forgive me." He pushed her away and straightened his cravat. "I have some business to attend to and must leave you here in Florence for a few days. Do you mind?"

"Of course not," she hastened to assure him. "Whatever you must do. Just . . ." Her voice dropped to a plaintive whisper. "Hurry back to me."

He kissed her hand. "Of course, my dear wife."

For two days Lili didn't leave the hotel. The weather was beautiful, but she was too anxious to stray far. What if Matthieu should try to contact her? What if he returned early and didn't find her waiting there?

He returned on the day and hour he'd promised, bringing with him a diamond choker in a velvet box and an armful of bloodred roses. They fell into each other's arms with renewed passion. "See how I hate to be parted from you?" he murmured into her cascading hair as he pushed the dressing gown from her shoulders.

Lili craved more assurances that he still loved her, that he didn't regret marrying a woman so far beneath him. But she bit her tongue. *Since he's willing to overlook it, I won't remind him of my shameful background,* she resolved. *The sooner we both forget about it, the better.*

"I know you're tired of hotels, my pet," Matthieu said on their return to Paris, "but we'll be comfortable here while we decide where to establish our residence."

Before their marriage Matthieu had entertained her often at his mansion in the city, and Lili knew he also owned a country estate she'd never seen. "I assumed we would live in the rue de Corbineau house," she said.

"No, no. I want something new. Something bigger." He squeezed her hand. "Something *ours*."

"Of course, Matthieu," she said, eager to please him. "Whatever you think is best."

The days passed slowly. Lili was usually alone at the hotel while Matthieu attended to his business interests. She longed for companionship but knew she couldn't contact Babette. Whenever she suggested that they see Matthieu's friends, he dismissed the idea. "We're still newlyweds," he reminded her. "I don't want to share you with anybody right now."

One early autumn morning, a month after their return from Italy, Lili awoke to the sun streaming in the bedroom window. She put out a hand to touch the empty pillow next to hers. The hotel suite was quiet. She sighed. It wasn't the first time Matthieu had dressed and left for the day while she continued dreaming.

Lili rose, slipping into the deep pink dressing gown Matthieu had given her as a wedding present. She went to the bedroom door and opened it, expecting to see her breakfast tray resting on the table in the antechamber.

There was no tray. Lili frowned. "Louise?" she called. Her maidservant didn't appear. Lili stepped back into the bedroom, rubbing the sleep from her eyes. She went to the ornately carved armoire, searching for her slippers. When she opened it, she gasped at what she saw. Or rather, at what she didn't see.

All of Matthieu's belongings were gone.

Lili stood for a moment, staring into the empty cupboard. Then she recovered herself. Quickly she searched the rest of the room. Not a single possession of her husband's remained—not one shoe or handkerchief, not his favorite quill pen or snuff box.

Lili raced into the hallway. Louise had been occupying a room next to Matthieu's manservant, Albert. Lili pounded on both their doors. "Louise! Albert!" she shouted. When there was no answer, she turned the knobs. The doors were unlocked and it took only a moment to verify that Louise and Albert were gone as well.

The blood pounded in Lili's temples. Breathing hard, she retreated to the suite she'd shared with Matthieu. Closing the door, she sank to the floor, suddenly unable to support herself for an instant longer.

She couldn't fail to read the signs all around her.

She had been abandoned.

The cold November wind rattled the papery brown leaves on the trees in front of the Fouchettes' house. Lili stood on the walk, frozen in indecision. She couldn't bear the thought of exposing herself to prying, curious eyes, but the Fouchettes were her last resort. *They must have some information,* she thought desperately.

For weeks she'd waited for her husband to come back to her, reluctant to stir from the hotel for fear that she might miss a visit or communication from Matthieu. There had to be an explanation for his sudden disappearance—surely he wouldn't just desert her! Then she'd learned from the hotel management that her rooms had been paid for through the end of the month only. Piece by piece she began pawning the jewelry her husband had given her, calculating that she had enough to live on for another month or two. But what then?

At last she'd swallowed her pride and gone in search of the count. But everywhere she went—his place of business, his city residence, the homes of his friends—she was rebuffed. Time after time, at one acquaintance's after another, people who'd received her with pleasure when she was on Matthieu's arm now informed her, through their servants, that they were "not at home." It was as if the count no longer existed, as if *she* no longer existed.

Lili had plunged into despair. Now, clinging to her last shred of hope, she knocked on the Fouchettes' door. The butler viewed her with suspicion. Lili knew she looked wild-eyed, and she struggled to keep panic from getting the best of her. "Please tell Madame Fouchette that the Countess de Bizac would like to speak with her," she requested tremulously.

The butler was gone for what seemed an eternity. Lili clasped and unclasped her hands, her throat tight with tears. If Madame Fouchette turned her away, she was sure she would just crumble in a heap on the pavement. For days she'd felt faint and nauseous, unable to swallow more than a bite or two of food.

At last the butler reappeared. "This way, madame."

He showed Lili to the parlor. Madame Fouchette didn't rise and greet Lili with a kiss as she used to do. Instead she gestured to a chair. "Sit down, Lili, and tell me what I can do for you," she said briskly.

Lili sank into the chair and burst into tears. "It's Matthieu," she sobbed. "You must tell me where I can find him!"

"I don't know for certain." Madame Fouchette frowned at Lili's emotional display. "But I believe he's in the country with his wife."

"His wife?" Lili dug her fingernails into the chair's upholstery. "But *I'm* his wife!"

"Oh, my dear." Madame Fouchette clucked her tongue. "Don't tell me he played that old trick on you."

"W-What trick?"

"But you knew he was already married to another woman!"

Lili shook her head. "No," she whispered.

"I am very, very sorry," said Madame Fouchette, with what appeared to be genuine sympathy. "Matthieu has always been a notorious philanderer. We all thought you understood what you were getting into."

Lili struggled to grasp the terrible implications. "So you're saying that our wedding—my marriage to Matthieu . . ."

"If there was a ceremony, it was a fraud," Madame Fouchette stated. "Matthieu isn't the first man to ruin an innocent girl in that fashion."

Lili twisted the gold ring on her finger. "But there was a priest. And a marriage license! We went to Italy for our honeymoon!" Her eyes brimmed with tears. "He loved me."

"I'm sure he did. He wouldn't have gone to so much trouble otherwise. But feelings fade. Most likely the real countess grew impatient for him to cease his dallying and return home."

Madame Fouchette escorted Lili to the door. "My dear, if I can do anything for you . . . some cash to tide you over?"

Lili shook her head numbly. "No. *Merci.*"

The door closed behind her. In a fog Lili trudged back to the hotel. *I can sell what remains of my jewelry, but I'll still have to find another place to live,* she thought as she sat in the room she'd shared, for a brief time, so happily with Matthieu. *I need to be more frugal. I must save every franc.*

Abruptly a wave of nausea washed over her. Lili lurched to her feet, rushing to the basin on her dressing table. She retched into the bowl.

Straightening, she wiped her face with a towel. She stared at her reflection in the mirror. The change wasn't visible . . . yet. For a few months she'd only suspected. Now she was certain. She had to find a safe, affordable room to rent and some sewing work. Because soon she'd have another person to take care of.

Her husband had never really been her husband, but they'd lived together as man and wife. Lili was pregnant.

8

The winter was the longest and most miserable Lili could remember. She did all she could to keep bread on the table and coal in her stove, taking in sewing in her new cramped quarters over a *boulangerie* in a grimy part of the city. But at times she was overcome with loneliness and fatigue. She knew Babette and her old friends would have welcomed her back with open arms, but she was too ashamed to turn to them. How could she let them see how far she'd fallen?

It was January, a new year, but despite the life growing inside her, Lili felt no hope for the future. One cold, gray morning she wrapped herself in her only warm garment, a heavy wool cloak. She ventured outdoors, heading for a dress shop in a more prosperous quarter of the city—the proprietress had promised her some work. She trudged along, the cloak pulled close at her neck. It was snowing, and she paused for a moment to catch her breath and watch the street turn white.

Just then a cavalcade of soldiers rounded the corner, their horses at full gallop. Behind them a cart clattered along the cobblestones. A bound man stood in the cart, dressed in the plain white garments of someone destined for execution.

Lili's heart throbbed with pity. The bloody work of the Revolution was still not done, and the reign of terror conducted by France's current leaders continued to keep the guillotine busy. *What was his crime?* Lili wondered. Looking at the face of the condemned man as the cart careened by, she gasped in disbelief. She'd seen him once or twice before, when she was a young girl, and though he had aged, she could not fail to recognize him. It was Louis XVI, the king of France.

The cart and the riders disappeared, leaving the streets once more silent and cold and drifting with new snow. Shivering, Lili resumed her journey. *So, the king is finally to die,* she thought. She supposed she shouldn't be surprised. For years now the world had been turned upside down. She'd thought she could find her way through the jungle of new social rules, but she had been wrong. After her betrayal by Matthieu, she was worse off than ever. A hot tear trickled down Lili's cold cheek. She almost wished she could trade places with the king. What was the point of struggling like this, day in and day out, when she had no prospects? Why hadn't she died when the rest of her family had perished?

The March wind howled outside Lili's window apartment and rain poured down the window-panes. Lili sat at the kitchen table, her hands cupped around a warm potato, roasted in its skin. It was all she had to eat that night, and she planned to savor every bite. It wouldn't be enough, though. She was seven months pregnant and her body craved nourishment. She placed a hand on her round belly. "I'm sorry," she whispered to the unborn child kicking vigorously inside her. "I'll try to do better tomorrow."

When the potato was gone, she prepared to wrap herself in her quilt and try to sleep. A knock on the door stopped her. Startled, Lili crossed the room. "Who is it?" she asked.

"Marie Chardin," a woman responded, "from the *boulangerie* downstairs."

Lili opened the door. A short, plump woman in a plain brown dress stood before her, a cloth sack in her arms. "Come in, Madame Chardin," she said shyly.

"You must call me Marie," the woman insisted, giving Lili a warm smile. "We've been neighbors for some months now. It's time to be friends as well, *n'est-ce pas?*"

Lili ducked her head, embarrassed. She did

70

much of her shopping in the *boulangerie*—the prices were fair and the bread good. But though Marie and her family seemed kind, she'd hesitated to strike up an acquaintance. She couldn't hide what she was—a pregnant, unmarried woman. Why would upstanding people like the Chardins want to associate with her?

Marie seemed to sense Lili's discomfort. "My dear, I won't force myself upon you if you'd prefer privacy," she said gently. "But I worry about you. A woman in your condition shouldn't be alone so much." Marie emptied her sack on Lili's table. There was a loaf of fresh bread, some vegetables, and a chunk of cheese. "I'll come to see you again tomorrow evening," she promised.

Lili nodded, speechless at the other woman's generosity.

Marie bustled out, and Lili was alone once more. But she didn't feel alone. She'd made a connection—the Chardin family was right downstairs. *I once had a friend named Marie,* she remembered, tears streaming down her thin, pale cheeks. *And now I do again.*

Weeks passed, and nearly every night brought a visit from Marie Chardin. If her children were already in bed, Marie would bring some sewing or a book to read while Lili prepared a meal with the food Marie provided. Then the two women talked for hours.

71

Lili quickly grew to think of Marie as the older sister she'd never had. "You must wonder how I came to be in these circumstances," she said one night.

Marie nodded. "Of course, but I don't like to be nosy. I give the bread freely—you don't owe me anything in return."

"But I want to tell you." Lili pulled up a stool near Marie's chair. "I want you to know who I am." Lili told Marie about the horrible night in 1789 when her family's château was raided and her father and brothers put to death. She detailed her years as a seamstress, her friendship with Babette. "I look back on that as one of the happiest times of my life," she said, her eyes misty. "I worked hard, but I made a decent living. I was independent. I could be proud of myself."

"What happened, my friend?"

"I met . . . a man." Lili's cheeks flushed. "A wealthy, powerful man. A handsome, charming man. Oh, I was such a fool!"

"You fell in love," Marie stated.

Lili nodded. "I should have known I was playing a game I couldn't hope to win. But when the count began paying attention to me, I was so flattered!" She told Marie about the sham marriage and de Bizac's desertion. "It was all my own fault. My vanity blinded me to his true character and motives."

"What a cruel, heartless man," Marie exclaimed,

72

her eyes flashing. "To abandon you, knowing you might be with child!"

Lili sighed. "I did not choose well."

"Don't blame yourself for being trusting," Marie said kindly. "Though you would have done better to settle for a solid, dependable man like my Jean-Luc."

Lili smiled. Jean-Luc was as short and round as Marie, and just as lovable. It was hard to imagine them experiencing a grand passion. But maybe they had something better, something deeper and more lasting. "I was in love one other time before," Lili confided. She described how Georges had rescued her from the guillotine only to leave her in Paris to fend for herself.

"You still think about him?"

"Yes." Lili's eyes were wistful. "I can picture him, hear his voice, as if it were yesterday."

"But when you were together, before the Revolution, you didn't deem him suitable as a lover, a husband," said Marie.

"No," Lili admitted. "But I've changed. I know better now." She gazed earnestly at Marie. "Experience has taught me that we are all just people, whether we're born in a castle or a cottage. It's our actions, the way we treat others, that elevate us. If only I could turn back the hands of time!"

Marie smiled. "Ah, don't we all wish that sometimes?" They sat for a few minutes in silence. Then

73

Marie held up her knitting to show Lili. "See how these booties for the little one are coming along."

Lili put out a hand to touch them. "Soft as a cloud."

"You have much to look forward to," Marie reminded her.

Lili looked to the window and nodded. Outside, the night was balmy, the breeze fresh and scented with blossoms. Spring had arrived. Though she was still poor and unmarried, hope blossomed in her heart like a fragile flower. She'd made so many mistakes, but now she had a chance to do one thing right. *I'll be a good mother,* she vowed.

Lili had never imagined such pain. For one endless stormy night and day contractions racked her body, threatening to snap her slender frame in two. The pain went on and on and her labor didn't seem to progress, no matter how hard she breathed and strained. Now it was night again and still raining. *Twenty-four hours,* thought Lili, panting and dazed. *How much longer can I take this?*

Marie, acting as midwife, had been at Lili's side the entire time. A few hours earlier she'd summoned her younger sister Nadine to help. Now Marie wiped Lili's sweating forehead with a cool damp cloth. "Your body's ready—it's time to push. When the next contraction comes, bear down with all your might."

The contraction came and Lili tried to push,

but she was too weak. "I can't," she sobbed. "I have no strength."

"You must," said Marie, gently but firmly. "This baby wants to be born!"

Lili endured another hour of agony, pushing as hard as she could while Marie and Nadine urged her on. "You're almost there, Lili!" Marie cried.

Lili slipped in and out of consciousness. At one point, through the fog, she thought she heard Nadine say, "I've never seen such a difficult labor. She's lost so much blood. What if we lose her and the baby too?"

Lili clutched Marie's hand. "My baby," she moaned. "Don't let my baby die."

"Hush," Marie replied. "You'll both be fine. One more push, Lili. You can do it."

Lili squeezed her eyes shut, tears streaming down her face. A scream ripped from her. And then there was another sound in the room, the happiest sound of all. The first wails of a newborn baby.

Lili felt no more pain. Her body felt numb and light, as if it were floating. Her vision was hazy, but dimly she could see Marie's beaming face. "You have a daughter, Lili."

"A daughter." Lili's failing heart gave one more strong beat. Joy and peace filled her soul. "Promise me," she whispered, grasping Marie's hand and squeezing it as hard as she could. "You'll raise her as your own."

Marie bit her lip, fighting back tears. "Of course, Lili."

Lili tried to hold out her arms but couldn't lift them. Marie laid the swaddled infant on the bed next to its mother. Lili managed to move her hand enough to stroke the tiny girl's downy blond hair. Tears spilled from Lili's eyes. "She's so beautiful, so perfect," she whispered. "It's a miracle."

She lifted her eyes to the window next to her bed. Nadine had pulled back the curtain. The storm had passed and the predawn sky was filled with twinkling stars. Lili looked back at her baby. With what little strength remained to her, she uttered her last words. "Her name," she said, gazing into her baby's eyes, which were as clear as the starry heavens, "will be Celeste."

9

1800. The Loire Valley, France.

The first day of a new century, reflected Georges
Oiseleur. *What a thing for a man to live to see!*

He stood on a balcony of the gracious manor
house that was now his and stared, brooding, at the
acres of perfectly tended vineyards that stretched
across the rich soil of the river valley. Ordinarily,
surveying his property gave him great pleasure.
But on this New Year's Day he felt only sorrow and
emptiness.

As a youth working on the de Beautemps estate
Georges could only dream that one day he might
be as wealthy as his masters. Now his dream had
come true. In the wake of the Revolution he'd ful-
filled his potential: pursued an education, entered
the world of trade, and made a great fortune in

textiles. The name of Oiseleur now commanded respect. Georges had formed alliances with all the powerful families in the region, including the Marquis de Bocage, who'd helped him get his start in business, and he'd bought a large estate adjacent to that of his former masters. It should have been enough, but it wasn't.

"I'm alone," Georges said to himself. In the distance he could glimpse the ruins of Winterthorn. "Without Lili it means nothing."

He'd spent the last half dozen years in search of his first and only love. At the time of the Revolution, it was unthinkable for a man of his lowly station to ask a noblewoman like Lili to be his wife. Now that he finally felt almost worthy of her, he despaired of ever finding her.

Grabbing his greatcoat, Georges strode out of the house and down a dirt road that marked the property line between his land and Lili's family's old estate. As he walked along it he studied the fallow fields with a critical eye. He wanted to find Lili in order to make her his wife, but that wasn't the only reason. During the peasant uprisings of 1789 many property deeds had been destroyed and the land confiscated. The Winterthorn deed, however, had been preserved, and some of the land and dwellings were still intact. Not the wealth of old— the château was a pile of rubble—but a substantial holding, and Georges had done the groundwork to restore the estate to Lili, its sole heir.

But where is she now? he wondered. Long ago he'd gone door-to-door in the Paris neighborhood where he'd left her that wild July night. He'd scoured city and village record books all over France. All to no avail.

Georges dug his hands deep in the pockets of his coat. His breath made clouds in the cold winter air. As he kicked a rock in the dirt road with the toe of his boot a smile creased his somber face. *It was right around here that I caught her runaway horse that day, while that fop Saint-Germain stood by uselessly,* Georges remembered. He'd held Lili in his arms for the first time. *And the next time I touched her . . .* He clenched his jaw. "Why did I let her go?" he muttered.

He'd often berated himself for abandoning her that dangerous night in 1789. But he'd always felt sure, deep in his bones, that Lili had made her way to safety. She was pampered and selfish, but she was also feisty and iron willed. "I'll find you yet, Lili de Beautemps," Georges promised, reaching down for a handful of dark, rich earth. "And I'll give you back what's yours." *And offer you myself too,* he added silently. *If you'll take me.*

Six months later a carriage rattled along the cobbled streets of Paris behind a pair of galloping black horses. Georges gazed out the window at the passing cityscape, his eyes glittering. At last, after years of fruitless searching, he had a lead on Lili's whereabouts!

It was pure coincidence. A friend of his house-keeper's had been traveling with her employers. At a hotel in Paris the woman had started up a conversation with a maid named Simone. When the woman complimented Simone on a hair orna-ment, Simone said it had been a gift years earlier from a kind and beautiful young woman who'd stayed briefly at the hotel. A woman with dark flowing curls and striking violet eyes. A woman named Lili . . .

When Georges spotted the address, he shouted at the coachman, "Here! Pull up." Before the wheels even stopped rolling, Georges was out of the carriage and dashing into the hotel.

Simone was waiting for him in the lobby. Before he could say a word, she blurted, "I didn't steal the ornament, sir. It was a gift. And I didn't ask for it either." She twisted her hands nervously in her apron. "I simply admired it one day, and she took it right from her hair and said, 'Why, here, then. It's yours.' Because my hair was the same color as hers, sir, and—"

"I'm not accusing you of stealing," Georges interrupted. "I came only for information. Anything you can tell me about this Lili . . ." He took a deep breath, trying to slow the frantic pace of his heart. "Her full name," he continued. "Was it de Beautemps or something else? Was she alone?

Where did she go after leaving the hotel?"

"I don't know where she went, but she wasn't alone. I remember it quite well, you see, because he was such a rich man. So much money flashing around, and plenty of nice extras for the staff. While it lasted, that is. He left rather suddenly. Her too."

"He?"

"Why, her husband, of course. They were newlyweds."

"Of course." Georges sank onto an upholstered Louis Quatorze chair. Of course a beautiful woman like Lili had married. He laughed bitterly at his long-cherished, utterly foolish hopes, muttering, "Did you think she would be waiting for you?"

"Sir?" asked Simone, her brow furrowed.

Georges recollected himself. "Her husband's name," he said, his manner once again businesslike. "Do you remember it?"

"Yes, sir. It was the Count de Bizac."

Wasting no time, Georges directed the carriage to city hall. He'd heard of de Bizac but didn't know how to locate him. The Department of Records would have an address if the count and his wife lived in Paris.

He was escorted to a musty, cold room in the dim recesses of the old stone building. "Any documents relating to a Lili de Bizac," he requested of the clerk. He put some coins into the man's hand. "And hurry."

For what seemed an age he could hear the clerk rustling pages and shifting heavy volumes. All the while images flickered dizzily through Georges's brain. Lili, that night in the garden after her first ball, in her green dressing gown. Laughing and teasing him, her hair loose and her eyes bold. Lili with her sketchbook, Lili on horseback. Chattering with Marie or strolling arm in arm with her doting father. Lili wrapped in his cloak, riding on the saddle in front of him, away from the blood-thirsty mob and the burning château. Their unforgettable kiss. *She's another man's wife,* Georges reminded himself. *She'll never be yours.* But did it matter? He'd sell his soul simply to see her once more. It would be his life's greatest happiness to restore her to her property and title.

The clerk shuffled back into the anteroom, a cumbersome leather-bound book in his arms. He laid it open on the oak table, pointing to an entry. "This is all there is."

Georges bent, squinting in the gloom. There indeed was her name, recorded in neat tiny script. But the heading at the top of the page . . .

The column was labeled "Deaths."

Georges traced the words with his index finger, reading them out loud. "Lili de Bizac, the fifth of May, seventeen ninety-three, in childbed." His voice cracked. "Oh, Lili." Ashamed of the tears that filled his eyes, he turned away and stumbled from the room.

Outside, he spurned his carriage. He had to walk and walk and walk, until his body was too tired to feel anything anymore. The tragedy overwhelmed him. *She's gone, my only love. For what purpose have I been living, then?*

The sunny summer day seemed like an insult. Georges wished it would rain and storm, echoing in nature the torment that filled his soul. Instead the birds were singing their hearts out and the parks were a riot of flowers and greenery. At last, worn out, he dropped onto a bench and let his head fall into his hands. When he looked up again, he spotted a young girl on a nearby bench, a sketchbook on her knee. She sat primly, her back straight as a rod, her pencil moving light and quick over the paper. *Oh, Lili,* Georges thought, his heart breaking. *Why did you have to die so young?*

He stood up to walk back to the carriage. Then he glanced again at the girl on the bench. Lili had died in childbirth. She was beyond his reach, but she'd left behind a son or daughter. There was only one thing Georges could do for Lili now. He could find the child and restore his or her birthright.

10

1809. Paris.

"Blow out the candles, Celeste!" voices urged gaily. "Make a wish!"

Celeste Chardin looked at the smiling faces crowded around her in the room behind the *boulangerie:* her adoptive mother and father and six brothers and sisters. "Yes, please hurry," said nine-year-old Gigi, the baby of the family. "I want a piece of cake!"

Everyone burst out laughing, including Celeste. She took a deep breath, then exhaled with all her might, extinguishing all sixteen candles on the cake. The Chardins clapped. "Now, who wanted the first piece of cake?" Celeste teased. "Was it you, Thomas?"

"No, no!" squealed Gigi, pushing past her brother and holding out her plate. "It was me!"

Marie handed Celeste a knife. "It seems a shame to

cut it," Celeste said. "I've never seen such a beautiful cake. Those sugar flowers! You're an artist, *Maman*."

"I only hope it tastes as good as it looks." Marie smiled fondly at her daughter. "Let's find out."

Soon the whole family was happily devouring the birthday cake. Then they showered Celeste with gifts. There was a summer-weight cloak, hand stitched by her mother; a new bonnet from her sisters; a necklace from her brothers. Even Gigi had made her a keepsake book of pressed flowers. "You are all too generous," Celeste declared, her deep green eyes sparkling with grateful tears. "This is the nicest birthday I can ever remember."

"How often does a girl turn sixteen?" said Jean-Luc, planting a paternal kiss on her cheek. "Congratulations, my child."

"Come, try on the bonnet," said Celeste's older sister, Natalie. "I can't wait to see it on you!"

Celeste stood in front of the looking glass with her sisters clustered around her. The green taffeta bonnet fit close to her head, its brim framing her fair curls. She tied the paler silk ribbon under her chin with a large bow. "What do you think?"

"It suits you perfectly!" cried fifteen-year-old Margaret.

"Just as we knew it would," agreed Natalie.

Celeste smiled at her sisters in the mirror. She couldn't help enjoying her reflection. The bonnet *was* becoming. Bright and summery, it made her eyes look even greener and more lustrous.

With her sisters right beside her, Celeste couldn't help reflecting on the contrast in their appearances. Though she went by the name Chardin, she knew, as did the others, that she wasn't related by blood to the people she considered her family. Physically she was like a swan among more humble fowl—tall, willowy, and exceptionally pretty with fair skin and golden hair, whereas the Chardins were plain and dark, stocky and short. *But good as gold in their hearts,* thought Celeste. *Raising me as their own, all these years* . . .

Her birthday always made Celeste slightly sad, though the Chardins made it a festive occasion. Of her real father she knew nothing, and the only memento she had of the mother who died giving birth to her was a locket with a miniature portrait. The Chardins never spoke of the events that brought Celeste into their home, but Celeste sensed they were somehow shameful.

Celeste tucked the new bonnet back into its box. "It's lovely, sisters," she said, giving them each a kiss on the cheek. "Promise you'll walk with me in the park tomorrow so I can show it off."

Her parents had been looking on indulgently. Now they beckoned Celeste over to them. "My dear, we have some news for you," Jean-Luc announced.

Celeste took a seat at her father's side. Folding her hands in her lap, she looked at him expectantly. Jean-Luc cleared his throat, then nodded to his wife. Marie too suddenly seemed at a loss for words. "What is it?" Celeste prompted.

"You're sixteen today," Marie began at last, taking her daughter's hand. "A woman. And though I wish I could keep you with me forever, it's time for you to make your own way in the world, as your older sister and brother have."

Celeste nodded. "I'm ready to work, *Maman*."

"There's a job for you, a very good one," Marie told her. "In the household of the Marquis de Bocage."

"Poplars is one of the great manors of Paris," contributed Jean-Luc.

"My cousin knows the housekeeper there," Marie went on. "Madame Lafitte is looking for a new maidservant, and when she heard of you from Claire, she thought you would satisfy admirably. You begin the day after tomorrow."

Celeste's heart contracted painfully. With difficulty she mustered a weak smile. "So soon, *Maman?* And such a grand house. How will I know what to do?"

Marie squeezed Celeste's hand. "You're a sensible, well-mannered, and hardworking girl. You'll be just fine."

"It's an excellent position," her father said.

Celeste couldn't help herself. She burst into tears. "But I don't want to leave you!" she sobbed.

Marie folded her in a warm hug. "Shhh. You can come home whenever you have a day off. Nothing will really change—the *boulangerie* will always be here. Do we not see Natalie and Richard frequently?"

Celeste nodded. "I'm sorry," she said, wiping

her tears on her handkerchief. "It sounds like a very good job. I'll make you proud of me," she promised, smiling tremulously at her parents.

Jean-Luc patted her smooth cheek with his rough hand. "We already are, my child."

At the de Bocage residence on the outskirts of Paris, Celeste's brother Richard unloaded her suitcase. After hugging her quickly, he jumped back into the wagon and cracked his whip. The team of horses plodded away down the poplar-lined drive.

Celeste stood where her brother had left her, staring up at the enormous brick-fronted house. She gulped, her throat dry as sawdust. *So many windows! It is as big as a cathedral!*

An elderly woman with a stooped back opened the front door and peered out at her. She wore a plain black dress and a white apron and cap. "You must be Celeste," she called. "I've been waiting for you. Come in, come in."

Suitcase in hand, Celeste trotted up the steps of Poplars. The two women exchanged curtsies. Then Madame Lafitte bustled down the wide hall, waving Celeste after her. "I'll introduce you to the other servants," she said, "and then the mistress. This way."

Celeste hurried after the housekeeper, her eyes darting from side to side. Through what seemed like countless doorways she glimpsed one splendid room after another. There were paintings on the walls in heavy gilt frames, elegant furniture covered with rich fabrics, curtains of velvet and lace, and carpets on every floor. Light poured through the tall windows, glinting off crystal chandeliers and china vases and statuary. *And ceilings three times as high as those at the* boulangerie! marveled Celeste.

The walk to the kitchen at the back of the house seemed about a mile long. Madame Lafitte clapped. In seconds five uniformed servants materialized and stood in a line, their manner formal and attentive. "Madame Roche, the cook," Madame Lafitte said briskly. "Genevieve and Annette, the maids. Claude and Guy, the under-butlers. My husband, Monsieur Lafitte, is the butler—you'll meet him later."

Celeste dropped a curtsy. The other servants stared appraisingly, but not one uttered a welcoming word. Genevieve and Annette, who appeared to be sisters, looked down their long noses in a superior fashion. Madame Roche frowned, eyeing Celeste from head to toe. "I hope she's not as picky about her meals as the last one," she said to Madame Lafitte with a sniff. "Some of these working girls put on the fanciest airs."

"I—I—I'm not in the least bit—" Celeste began, stuttering.

"Come along, I'll show you your room," Madame Lafitte said, whisking Celeste onward.

They climbed four flights of steep stairs, and Celeste got a quick look at a tiny, charmless room in the attic, furnished only with a narrow bed and a small chest of drawers. They returned to the ground floor by way of the main staircase. "The marquise is in the morning room this time of day," Madame Lafitte told Celeste, continuing at a breathless pace.

They halted outside a gracious, well-proportioned room. Celeste blinked at the rich beauty of the scene within. Warm morning light filtered through gauzy white curtains. An elegantly dressed woman sat at a mahogany writing desk while a girl about Celeste's age lounged on a velvet couch, stroking the head of a silky spaniel.

Neither woman rose when Madame Lafitte and Celeste entered. "This is Celeste Chardin, the new maidservant," the housekeeper announced respectfully. "If you need me, I'll be in the dining room, completing my inventory of the silver."

Celeste dropped a curtsy and then stood, silent and deferential. After an incredibly long pause the marquise spoke. "Madame Lafitte will outline your responsibilities," she informed Celeste in a sharp, frosty voice. Like the cook, she too seemed to find something objectionable in Celeste's appearance, though Celeste wore an unadorned gray dress with long sleeves and a modest neckline. "I insist that servants in my household perform their duties in near-invisible fashion," she continued. "You'll wear the uniform that Madame Lafitte provides for you. I do not want to see or hear you. Though of course when you are summoned, you will respond promptly."

Dumping the dog on the carpet, the girl on the

couch sat up. "I thought she was to be *my* maid, *Maman*," she said petulantly.

The marquise nodded. "Among other things you will attend to my daughter Emilie's wishes."

"There's a braided rope in my room," Emilie told Celeste, her tone haughty. "It rings a bell in the attic. You will come when I call. Instantly."

Celeste bowed her head in assent. Shifting her weight from one foot to the other, she waited to be dismissed. At last the marquise waved a bejeweled hand. "That's all. Get to work."

Celeste curtsied, then backed out of the room. As she ran in search of Madame Lafitte her heart was heavy. *The house is beautiful,* she thought, biting her lip to keep from crying. *But the people in it are cold as ice.*

Late that night Celeste sat on a hard wooden chair in the kitchen, nibbling a meal of cold meat and bread. The other servants had eaten long ago and retired to their own rooms. Celeste, however, had been running around, attending to Emilie all evening. The bell had jangled without ceasing. *I'll be hearing it in my dreams,* Celeste thought tiredly.

The sound of a footstep made her jump. When she saw it was only Madame Lafitte, she sank back in her chair with relief. "You did nicely today, Celeste."

Celeste forced a smile. "Thank you, ma'am."

"Mademoiselle Emilie is . . . high-spirited."

91

You mean a spoiled brat! Celeste thought. Out loud she said, "Yes, ma'am."

"Her older brother is away at university," commented Madame Lafitte.

Thank heavens. One less member of this terrible family to deal with! "Yes, ma'am," Celeste said again.

Madame Lafitte started to leave, then turned back for a moment. "I know it's hard, being away from home for the first time," she said, her usually brisk voice softening. "If you're ever lonely for your mother, come to me."

"Yes, ma'am," Celeste whispered, her throat tightening.

When she was alone once more, she could no longer hold back the tears. Madame Lafitte's kind words were meant to comfort her, but instead they had pushed her over the edge. Shoving back her chair, Celeste ran upstairs to her room. She threw herself down on the bed and buried her face in the pillow, sobbing.

Just days earlier she'd blown out the candles on her sixteenth birthday cake and the world had seemed like a beautiful package just waiting for her to open it. Now the future that stretched before her looked cheerless and lonely. "Why did I ever have to leave the *boulangerie*?" she cried.

11

"After dinner, Oiseleur, you must come out to the stables to see my new stallion," the marquis de Bocage said to his friend and business associate, Georges Oiseleur, who was dining with the family one Thursday night. "I want your opinion—I'm sure he is the finest animal I've ever laid eyes on."

Georges smiled. "If you're so certain of his quality, then you hardly need my confirmation."

The marquis laughed. "But you're an uncommon judge of horseflesh. I've never found a pair to match the bays that pull your curricle."

"I'll gladly tell you what I think of the beast," Georges declared. "But I want your word that if I pronounce him second-rate, you won't lose your temper and refuse me further invitations to dine at Poplars."

The marquise fluttered her eyelashes. "Monsieur

Oiseleur, you will always be welcome at our table. For in addition to horses, you are an enviable judge of wine. How else would I know what to serve my guests if you weren't here to advise me?"

Georges lifted his glass to her. The marquise was a snobby, conceited woman, and he knew that despite her flattery, she scorned his humble origins. But in polite society one never said what one really felt. Over the years Georges had become as adept as anybody at making gracious, meaningless conversation.

He did have a genuine affection for the marquis, a genial man fifteen years his elder. The marquis had given him his start in business and had always treated him like a favorite son. Georges's own parents were dead and his siblings scattered. *Despite the marquise and her insufferable daughter, I enjoy these meals*, Georges reflected. *This is the closest thing to a family I know.*

As one maid took away the soup plates two others carried in platters from which they began to serve the entrée and side dishes. Immediately Georges's eye was caught by one of the girls. She was tall and willowy, and her plain uniform couldn't disguise a stunning figure. Bright blond curls peeped from beneath her white lace cap. Her eyes were lowered respectfully, but when she glanced up, he glimpsed spectacular deep green eyes. He couldn't help but smile at her, and she smiled shyly back.

His gaze followed her as she left the room with her empty platter. *What is it about her?* he wondered. Her manner was that of a servant, not intended to draw attention. But her appearance was far from servile. Her posture was graceful, her step light. He didn't think he'd ever had the pleasure of observing such a beautiful creature. Except once. *That's it,* he realized, surprised. *Somehow she reminds me of Lili.*

Georges looked down at his wineglass, turning his gaze inward. Despite the passage of years he still couldn't think of Lili without pain. As he recalled his search for her, his fingers tightened on the stem of his glass. Nine years ago, on learning of her death in childbirth, Georges had gone to her husband, the Count de Bizac, only to hear the other man's sordid and cynical tale of his sham marriage to Lili, whose innocence and virtue he'd thoughtlessly destroyed. As for Lili's child, the count claimed to know and care nothing of its fate.

In his fury Georges had challenged de Bizac to a duel. Georges had wounded but not killed the scoundrel—small satisfaction. Then he'd spent nearly a decade looking all over Europe for Lili's child. At last he'd been forced to accept that he would never know what became of it.

"Yes, Oiseleur," the marquis was saying. He gestured with his fork for emphasis. "We count on you to choose our wine, rate our livestock, and generally keep us entertained." His eyes crinkled.

"It's our good luck that you're a confirmed old bachelor with nothing better to do."

Georges smiled. "Yes, my friend," he agreed. "Until I'm fortunate enough to find a partner who is in all ways as accomplished and admirable as your own, I'll remain eligible." He spoke lightly, knowing that the marquis couldn't guess how his teasing remark had stung. In his forties, Georges was still a handsome man, but there was a bitter sadness etched in the lines of his face. While the new maid, the one who reminded him of Lili, served cheese and fruit for dessert, Georges thought about the cold comforts of his own home. *I will always live alone,* he imagined, stifling a glum sigh. The manor would never be graced by the presence of a wife or brightened by the laughter of children.

"I'm very interested in your proposal," the marquis told Georges a few days later as they discussed business matters in the library of Poplars. "Leave the papers with me and tomorrow we'll discuss the amount I'd be willing to invest."

The two men talked for a few more minutes, then shook hands and bid adieu. As Georges was showing himself out, he saw a girl at the other end of the hall. Immediately he recognized the new maid with the blond curls. "Excuse me," he said, seizing the opportunity to exchange a few words with her.

"Sir?" she responded.

"I was wondering if . . ." He touched his cravat. "If I might trouble you for a glass of water."

"Certainly." She dropped a curtsy. "If you'd please to sit in the front parlor, I'll bring it to you right away."

Georges made himself comfortable in a wing chair in the sunny parlor. The maid returned with a glass. She was about to duck out of the room but stopped when he cleared his throat. "Thank you, um, er . . ."

She blushed prettily. "Celeste, sir."

"Celeste," he repeated. He gave her a friendly, encouraging smile. "So, Celeste. You're new to the household. This is a good place of employment, I trust?"

She lowered her eyes. "Yes, sir."

I imagine the marquise is a dragon to the servants, thought Georges. "What are your duties, child?"

"I help with meals and general housekeeping," Celeste told him. "And I wait on Mademoiselle Emilie."

Ah, Emilie. He sipped his water. *The little dragon!* "You have time to visit with your own family occasionally? To study, to exercise outdoors?"

"A little time. I haven't much schooling, sir," she confessed. "It's not necessary in my station in life."

"Hmmm." Georges contemplated her smooth,

youthful face. She was pretty and articulate but completely untutored—a blank slate. *I could give her one of my speeches,* he thought, *about the importance of universal education, but I'll spare the child!* "Thank you, Celeste. You may return to your work."

As he prepared to leave Poplars, Georges again found himself inexplicably thinking about Lili and about the children they might have had together—perhaps a daughter as lovely as Celeste. *Her life must be a hard one,* Georges imagined as he donned his top hat in the front hall, *with little leisure and few comforts.* For some reason he felt a fatherly concern for the young maidservant. *Perhaps I could do something for her,* he speculated. *I'll have a word with the housekeeper.*

Aching from exhaustion, Celeste walked slowly upstairs to the attic. It had been another long, discouraging day. She'd polished silver and swept floors, served meals and washed dishes. And whenever she had a moment to sit down and rest, Emilie rang the bell or shouted her name. Celeste had helped Emilie change her dress and hairstyle three times. She'd accompanied her on a stroll in the lane, carrying a heavy wool blanket for her to sit on as well as an armful of prickly holly branches Emilie had collected along the way.

She'd only been at Poplars two weeks, but it felt like two years. Celeste fought back tears. She wanted nothing more than to pack her box and run home to the *boulangerie* and the loving arms of her parents. She couldn't bear to disappoint them, though.

She pushed open the door to her room. As she set her candlestick on top of the chest of drawers, she blinked in surprise. "Somebody's been here," she said aloud. Three books lay on top of the chest, neatly stacked. Next to them a flaky pastry was wrapped in a linen napkin. Celeste stared at the pastry suspiciously, as if it might be poisoned. "What on earth . . . ?"

Whirling, she looked around her shadowy, cold room. In place of the plain, rough blanket that used to be on her bed, a quilted comforter billowed. Celeste walked forward. Tentatively she sat down on the edge of her bed, sinking deep into the fluffy, cloud-soft goose down.

Slowly a smile spread across her face. Springing to her feet, she ran back to the dresser and grabbed the napkin and its contents. She took a big bite of the sweet, fruit-filled pastry. It melted in her mouth—she'd never tasted anything so delicious. When it was gone, she licked every last crumb from her fingers. *It's like Christmas morning,* she thought. *Who did this?*

After washing her hands and face in the cold water in her basin, she put on her nightdress and let down her hair. She carried one of the books to bed. Snuggling under the comforter, she stroked the volume's rich leather binding. The Chardins had taught her the alphabet and how to write her own name, but they were not themselves literate, so Celeste had never learned to read. At that moment, however, she didn't care that she couldn't even decipher the book's title. *It's mine,* she thought with sleepy happiness, placing it on the mattress beside her.

"It's your afternoon off, you wretched thing," Genevieve said ungraciously one Wednesday. "All the more work for me and Annette."

Celeste could have pointed out that Genevieve and Annette both had already enjoyed afternoons off that week. "At least Mademoiselle Emilie is not at home," she reminded the other maids instead. "Your job will be easy without her to wait on."

She only had a few hours—not long enough to go home to visit her family. Putting on her cloak and bonnet, she hurried out of the house before anyone could think of one last chore for her to do. With a giddy feeling of freedom she ran into the wooded lane that separated Poplars from the neighboring house. It had rained that morning, and the grass was still dewy. Celeste drew in deep breaths of fragrant summer air as she strolled briskly along, swinging her arms.

Refreshed by her walk, she returned to the house with pink cheeks and bright eyes. Just a week earlier, the last thing she would have wanted to do on her free afternoon was retire to her gloomy chamber. But today she took the stairs to the attic three at a time.

Her room had become a bower of small luxuries. Celeste lounged on her bed, admiring her pretty surroundings. The room had been so bare when she first arrived at Poplars, like a prison cell! Now she possessed six books, a few with pictures that she looked at again and again. There were curtains of fine muslin at the window. A soft floral-patterned carpet covered the hard wood floor. Every day brought a new surprise. This afternoon's offering was a plump, fresh-baked muffin studded with currants. She ate it daintily, relishing every bite. *If only I knew who I ought to thank! Who is my benefactor or benefactress?* It was a baffling mystery, but a pleasant one. Whoever it was meant her no harm.

"I think it's Madame Lafitte," Celeste decided as she opened one of her books, an illustrated collection of verse. She recalled the housekeeper's expression when she asked about it. Madame Lafitte had denied any knowledge, but her eyes had darted away and a tiny smile pursed her lips. "Then again, maybe it's not." Some of the secret gifts had been lavish and expensive, beyond a housekeeper's means.

She was admiring the embroidery on the small pillow that had mysteriously appeared on her bed yesterday when a bell began to ring. Celeste smiled. *Emilie is home. Too bad for Genevieve!*

The bell rang again and again. It wasn't Celeste's duty to respond to the summons, so she didn't budge. The bell continued its insistent clanging. Then, after a minute's silence, Celeste heard footsteps pounding up the staircase. Without knocking, Emilie burst into Celeste's room. "You wicked girl!" Emilie shrieked, placing her hands on her hips. "How dare you laze about when I—" Emilie bit off her sentence. Blue eyes narrowed, she raked the small room with a penetrating and critical gaze. "Why, where did you get these things?" She grabbed the embroidered pillow off Celeste's bed.

"That's mine!" Celeste cried, snatching it back.

Emilie stomped over to the window and gave the curtain a tug. "This fabric. It's much too fine for a servant's room. You're stealing from us!"

"I am not!"

Emilie kicked at the new carpet. "Then you've taken a lover," she accused. "Somebody well-to-do. Do you expect him to carry you off on his white horse? Is that why you're lolling about up here, shirking your duties?"

Celeste's cheeks flamed. In the past, when her arrogant young mistress overstepped her bounds, Celeste had bitten her tongue. Now, for the first time, she found herself talking back. "I'm not shirking my duties," she declared. "This is my afternoon off, and if you need something, you can ask Genevieve or Annette. As for the rest, for your information feudalism is dead. I may be your servant, but I'm not your slave. I have a right to comfort and beauty, same as you."

Emilie stared at Celeste, her jaw hanging slack. She started to say something, then snapped her mouth shut. Spinning on her heel, she flounced out of the room, slamming the door behind her.

Celeste sank back onto the bed, one hand on her pounding heart. She was shaking, not so much from Emilie's remarks but from her own bold response. A shy, proud smile crossed her face. *I meant what I said,* she realized, amazed at herself. *I do* have rights, *and there are lines even my employers can't cross.* Until only recently she'd been cowed by Emilie and Emilie's even more intimidating mother. Where did this new self-esteem come from?

Celeste looked around the room at her new possessions. They were just material things, but they seemed to stand for something greater than themselves. They promised that her menial position at Poplars didn't have to be the end of her life's road. There was something better around the bend.

12

"Did you translate the Latin passages I assigned yesterday?" an attractive young woman in her midtwenties asked Emilie.

The family was in the drawing room after dinner. As was his frequent habit, Georges had joined them for the meal and now was savoring a glass of port and a pipe with the marquis. The two men sat in deep easy chairs, looking on as Emilie's tutor struggled to make headway with her uncooperative student.

"I did not," replied Emilie without a hint of apology in her voice. "I *hate* Latin. I see no point in it!" She appealed to her father. "Papa, no other girls of my acquaintance must study Latin."

"You study what Mademoiselle Grandet tells you to study," said the marquis, an indulgent smile belying the command.

"Then your poetry," attempted Solange Grandet,

unruffled. Georges couldn't help admiring her serenity . . . *and* her elegant figure, plentiful chestnut hair, and clear blue eyes. "Surely the other girls don't turn up their noses at romantic verse."

"I didn't read my poetry, and I didn't do my sums, and I didn't practice the piano." Emilie glared at her tutor defiantly. "I'll stop wasting your time if you stop wasting mine."

Surely Mademoiselle Grandet will lose her temper now, expected Georges. But Solange just smiled grimly. "We'll read poetry together, then."

"I lost my book," said Emilie.

"But I have another copy," countered Solange.

Emilie rose as if about to attempt an escape. Book in hand, Solange cornered her. Georges gave a silent cheer. *Bravo, mademoiselle!* The scene both amused and troubled him. *A private tutor, her own musical instruments, and so many books,* he thought. *Yet the spoiled child takes it all utterly for granted—nay, she outright scorns the privilege of learning!* When he himself was young, reading had inspired him to aim high. He recalled Celeste's confession. What did she make of the books Georges had asked Madame Lafitte to place in her room?

By providing her with some physical comforts, Georges had felt he'd done all he could to help Celeste. Now he studied Solange Grandet's calm, lovely profile, a new scheme forming in his mind. Emilie cared nothing for education. What would Celeste do with the same opportunity?

❋   ❋   ❋

Dressed for sleep, Celeste sat at the writing desk and chair that had mysteriously appeared in her room two days earlier, along with a quill pen, an inkstand, and a stack of white paper. One of her books lay open on the desk. Painstakingly she copied words from the book onto a sheet of paper, trying as she did to decipher their meaning. Just then there was a knock at the door. Quickly Celeste closed the book and covered up her unskilled handwriting. "Come in," she called.

She braced herself, expecting the rude and imperious Emilie. Instead a slender woman in a fawn-colored gown entered. She smiled kindly, her face framed with glossy chestnut curls. "I'm sorry to intrude," said Solange Grandet, eyeing the books and paper on Celeste's desk. "But perhaps I've chosen an opportune moment."

Celeste blinked. *"Pardonnez-moi?"* she managed to squeak.

Solange deposited her satchel on Celeste's bed. She shook it upside down, and a number of books tumbled out. "If you're not too tired, we might as well get started right away."

Celeste was still baffled. "Get started on what?"

Crossing to the desk, Solange placed a hand on Celeste's shoulder. "I've been sent," she said, "to teach you how to read."

A few weeks later Celeste and Solange were curled companionably on the plump couch in

106

Solange's apartment on the second floor of Poplars, a book propped between them. Celeste read haltingly, tracing the words on the page with her index finger. When she reached the end of the page, she looked up at Solange, her expression hopeful. Solange clapped. "Wonderful, Celeste! Not a single stumble. It's all coming together, isn't it?"

Celeste flushed, her heart swelling with joy and pride. "It's coming together," she agreed. "It's coming alive. Oh, Solange, I never imagined that books, which look so dull on the outside, could be so colorful on the inside!"

Solange gave her a quick hug. "Reading will open up a whole new world for you."

It already had. In just a few weeks Celeste's life had changed immeasurably. Her new books brought her more pleasure than anything she'd ever known, and she'd come to love Solange like a sister. She wasn't nearly as homesick for the *boulangerie*, and she found it much easier to tolerate the incessant demands of her employers.

"But Solange," said Celeste, closing the book. "I worry that tutoring me takes up too many hours— you have no time left for yourself."

"I enjoy our lessons," Solange replied sincerely. "Add to that the fact that I'm receiving a salary for tutoring you, and I have no reason for complaint."

"Who's paying you?" Celeste asked, devoured by curiosity.

"I'll answer as on the other occasions when

you've asked the same question. I can't tell you."

Celeste bounced on the sofa. "But I'll die if I don't find out!"

Solange laughed. "I'm sorry to hear that, for your sponsor wishes to remain anonymous."

"It can't be my master and mistress," Celeste mused. "They treat me like a piece of furniture. Then who?"

Solange just smiled.

They returned to their reading. Celeste made many mistakes, however, as she continued to puzzle over the mystery. *Will I ever know the truth?* she wondered.

There was definitely something different about Celeste. As he dined with the marquis, Georges noted it with secret satisfaction. *She carries herself with more confidence,* he decided. Her eyes weren't always glued to the floor—they sparkled with life. She looked happy.

After dinner, when the group retired to the drawing room, Georges took a turn about the room with Solange. When they were out of earshot of the others, he inquired in a low voice about Celeste's progress.

"She's doing remarkably well," Solange told him. "She's the most talented, delightful pupil I've ever had."

Georges smiled. "Especially in contrast to our Mademoiselle Emilie?"

Solange didn't reply, but her blue eyes twinkled.

"You'll continue to work with Celeste, then," said Georges.

"As long as she's willing," said Solange.

The marquis waved them over to the card table, putting an end to their private conversation. Solange declined a game of cards and, bidding the others good-night, retired to her apartment. Georges watched her go, his gaze appreciative. His first impression of Solange had been of loveliness and intelligence, and now to those he added the qualities of sweetness and generosity. He was gratified that he'd been able to improve Celeste's lot . . . and didn't mind at all that in so doing he'd improved his acquaintance with the charming Mademoiselle Grandet.

The summer day was warm. Celeste sat under a pear tree in the orchard behind Poplars, her back against the gnarled trunk. Cicadas buzzed in the leaves, butterflies fluttered among the tall grasses, and the air was ripe with birdsong, but she was aware of nothing but the words on the page before her. She had the afternoon off and planned to spend every free minute reading *Gulliver's Travels*.

She turned a page, too absorbed to notice the rattle of pebbles in the dirt lane running between the rows of fruit trees. A young man had tethered his chestnut horse nearby and was walking up to her. Celeste jumped to her feet, mortified at being caught in her master's orchard. "I—I was just leaving," she stammered, holding the book behind her back. "Excuse me, sir."

She hurried past him into the grassy lane. "You needn't go," he called after her. "It is you who should excuse me, for intruding upon your privacy. Please don't let me chase you off."

Slowly Celeste turned back. The stranger stood with his hat in his hand, an amiable smile on his face. He was so polite—and so handsome—it was impossible not to smile back. "Well . . . ," she murmured.

He gestured to the book in her hand. "What are you reading?"

"*Gulliver's Travels.*" Celeste eyed him shyly. He was dressed in a plain, dark suit of clothes—not a laborer, but not a nobleman either. *A clergyman?* she wondered. *A merchant, a clerk?* "In translation, of course. Do you know it?"

"Yes," he replied, "and I thought it the most remarkably interesting piece of literature I'd ever read."

"Oh, I feel just the same!" Celeste exclaimed. "The author's imagination—it is incredible."

"And the story works on so many levels. Entertainment, satire . . ."

They walked along the lane, side by side, chatting. Celeste found herself pouring out her opinions to this attentive young man. His comments were thoughtful and good-humored. As he asked her questions about her reading they discovered they preferred many of the same writers. "You know, I have a book in my saddlebag you might enjoy," he said when they turned to walk back the way they'd come. "I hope you'll let me—"

He broke off his sentence abruptly. In the distance they could hear the sound of a cart coming down the lane. "Forgive me, mademoiselle, but I must go." Seizing her hand, he lifted it swiftly to his lips and then, with a bow, strode off. Swinging up onto his horse, he kicked the animal into a canter. *"Au revoir,"* he called back to Celeste.

Horse and rider disappeared into the trees just as a team of oxen pulling a cart came into view. Celeste stood beside the lane, staring at the spot where she'd last seen the young man. Her cheeks were flushed and her eyes bright. He'd been so literary, so pleasant . . . and so remarkably good looking. Who was he?

That evening, just before dinner, Celeste watched Madame Roche taste the cream of celery soup for the tenth time. The cook wrinkled her nose. "The seasoning is still not right," she cried. "I am in despair!"

"But it's time to serve," said Madame Lafitte. Seizing a spoon, she sampled the soup herself. "It is delicious. What are you fussing about?"

"The young master is home from university," the cook reminded the housekeeper. "The food must be better than merely delicious. It must be perfect."

Genevieve and Annette, who like Celeste were waiting to serve the meal, rolled their eyes at each other. "Supposedly he's been Madame Roche's

111

special pet since he was an infant and she served him his porridge with a solid gold spoon," Annette whispered to Celeste.

Madame Roche carefully seasoned the soup, then tasted it again. At last she pronounced it acceptable. As Genevieve hoisted the soup tureen and Annette wielded a ladle, Celeste picked up a silver platter piled with breads. *All this bother because of one stupid boy*, she thought with a sigh. It certainly looked like Marc de Bocage was as spoiled as his younger sister, Emilie.

As she followed Genevieve into the dining room Celeste could hear that the family's conversation was more animated than usual. They all seemed to be talking at once. Emilie's laughter rang out frequently.

The other girls carried the soup to the foot of the table to serve the marquise first. Celeste walked forward, intending to set the platter in the center of the table. Curious, she shot a glance at the new arrival, only to find him looking at her too. As their eyes met, Celeste gave a start. The platter slid from her fingers and crashed to the floor.

His face was not unfamiliar to her. Marc de Bocage, son of the marquis and marquise, heir to Poplars and the rest of the family's immense estate, was the young man she'd met in the orchard that afternoon.

13

After dinner the family retired to the drawing room. Marc de Bocage leaned against the mantel, a glass of cognac in his hand. "It's good to be home," he remarked.

"I wish you were here all the time," complained Emilie. "It's so dull without you. But education is making you *much* too serious. Wherever did you get that horrible suit?"

Her brother laughed. "I'm at university to improve my mind, not worry about my wardrobe."

"I didn't know that in order to be smart, one also had to be ugly." His sister sniffed.

"One doesn't," he agreed. "But I've observed that people preoccupied with fashion usually have little else to recommend them."

Emilie tipped her head to one side as if trying to decide whether he'd just complimented or insulted her. *Too bad* she *can't go to university,* Marc thought, amused. If anyone needed mental improvement, it was Emilie. Not that a girl required a university education to be thoughtful and interesting. Marc's smile faded as he recalled his astonishment at the dinner table. The girl who'd captured his heart in a few quick minutes that afternoon in the orchard was one of his family's servants! *Poor thing got quite a scolding when she dropped that platter,* he thought, chagrined. *She was just as shocked as me. I'd have spared her the surprise, if only I'd anticipated it.*

"Father, I want to sit down with you later and catch up on the news of the estate," Marc said.

"Not much is new," the marquis replied, swirling the cognac in his glass. "I'm investing some capital in a textiles venture of Oiseleur's. You might be interested in hearing about that from him directly."

"Yes." Marc stroked his chin, trying to think of a roundabout way to ask what he wanted to know. "As for the household, it appears . . . rather, I noticed . . . ahem. You've hired a new servant or two?"

"We replaced a pair that left," his mother informed him. "That wretched Monique who continually scorched the linens when ironing and her good-for-nothing husband."

"The new girl," said Marc. "She is, uh, working out satisfactorily?"

"I think Celeste is as useless as Monique," Emilie contributed. "She's stubborn and slow. She never gets my bathwater hot enough, and she has no skill at hairdressing. She reads books in her room, you know!"

The marquis chuckled. "A capital crime, I'm sure."

"I've had no complaints from Madame Lafitte," his wife drawled languidly. "She seems neat and quiet enough to me and tolerably efficient, despite that unfortunate incident in the dining room this evening."

Emilie scowled. "Well, *I* dislike her. She's . . . she's . . ."

Everything you're not, Marc could have said. He bit his tongue.

Later, when his family had retired, he remained in the drawing room, a book open on his knee. He couldn't concentrate on his reading, however. *Celeste.* The name ran through his mind like water in a brook, light and lilting. He kept conjuring up visions of her exquisite face. And she was not only pretty—she was intelligent and charming too. And sweet and unpretentious and . . .

Stop right there, Marc commanded himself sternly, slamming his book shut. He'd made a mistake in the orchard that afternoon. Now that he knew the truth about Celeste, he mustn't indulge this attraction. *No more foolishness. She's a servant—she isn't for you.*

115

*   *   *

In the kitchen two days later Celeste dropped a crystal goblet she'd been drying, catching it just before it hit the floor. "You're absentminded today," Madame Lafitte scolded, but not harshly. She took the goblet from Celeste. "Here, let me finish. You get started on the sweeping."

Broom in hand, Celeste retreated from the kitchen, thankful to be out from under Madame Lafitte's eagle eyes. For two days she hadn't been able to do anything right. She'd placed the spoons where the forks should be when setting the table and knocked over a vase of flowers while dusting. Curling Emilie's hair with a hot iron, she'd burned a lock right off her mistress's head. She couldn't stop thinking about Marc, and she was in such a spin simultaneously trying to avoid him and hoping to run into him that she couldn't walk straight.

She'd relived their meeting in the orchard a hundred times. *I should have guessed his identity,* she thought now as she swept out the back hall. But how could she? He was so different from the rest of his family—so understated in his dress, and not at all pompous or lordly. He was interested in books and ideas. And he was funny too—he'd made her laugh.

Celeste lifted a hand to her forehead, brushing the curls from her face and blushing as she remembered how freely she'd spoken with him before she knew who he was. Marc had clearly

116

been surprised to see her in a maid's uniform, serving dinner. *He must think me shamelessly bold, wandering about his father's property and making conversation with strangers,* thought Celeste. She sighed. There was one thing to be thankful for—apparently he hadn't mentioned the encounter to anyone. She hadn't gotten into trouble over it.

Celeste made her way to a side wing of the house, where the music room and some sitting rooms were located. Bent over her broom, for a moment she didn't realize she wasn't alone in the hall. "Good morning, Celeste," someone greeted her.

She jumped, the broom flying from her hands. Marc hurried to retrieve it, returning it to her with a bow. "Sorry," he said with a rueful smile. "I keep startling you, don't I?"

Celeste ducked her head as she took the broom. "Thank you, sir."

She expected Marc to go on his way. Instead he rocked back on his heels, hands in his trouser pockets. "I hope you don't feel . . . what I mean is . . . I liked talking to you about books the other day," he finally blurted.

Celeste blushed. "I did too," she said softly. "But I know I shouldn't have been in the orchard."

He waved a hand dismissively. "You live at Poplars, don't you? You have the same right as any of us to walk the grounds. I assure you, I didn't think anything of it."

"Thank you, sir."

"Well. I'll let you get back to your work. But I hope next time I see you," he said with a smile, "you'll have a book in your hand."

Celeste couldn't help smiling back. "Thank you, sir."

They were still standing awkwardly in the hall, not looking at each other but somehow unwilling to part, when Emilie appeared, a sheaf of piano music in her hand. At the sight of his sister Marc bowed to Celeste and hurried off.

Emilie looked after her brother, her eyebrows arched quizzically. Then she turned to Celeste. In one quick glance she took in the servant girl's flushed cheeks and shining eyes. "What were you doing just now?" Emilie demanded.

"Nothing, ma'am," mumbled Celeste, vigorously plying her broom.

"Stop that sweeping," Emilie ordered. "I'm speaking to you!"

Celeste obeyed, her eyes on the floor.

"You should be working, not flirting with my brother, you lazy girl," Emilie berated Celeste.

"I wasn't—"

"And don't talk back to me!" Emilie's eyes flashed with fury. "Perhaps you think you're a fine lady, *Mademoiselle* Celeste," she said with heavy sarcasm, "sleeping on goose down and satin and learning your ABCs. But you are not and never will be mistress of the manor. Don't you dare forget your place!"

118

Celeste bit her lip.

"Did you hear me? Did you *hear* me?" Emilie shrieked.

"Yes, ma'am," Celeste said, almost inaudibly.

Emilie stared at her for a long moment. Then, apparently satisfied by Celeste's submissive attitude, she stomped off into the music room.

When Emilie was gone, Celeste lifted her eyes. They were brimming with tears. She remembered how quickly she'd retorted the other day, when Emilie barged into her room and accused her of stealing. Today Celeste had been speechless, too confused by her own feelings to defend herself. *Besides, maybe Emilie is right,* she thought. *Maybe I am forgetting my place.*

"You're not concentrating," Solange observed as Celeste stumbled over vocabulary that she usually didn't find difficult. "Is something bothering you?"

Celeste couldn't lie to her beloved tutor. "Yes," she confessed. "Something's happened and I don't know what to do."

"If you tell me about it, perhaps I can help," offered Solange.

Celeste bit her lip. "It has to do with . . ." She couldn't come right out and say that she'd fallen head over heels in love with the young master of the house. "I've been thinking about the Revolution."

Solange laughed. "My. How serious!"

"I know it changed society tremendously,"

Celeste said. "There's something I don't understand, though. If the Revolution made all men and
women equal, why are there still rich people and
poor people? Masters and servants?"

Solange looked grave. "Society *did* change, but
it didn't start over from scratch. We can't return to
the Garden of Eden. Maybe it's more accurate to
say people are *more* equal than they were. The
boundaries of class are still there, but they're more
fluid. Take our friend Georges Oiseleur. He was
born a peasant and now he's the best educated,
most successful man of my acquaintance."

Celeste nodded, though Solange's remarks hadn't
cheered her up. *It's nice that Monsieur Oiseleur
has done so well, but if you ask me, the Revolution
didn't make a difference for the rest of us,* she
thought, miserable. The Chardins would spend the
rest of their lives working hard just to make ends
meet. Meanwhile Marc and Emilie had been born
to wealth and comfort, as had countless generations of de Bocages before them.

They continued the lesson, but Celeste's heart
wasn't in it. What good would it do her, learning to
read and write? There would always be an unbridgeable gulf between her and Marc de Bocage.

Marc sat at the dining-room table, trying to
catch Celeste's eye as she served dessert, a pear
tart with sweet whipped cream. But Celeste's eyes
remained downcast, her face expressionless. *Good*

girl. She knows her place better than I know mine, he thought glumly. *Dash it, though, I just want one of her pretty smiles. Why doesn't she look at me?*

He'd tried everything he could think of to rid himself of this infatuation. He'd spent the past ten days busy about the estate, riding and hunting, calling on neighbors and friends, accepting each and every social invitation that came his way. The highlights of every day, though, were his chance encounters with Celeste. Not that chance had anything to do with it—he sought her out on purpose. *And why wouldn't I?* he asked himself. *She's the brightest, sweetest, most poised and beautiful young woman I've ever met!*

Marc knew that in the old days, a man in his position wouldn't have hesitated to exercise his *droit de seigneur* and seduce such a girl, then cast her aside when his fancy passed. But Marc valued honor above all other virtues. He could never take advantage of Celeste's innocence and relative powerlessness.

Celeste had left the room. Marc took a bite of the tart, not really tasting it. "I want to throw a ball, Papa," Emilie was saying. "Twice as big and ten times as grand as the one at the Thibaults's the other night. May I?"

"Twice as big and ten times as grand." Her father's eyes twinkled. "That adds up to twenty times as expensive, wouldn't you say?"

"Oh, Papa, don't be stingy," cried Emilie. "I *will*

give a ball and it *must* be the most elegant and talked-of social event of the season. Why bother otherwise?"

"Well, if you will and it must, then far be it for me to stand in the way," the marquis said agreeably.

Marc hadn't been paying attention to his sister's idle chatter, but now his attention was arrested. A ball . . . "I think it's a fine idea, Emilie," he spoke up. "I'll tell you what—I'll help you host it. We'll invite absolutely everyone."

His sister clapped. "We'll have such fun!" she squealed.

"Such fun," Marc agreed. He didn't explain why he was really volunteering to help with Emilie's party. *It will be the perfect occasion,* he decided. *I'll pick the prettiest girl there . . . and forget Celeste Chardin forever.*

14

"I've never polished so much silver, "Genevieve groaned.

"Or washed so many goblets and plates," said her sister.

"Or prepared so much food, or mopped so many floors, or ironed so much linen," contributed Celeste.

The household had been in a flurry for days preparing for the ball. The guests would start arriving in just a few hours. The three maids were in the kitchen, snatching a moment's rest and nibbling a quick meal since they knew they wouldn't have time for dinner later. Just as Celeste plucked a grape from a juicy cluster, someone shouted for her. "Celeste!" Emilie shrieked. "Come here this minute! You still need to do my hair. And where are my clean petticoats and stockings?"

"Lucky Celeste," said Annette with a giggle.

Genevieve smirked. "To be chosen to dress Her Royal Highness!"

Reluctantly Celeste dragged herself upstairs to Emilie's chamber. Emilie was rushing around the room in her dressing gown. "Now, Celeste," she lectured, shaking a hairbrush for emphasis, "make sure you curl my hair right this time. Last time it was too much and I looked an awful fright."

Mustering all her patience, Celeste attended to Emilie's many demands. It seemed Emilie couldn't make a single decision about her attire, button a single button, tie a single bow without Celeste's assistance. The whole time she prattled excitedly about the upcoming festivity. "It's my ball and so I'll need to make sure everyone's having a good time, but I don't intend to miss a single dance," Emilie announced, adjusting the froth of lace at the neckline of her blue high-waisted gown. "I don't know, though. Should I give the first two dances to Robert or Claude? Robert is richer, but Claude is handsomer. Then of course there is Alain." Emilie preened in front of the mirror. "*He* has had his eye on me forever. And I used to think he was boring, but ever since he took his world tour . . ."

Celeste tuned Emilie out. A few minutes later, though, a remark of Emilie's grabbed her attention. "It will really be so much fun, hosting this party with my brother," Emilie mused. "He's as fine a dancer as any I've seen and will never lack for a partner. The girls always flock around him like butterflies. I wonder who he'll favor tonight? Maybe he's finally ready to choose a wife." Emilie tipped her head to one side, considering. "Will it be Josephine or Michelle? Perhaps Paulette. She has a considerable fortune and the prettiest figure imaginable. But Madeleine is pretty *and* smart. Yes, Madeleine will be the one."

Emilie sat on the edge of the bed, extending her feet one at a time so Celeste could put on her shoes. Celeste bent her head, glad to hide her face from her mistress. She didn't want Emilie to guess how close she was to tears at the thought of Marc dancing with a string of admiring women, each one richer, prettier, and more accomplished than the last. *I might as well face facts—he'll dance with all the girls,* Celeste told herself mournfully, *and maybe even marry one of them.* Marc de Bocage would never be hers.

Celeste paced her room, an unopened book in her hand. It was warm in the attic and she'd opened her window to get a breeze. The sound of music and muted laughter wafted in on the cooling night air. Throwing her book on the bed, she ran to kneel by the window. Looking down, she saw some people in the garden, the three women in pale, shimmering dresses. The windows of the adjacent ballroom blazed with light. There was more conversation and laughter, then the men took the women's arms and escorted them back inside. The courtyard was empty.

On an impulse Celeste jumped to her feet. She ran down to the ground floor, her steps light and soundless. Outside she tiptoed through the garden, careful to stay in the shadows. *If anyone should catch me out here in my maid's uniform!* she thought, her pulse racing. *I'll just take one quick look.*

There was a window at the edge of the courtyard where she could stand hidden by some shrubbery. Easing closer to the house, she put her face near the panes of glass. What she saw took her breath away. The ballroom was filled with people, all brightly and richly dressed. Celeste stared at the gowns, fingering the fabric of her own plain cotton dress. Silks the color of cream and butter and satins in rich jewel hues. *And gold and diamonds in their hair and on their wrists and at their throats,* Celeste marveled. *Oh, how lovely!*

She glimpsed Emilie, smiling flirtatiously as she danced with a dashing young man in a blue coat. Then Marc came into view. Celeste's heart throbbed. There were many elegant men in the room, but without question Marc was the handsomest. He wore close-fitting, light gray trousers, a plain black coat, and a vest with little ornamentation. The simplicity suited him.

Marc stepped through the dance sedately,

smiling down at his partner. With wistful envy Celeste gazed at the lucky girl in his arms. *Such bright red hair—it's not at all pretty,* she thought, eager to find fault. *And she's very short. Dumpy too!* Then Celeste sighed. Why did she kid herself? The girl was attractive, plump and rosy, beautifully dressed, and probably rich and clever to boot.

A lump formed in her throat. What had these people done to deserve their good fortune? Why was it her lot to be on the outside, looking in? "It's not fair," she whispered, dashing a tear from her cheek.

"I do believe your sister is the prettiest girl here," Michelle du Pont said to Marc as they danced. "I wouldn't be at all surprised if she finds a husband soon."

"She's only sixteen," Marc said. "I think she has some growing up to do first."

"I suppose *you* have ideas as to how she might improve herself," Michelle teased.

"Through reading and reflection," Marc replied seriously. Michelle's tone was lighthearted, but for some reason he wasn't in the mood to answer in kind. "A pretty face isn't worth much if it masks an idle mind."

Michelle laughed. "You're very stern. Your own wife will be a bookworm, then, always quoting Scripture and the like?"

Marc made an effort to smile. "I hope she'll be

well read," he responded, "but of course I'll only expect sermons on Sundays."

As they continued to dance Marc wondered impatiently when the music would end. His feet felt heavy as lead, and he'd never been so restless and distracted at a party. His own party, no less! Michelle was very pretty, with plentiful auburn hair and lively blue eyes, and her conversation was amusing. An only child, she'd inherit a sizable fortune one day. She was just the sort of girl he knew he should be looking for. *But I'm only going through the motions,* Marc realized. *Her beauty is utterly wasted on me. She might as well be an ugly old crone—I'm not the least bit attracted to her.* As far as he was concerned, the ball was a complete failure. Not one of his partners had pleased him. Not one lived up to the secret standard he'd set for himself.

He'd engaged Michelle for two dances. Now the music changed to a waltz. As they whirled around the room Marc's gaze wandered. Suddenly his heart leaped. In the far corner of the ballroom an angelic face peeped forlornly through a window. Marc blinked, thinking he must be seeing things— that his buried desire had conjured up this vision. But no. It was really her. "Celeste," he exclaimed.

"Pardon me?" said Michelle, startled.

Marc had stopped dead in his tracks. He gave Michelle a quick bow. "Forgive me. There's something I must attend to." Abandoning his partner in the middle of the dance floor, he raced for the door. The face at the window had disappeared, but he knew she couldn't have gone far. *I must find her,* he thought. He'd denied his feelings long enough.

Celeste stumbled away from the window, clutching her skirts to keep them from tangling in the shrubbery. *You fool!* she berated herself. She hadn't meant to stand there so long, but she'd become entranced. Now her young master was coming after her, no doubt to lecture her for her impropriety.

Celeste ran through the garden. "Wait!" Marc called. She kept running. He caught her just as she ducked under the grape arbor. "Celeste," he said, putting a hand on her arm. "Please don't run away from me."

They stopped at the edge of a small pool, dappled with water lilies and moonlight. At his touch a warm flush stole up Celeste's throat to her face. "I—I'm sorry," she stammered, her eyes turned away. "I didn't mean to intrude. I only wanted—"

"Shhh," Marc murmured. "It's all right." They were standing so close, she imagined she could hear his heart pounding as fast as her own. Finally she summoned the courage to look at him.

He was gazing at her not with anger but with love. For a long, breathless moment they stared into each other's eyes. Celeste knew she should have kept running. She didn't belong here. But before she could move, Marc pulled her to him, wrapping his arms tightly around her.

She did the only thing she could . . . what she wanted more than anything she'd ever wanted in her life. She tipped her face and he brought his mouth to hers in a fierce, hungry kiss. It was a kiss that set her whole body on fire, a kiss that took them out of themselves and made the rest of the world disappear.

15

The afternoon sun filtered through the leaves of the fruit trees, speckling the orchard with gold. Celeste stood under the pear tree where Marc had found her reading a few weeks ago, twisting her apron nervously in her hands. Her eyes were glued to the lane that led back to the manor. *Will he come?* she wondered.

She should have been exhausted—she hadn't slept a wink the night before—but adrenaline coursed through her veins, invigorating her. After the kiss in the garden Marc had whispered in her ear, "Tomorrow at three, in the orchard. Our place. I'll meet you there," he'd promised.

She'd lain awake in her bed until the sounds of the party faded and the night grew quiet. As the sky brightened with dawn, her eyes remained wide open. She could still feel the warmth of Marc's arms around her, the exciting pressure of his lips on hers. Was he lying awake too, thinking of her?

She was so full of her secret, she'd barely been able to attend to her chores that day. What if she saw him? How would she act? But their paths hadn't crossed, and now it was three o'clock, and she'd left her broom and feather duster to sneak off to the orchard.

The minutes passed. Soon it was a quarter past the hour. Celeste paced near the tree. *What could be keeping him?* she fretted, chewing a fingernail. All of a sudden a horrible possibility occurred to her. For her, the kiss in the garden had been a declaration of love. But what if Marc had just been playing games? Celeste's heart went cold. *Maybe to him it was just a stolen kiss with a servant girl. He never meant to keep our rendezvous at all.* A tear glittered in her eye. How could she have been so stupid? Of course he wasn't in love with her!

Her despairing thoughts were interrupted by the sound of galloping hooves. A horseman appeared in the lane. Celeste sank into the shadows of the pear tree, not daring to hope. But as the rider drew near she saw that it was really him.

Marc jumped from the horse, letting the reins fall to the ground. "Celeste," he said, his voice shaking with emotion. She went into his arms joyfully. The kiss was even more passionate than the one the night before. They drew apart just long enough to catch their breath, then kissed again, more slowly and sweetly.

Still locked in an embrace, they fell laughing

onto the fragrant green grass beneath the pear tree. "I can't believe I'm holding you," Marc said in amazement, tracing the lines of her face with his finger. "Beautiful, adorable Celeste."

"It's like a dream," she agreed, snuggling against him.

Marc propped himself up on one elbow. "I thought you wouldn't be here," he confided.

"I thought *you* wouldn't!"

They both smiled. "I hope you're not mad at me," he said. "I don't want you to feel I took advantage of you last night."

She shook her head. "I don't. I feel . . . happy."

Marc pulled her close again. "Oh, Celeste."

The moment was unbelievably tender. A lump formed in Celeste's throat. "We shouldn't be together like this," she managed to choke out. "If anyone discovers us—"

"I don't care if they do."

"But I'm just a servant and you're—"

"It doesn't matter," he insisted.

Celeste shook her head sadly. "You know that's not true."

At last Marc sighed. "You're right," he admitted. "You and me . . . it's crazy. But it's also wonderful."

She rested her head on his chest. "What are we going to do?"

"I don't know," Marc said, stroking her hair. "I don't know."

❖   ❖   ❖

As he entered the lane to the orchard Marc held his horse to a slow trot. He needed time to think. Every day for two weeks he and Celeste had met at their secret place by the pear tree. They'd kiss, then walk for a while, then kiss some more. They talked about everything under the sun. *Everything except the future,* Marc thought. *Because for us there* is *no future.*

"Today is the day I tell her," he said out loud. "We can't continue like this. It's not fair to lead her on since I could never marry her." His family was starting to wonder why his courtship of Michelle du Pont wasn't proceeding more briskly. The marquise made it clear she expected an engagement before summer's end. If they found out about Celeste . . . the scandal!

Marc tied the horse at the gate and entered the orchard on foot. He walked in from a different direction than usual to take Celeste by surprise. He saw her sitting under the pear tree, her back against the trunk and a book open on her knee. Her white lace cap lay in the grass—her blond hair shimmered in the sun.

Marc drew in his breath sharply. *Just as beautiful as she was the day I first saw her,* he thought. And something else hadn't changed since then. From that first conversation he'd been in love with her, deeply and truly. His feelings for Michelle du Pont weren't even a pale shadow of that love— they were nothing. *Celeste owns my heart*

134

completely, Marc recognized, *and she always will.*

She looked up then and saw him. Lifting her hand, she waved gaily. Marc hurried to Celeste's side, his resolution to break things off with her abandoned.

The next night Celeste sat before the mirror in her room, brushing her hair. When it was loose, it fell down to her waist in rippling golden waves. She gazed at her reflection, hardly recognizing her own face. The light in her eyes, her smile, the color in her cheeks . . . *I look so different,* she marveled. *Why doesn't everyone notice?* But of course she was on her guard around the staff, and especially in the presence of Marc's family. They must never, ever guess the truth.

Celeste put down the brush with a sigh. The secrecy was the hard part. She was filled with such joy, she wanted to tell the whole world. Instead she was sworn to silence. It was worth it, though. She remembered what she'd said to Marc the day after the ball, that their love was like a dream. When they were together, they looked ahead only as far as their next meeting, never speaking of the day after tomorrow. Past and future disappeared—they were suspended in a timeless present. *It* is *a dream,* thought Celeste, *and I never want to wake up because when I do—*

Her thoughts were interrupted by a quiet knock on the door. She stood, pulling her dressing gown closed at her throat. "Who is it?" she called out, startled.

"Celeste, it's me," a low voice said. "Marc."

Celeste hurried to the door, her heart racing. Marc had never been to her room before. "Come in," she whispered after a moment's hesitation.

Marc slipped into the room, shutting the door carefully behind him. Celeste took in his appearance: the passionate glitter in his eyes, the loosened collar, his disheveled hair. When he moved forward as if to embrace her, she instinctively stepped back. "W-Why are you here?" she stammered, her cheeks splotched with crimson. Did he want to take their relationship further than it had thus far gone? Since he couldn't be her husband, did he want to become her lover?

Her surprise grew when instead of reaching for her, Marc went down on one knee in front of her. Then he took her hands in his. "I'm sorry to intrude upon you like this, Celeste," he apologized, his eyes fixed hopefully on her face, "but once I made up my mind, I couldn't wait until morning to ask you. I've already waited too long. Release me from this torment—say you'll be my wife." Celeste stared, her eyes round with wonder. "I know this is unexpected," Marc went on. "My family will probably cast me off without a penny. But I don't care. I'll be happy if I have you."

Celeste sank down on the edge of her bed, moved beyond words. *He loves me even more than I ever imagined!* she realized. Tears filled her eyes. *And I love him too. So much.*

She put out a hand, lightly touching his hair.

136

Marc looked up at her expectantly. "Will you?" he asked. "Will you marry me?"

She found her voice and gave the only answer she could. "No."

Marc's footsteps receded down the hall. Celeste heard a ghostly creak on the staircase. Then dead silence settled over Poplars.

He had begged her to change her mind, but she'd insisted that he leave. Finally, his expression despairing, he'd said good night. Now Celeste paced her room, her eyes wild. *Did I do the right thing,* she wondered, *saying no to the man I love?* Second thoughts crowded in on her. She lay down but couldn't sleep. Rising again, she took her candle and crept out into the hall and down the stairs, following Marc's footsteps.

On the second floor she tiptoed past the room she knew to be Marc's. Entering another wing of the house, she stopped outside Solange Grandet's door. She had to knock a few times before Solange, who'd been asleep, heard her and came to the door. "Celeste, what is it?" Solange asked in a worried tone.

In response Celeste burst into tears. Solange slipped an arm around Celeste's shoulders and pulled her into the apartment. With a blanket wrapped around her and a cup of warm milk in her hands, Celeste felt strong enough to tell Solange the whole complicated story. Solange listened, her gray eyes full of sympathy. "I should have guessed," she interjected at one point. "Oh,

Celeste, you should have come to me sooner!"

"I'm not in trouble," Celeste assured her, wiping her eyes on Solange's handkerchief. "We never . . . Marc is too honorable. He wants to *marry* me, Solange!"

"It's like a fairy tale," Solange said.

"Yes, but fairy tales have no place in the real world." Celeste's chin trembled. "I love Marc and he loves me. But if I marry him, I'll ruin his life."

"He doesn't appear to see it that way," Solange pointed out.

"Because he hasn't really thought it through," Celeste argued. "He says he wouldn't mind losing his inheritance, but I know how hard life is for people who have nothing." She lost her struggle for composure and more tears spilled down her face. "How can I be the one responsible for depriving him of all he deserves?"

For a few minutes the two women sat in heavy silence. Solange stroked Celeste's hair. When Celeste was calm again, Solange said, "If you want my advice, I'll gladly give it. But I sense that you've already made up your mind."

Celeste nodded. "I have," she said, calm now and more determined than ever. "I'm sure in the morning he'll have thought better of his impetuous offer. He's a great man and I am merely a servant. It can never be."

Solange kissed Celeste on the cheek and bade her good night. Back in her own room Celeste snuffed the candle, crawled into bed, and cried herself to sleep.

16

For a week Celeste ran or hid every time her path crossed Marc's. Finally Marc cornered her in the back hallway. "I won't take no for an answer, Celeste," he declared. "I love you. Tell me you've had a change of heart—tell me you'll marry me."

"My heart is as it was," she choked out. "I love you too, but nothing else has changed. It's impossible. You must leave me alone. *Please*."

Shaking his hand from her arm, she ducked into the kitchen, with her apron pressed to her tear-filled eyes. Marc stomped in the other direction, raking a hand through his hair. "I can't bear this," he muttered. "When we love each other so devotedly, why should our happiness remain out of reach?"

Retreating to the music room, he sat down at the piano and struck a somber, minor-key chord. For a week he'd tried to persuade Celeste that marriage would bring them nothing but joy. She, however, remained convinced that his parents would disinherit him. *She's so sweetly unselfish,* Marc thought, picking out some more cheerful notes. *She thinks only of what's best for me.*

He'd had a week to change his own mind about wanting to marry Celeste, but with every passing day his love grew stronger. *My love is as deep as hers, but is my courage?* he wondered. It was time to put it to the test. He found his parents in the salon. "*Maman,* Papa," he began, "I must speak with you."

"What is it?" asked the marquise.

"I have decided to marry," he announced.

"Wonderful!" his mother cried, opening her arms for a hug. "Oh, I shall dearly love to have Michelle as a daughter-in-law."

The marquis beamed. "It will be a fine thing to join our two families. Congratulations, son."

"You misunderstand me," Marc said. "Michelle is not to be my bride."

"Not Michelle?" The marquise frowned. "Then who?"

"Celeste," Marc answered. "Celeste Chardin."

Both his parents gaped. "The maid?" exclaimed the marquis. "Are you joking with us?"

"I'm perfectly serious, Papa," Marc declared. "We'll be married as soon as I obtain her consent, and I'll be able to do that if you will bless our union first."

"Have you gone mad?" his father replied. "Bless the union between my heir and a *servant*?"

The marquise's complexion went from chalk white to a furious beet red. "That shameless girl!" she screeched. "What a devious scheme. She seduced you—is she pregnant? We'll take care of her, get her out of the way. But *marriage?* Out of the question!"

"She's not pregnant," Marc said. "I've treated her as I would any other well-bred young woman of my acquaintance—with honor and respect. And this was no scheme of hers. I fell in love with her naturally and inevitably because she is lovely, smart, and good."

The marquise clapped her hands to her ears. "I won't listen to this. Marc, you will never broach this subject again!"

"On the contrary, *Maman,* I won't drop it until I have my way."

The marquis strode across the room. Placing both hands on Marc's shoulders, he gave him a hard shake. "You'd better think twice about this, my boy. The match is disgraceful. Beneath you. I won't even consider it."

Marc shrugged off his father's hands. "I'll marry her with or without your approval," he persisted defiantly.

"It will be without, then," stated the marquis, his voice grim. "Without my approval *and* without a penny of my fortune."

Marc looked from his father to his mother and back again. Both their faces were set in implacable lines. "Fine," he said, trying to sound braver than he felt. "Good-bye, sir. Madame."

He bowed curtly. As he strode from the room his mother called after him, her voice small and choked. "Reconsider, Marc." He didn't turn back.

Outside in the garden Marc stood by a sculpted hedge, breathing deeply. The interview had gone even worse than he'd feared. His parents would never yield. *Celeste was right,* he thought. *If I marry her, I'll lose everything else.* He was still willing to make the sacrifice, but would she let him?

Later that evening Celeste was up to her elbows in soapy water, washing the dinner plates, when Genevieve burst into the kitchen. "Celeste!" she squeaked. "What have you done? The marquise wants to see you in her sitting room. Right this instant!"

Genevieve continued to pester her for an explanation, but Celeste kept her lips pressed tightly together as she rinsed the plate she'd been holding, then dried her hands on a towel. Straightening her cap and apron, she hurried to the marquise's sitting room. At the door her nerves failed. What could the marquise want? It couldn't be anything good. Marc had been absent at dinner that night, and the atmosphere between the marquis and marquise had seemed tense.

Celeste knocked timidly. "Come in," the marquise commanded. Celeste stepped into the room, standing just inside the door. The marquise beckoned her closer. "Over here," she snapped. "Don't pretend to be shy, Celeste, when I know for a fact you are not."

She knows, Celeste realized, going cold with

dread. She felt like a fox trapped by baying hounds, but she refused to let her terror show. She walked forward with her shoulders square and her chin high. "What can I do for you, ma'am?" she asked politely.

"You can tell me what you thought you were doing, seducing my son," the marquise spat out. "Did you really imagine you'd get your greedy little hands on his fortune?"

"I never—"

Fury contorted the marquise's aristocratic features, aging her into a hideous crone. "He says he plans to marry you, but it will never happen. Never, do you hear me? The estate will go to Emilie alone if he does. Now get out," she shouted, waving a clawlike hand. "Be gone from this house by daylight tomorrow. I never want to see your face again!"

Celeste ran from the room. Blinded by tears, she fled past the kitchen to the attic stairs, ignoring Annette and Genevieve's shouted questions. In her room she fell to her knees next to the window and buried her face in her arms, her whole body shaking. A minute later someone knocked on her door. Celeste knew who it was. "Go away," she called tearfully.

"I won't, Celeste," came Marc's voice. "We must talk."

"There's nothing more to say. Don't you see that?"

"You must let me in," he begged. "Hear me out!"

Celeste summoned all her willpower. "No, Marc. It's better this way."

At last he retreated. Celeste continued to kneel

by the window. Clasping her hands, she looked out at the clear summer night. Despite her heartbreak part of her was joyful. "He did want to marry me," she whispered to the starry sky. He'd risked his family's displeasure by making his desire known. It meant everything to know that his love was that deep, but it was clearer than ever that marriage was impossible. She couldn't—she *wouldn't*—tear Marc away from his family and his inheritance.

Celeste blinked. The stars grew blurry. *So now I have nothing,* she thought, tears sparkling on her eyelashes. *I've lost Marc, and I've lost my employment.*

She looked around her room. No, not nothing, after all. One by one she gathered up her books and some of the other small trinkets left by the secret benefactor whose identity she had never learned. She wouldn't quite be empty-handed as she returned to the *boulangerie*. Somehow she'd find the will to start over.

It didn't take Celeste long to pack her belongings. She considered going by Solange's apartment to say good-bye but couldn't bear the prospect of such a sorrowful leave-taking. Instead she waited until the house was quiet, then put on her cloak and slipped downstairs, a heavy valise in each hand. Outside she set the suitcases down on the pebbled path and paused to catch her breath.

The night was dark and full of the unknown. *But I can't go back,* Celeste thought. *This chapter of my life is over.* Before picking up the suitcases, she turned to take one last look at Poplars. Finding Marc's window, she put her fingers to her lips and blew a silent kiss. "Good-bye, my love," she whispered.

The road into the city seemed endless. Celeste stumbled through the dark, stopping often to rest. At one point she stepped into a pothole filled with muddy water, soaking her shoe and stocking. Tears stung her eyes and she wanted to sit down at the side of the road and cry, but she clenched her jaw and trudged on.

It was late and the road was for the most part quiet. A few carriages passed her and one or two horseback riders. To all their inquiries, polite or leering, Celeste made the same response. *"Non, merci.* I don't need any help."

She'd been walking for nearly an hour when a gleaming new carriage drawn by four matched bay horses reined in alongside her. A passenger leaned out the window. "Celeste," a man's voice called. "Is that you?"

Celeste peered apprehensively through the darkness. When she recognized the speaker, a wave of relief washed over her, weakening her knees. "Monsieur Oiseleur!" she cried.

Georges said a few words she couldn't hear and the footman jumped down, taking her suitcases and then handing her into the carriage. "You must let me offer you a ride to wherever you're going,"

Georges insisted. "It isn't safe for a young lady to walk the road alone at this hour."

Grateful, Celeste sank back against the richly upholstered seat. "Thank you." As she told him the address of the *boulangerie* her voice quavered. "I—I'm going home, to my family."

Georges's brow furrowed. "Celeste, what happened?"

She'd been trying to preserve her self-control, but now she burst into tears. "Oh, Monsieur Oiseleur, it's so awful," she sobbed. "We didn't mean to fall in love, but we couldn't help ourselves. And now I'll never see him again!"

The whole story spilled out: her first encounter with Marc, the kiss the night of the ball, their secret meetings, Marc's proposal, her confrontation that very night with the marquise. When she finally stopped crying, Georges gave her his handkerchief. "I am so sorry, my child," he murmured. "Marc's heart is in the right place, but he should have behaved more prudently. Alas, I know his parents well—they'll never relent."

"It's just so unfair!" Celeste cried. "We could have been so happy together if things were different." Another sob rose in her throat. "And I'm ashamed to go back to the Chardins. They've already done more than enough for me, considering that I'm not really their daughter. Marc doesn't know the worst about me," she explained miserably. "It's not only that I'm a servant—I don't even

146

know who my real parents are. My mother's dead and I never had a father. I'm nobody. Why should anyone love me?"

She buried her face in her hands, giving in to a fresh spate of tears. When she blotted her eyes a minute later, she noticed Georges looking at her strangely. "Celeste," he said, his voice vibrating with excitement. "The Chardins aren't your parents?"

"They raised me as their own—I've been with them since my birth. My mother died having me, you see. And my father . . ." Celeste sniffled. "He never claimed me."

"Do you know her name? Your mother's name?" George asked. "Where she came from, what she looked like?"

Celeste stared at him for a moment, startled by his urgency. Then, opening her cloak, she took the locket from around her neck. "I have only this," she said, removing the miniature portrait of the beautiful woman with lavender eyes and dark curly hair.

Georges took the drawing carefully. For a long moment he studied it closely. Then he turned it over to read the name that was written on the back in faded script. To Celeste's utter surprise, tears streamed down his face. "Lili," he whispered hoarsely.

🌿 *17* 🌿

Georges embraced a stunned Celeste. "I have so much to tell you," he said, fighting to control his surging emotions. "My home is closer than the *boulangerie*. Let us stop there first."

He said no more until Celeste was settled comfortably on a brocade sofa in the drawing room of the luxurious apartment he stayed in while doing business in Paris. "Monsieur Oiseleur, I'm in such suspense," she cried. "You recognized the picture of my mother! Did you know her?"

Georges took a deep breath. Then he directed her attention to a painting on the far wall of the room. It was a portrait of a young girl in the elaborate formal dress of the eighteenth-century nobility. Celeste focused on the girl's face. It was the face in her locket! "My *mother?*" she gasped.

"That painting was one of the few things I was

able to salvage from the ruins—only a few rooms of the château weren't damaged. She was probably fourteen or fifteen when she sat for it."

Celeste gazed at Georges, her eyes wide with wonder. "My mother . . . Lili . . . a *lady*?"

Georges sat next to Celeste on the couch. "Her family was one of the wealthiest in France. My own family worked on their estate." He colored slightly. "I . . . I was in love with her. But of course, it was a love that could never be expressed. She was too far above me."

"Like me and Marc," breathed Celeste. "Go on."

"During the Revolution there was an uprising in the village. Winterthorn was burned and Lili's father and brothers executed. Only Lili escaped, with my help."

Georges told Celeste what he'd pieced together of Lili's life in Paris: that she'd found work of some sort and then after a few years had fallen in love with a rich man who tricked her into a false marriage, then abandoned her, penniless and pregnant. He described his endless search for Lili's child. "I should have seen the resemblance," he declared, smiling at Celeste. "There you were, right in front of my eyes! But maybe I did recognize it, on some level. I knew that you were special, that you deserved a better chance in life."

Understanding dawned in Celeste's eyes. "It was you!" she exclaimed. "You gave me the books and the other things and arranged for Solange to tutor me!"

"Discovered at last," Georges said wryly.

Celeste shook her head, dazzled by the revelations. "I can't take it all in. My poor mother. Her story is so sad."

"But there's a happy ending." Georges squeezed Celeste's hand. "Your family's estate has been preserved, nearly intact. Lili's brothers had no offspring, so you, Celeste, are sole heir to an enormous fortune."

Celeste's head whirled. "Me?" she said, disbelieving. "Wealthy?"

"Beyond your wildest dreams." Georges explained that as trustee of the de Beautemps estate, he was legally her guardian. She was welcome to stay in his home until she could take possession of the property that was now hers. "You'll be well chaperoned by my housekeeper," Georges assured Celeste. "Stay the night, at least. We'll send word to the Chardins that you're here, and tomorrow I'll take you to Winterthorn to see your land."

Celeste was shown to a spacious guest bedroom. A maid had already unpacked her clothes. *Only today I was a maid myself,* Celeste marveled, *and now I'm being waited on by one!* She whispered Georges's words out loud. "'Tomorrow I'll take you to see your land.'" *My land.* She hugged herself. *Can this really be happening to me, Celeste Chardin?*

Her head was still spinning. It was too much to absorb all at once. She'd found Georges, who was now almost a father to her, and learned about the mother she never knew. *Marc,* Celeste thought suddenly. *And his parents!* In the shock of the moment she'd almost forgotten about them. How would they react when they heard the news?

"I can't go back there," Celeste told Georges at breakfast the next morning. "Not after the way the marquise treated me."

"Then I'll go on your behalf," Georges declared, "and clear the way for you to marry Marc."

Celeste shook her head stubbornly. "My fortune has changed, but I myself haven't. If they couldn't accept me as a daughter-in-law before, then they won't accept me now."

"I know this has been painful for you," Georges said sympathetically. "But you can't let pride get in the way of your happiness now that all other obstacles are gone." A sad, distant look shadowed his eyes. "I see in you and Marc a repetition of my unfulfilled love for Lili. It's too late for her, and for me. But it's not too late for you."

Celeste's eyes grew misty. "I do love him," she whispered.

Georges threw his linen napkin onto the table and flashed her a triumphant grin. "That's all I needed to hear. I'll waste no more time. Butler!" he shouted. "Order the carriage!"

* * *

"I don't believe it—not a word of it," cried the marquise, fluttering her hands. "Oh, Emilie, my smelling salts!"

The marquise swooned melodramatically. There was a flurry of activity in the drawing room. Emilie hovered over her mother, waving the bottle of smelling salts. Madame Lafitte ran in to see if she could help. Georges, meanwhile, continued his conversation with the marquis and his son. "The documents are at my house," he told the two men. "You'll find them most satisfactory."

"Astonishing," declared the marquis, his eyebrows lifted.

"Celeste . . . an heiress!" exclaimed Marc, still stunned.

The marquis looked at his son. "Of course, this changes everything. If you still care for the girl . . ."

Marc grasped Georges's arm. "I must see her. Where is she?"

Within minutes Marc was galloping across the countryside to Georges's residence. His heart pounded in his chest, keeping time with the horse's flying hooves. Just that morning, when he'd realized Celeste was gone, he'd thought he'd lost her forever. Now, perhaps, they had a second chance.

When he reached Georges's house, Marc jumped off his horse, leaving the reins dangling. He ran up the stairs to the front door three at a time. A startled housekeeper answered his urgent ringing of the bell. "Mademoiselle Chardin is in the library," she said. "May I show you the—"

Marc didn't wait for an escort. Racing down the hall, he burst into the library. "Celeste!" he cried hoarsely.

She rose to her feet, the book she'd been reading slipping from her fingers. Marc ran to her, and she met him halfway. Their embrace was giddy, joyous, and tearful. "You can't say no to me this time," Marc declared, showering her face with kisses.

"But your parents," Celeste said breathlessly. "They were scandalized. Your mother sent me out of the house!"

"They can't disapprove of you now that you're richer than we are," he replied, laughing. Then his expression grew serious. "But that's not what matters. Do you love me?"

Celeste smiled up at him. "I do."

"Then you'll take me as your husband, even though now you could choose any man in the land?"

"You wanted me when I had nothing to offer but myself," she said, her eyes shining. "I'll always love you as I did then, with all my heart."

Their lips met in a sweetly thrilling kiss. "We'll live happily ever after," Marc promised her.

Celeste nodded and kissed him again. She knew they would.

❖   ❖   ❖

"I've never seen two people so happy," Solange Grandet said to Georges Oiseleur, wiping a joyful tear from her eye.

The marquis had thrown a sumptuous ball at Poplars in honor of his son's wedding. After much dining, dancing, and toasting, the newly married pair had been whisked off in a coach pulled by eight white horses.

"They are," Georges agreed as he and Solange returned to the ballroom with the other guests. "I only wish her mother could have lived to see this day." The music was still playing—the party looked like it would go on far into the night. "Shall we?" he said, extending his hand to Solange.

Solange waltzed beautifully—she felt light as a feather in his arms. "I don't know how long it's been since I've danced like this," Georges confessed. "More years than I can count."

"I can't imagine why you avoid it," she responded. "You're an elegant dancer."

"I'm not as spry as I once was."

"You seem like a young man tonight," she observed.

It was true. Now that he'd finally done right by Lili's child, it was as if decades had fallen from him. *I'm not such an old fellow,* he thought, gazing down into Solange's glowing eyes. *My life isn't over. In fact, maybe it's just beginning.* "Solange. I may call you that? We've gotten to know each other well these last few months."

"Of course," she said. "I was so grateful to you for what you did for Celeste, even before you knew she was Lili de Beautemps's daughter." Solange blushed faintly. "I've enjoyed our talks."

"I have as well." Georges steered Solange to the far end of the ballroom. They were nearly alone. "And I wonder, if, well . . ." He cleared his throat. "We seem to have much in common, you and I. Intellectual interests, social concerns." He stopped.

"Yes?" Solange prompted.

"What I'm trying to say is . . ." Georges laughed at himself. "Listen to me. What a bumbler! Can you tell I've never made a proposal of marriage before?"

Solange smiled. "Is that what you are doing, sir?"

"Yes." They'd stopped dancing, but Georges kept her gloved hand in his. "I didn't see this coming," he admitted. "I thought happiness had passed me by. But you . . . you're an angel. I'd be a fool to let you go." He kissed her hand. "Would you be happy with a man like me, Mademoiselle Grandet?"

Her blush deepened, and for a moment she didn't speak. Georges held his breath. When at last Solange smiled, it was like the sun rising after an endless night. "Yes, Monsieur Oiseleur," she answered, her heart in her eyes. "I believe I would."

18

1865.

"I think she's the most beautiful baby I've ever seen," Celeste de Bocage said, tenderly cradling her newborn granddaughter in her arms.

It was baby Rose's christening day. The whole family was gathered for a celebration at Winterthorn. Since their marriage nearly half a century earlier, Celeste and Marc had lived in the rebuilt de Beautemps château.

Marc gently nudged aside the baby's white lace cap to better see her face. "She *is* beautiful," he agreed, turning his gaze to his wife. "But then, beauty runs in the family." To Marc's eyes, Celeste was as exquisite as when he first met her. She was in her seventies and her once golden hair was white, but her green eyes were still radiant, her skin soft and fair. Age hadn't diminished her beauty because its source was her inner strength and serenity.

"Look," said Celeste. "She has my mother's purple eyes."

The baby had been sleeping. Now she blinked and stretched, her tiny rosebud mouth stretching in a yawn. "But the flaming red hair," Marc observed, smiling, "and the feisty temperament. Where did she get that?"

As if on cue, Rose began to cry lustily. Laughing, Celeste quickly handed the baby to Lucie, the baby's mother, and the wife of Celeste's oldest child and only son, Claude.

"I think it's time to make a toast, before Rose cuts this party short," announced Claude, rising to his feet. He faced his parents, lifting his glass of champagne. "We wouldn't be here today if it weren't for my wonderful mother and father, Celeste and Marc de Bocage. You inspire Pauline, Marie-Rose, and me with your devotion to each other. Thank you for giving this family such a firm foundation. *A votre santé.*"

Everyone drank to Celeste and Marc's health. "I'd like to offer a toast too," said Marc, rising to his feet. Celeste gazed up at him adoringly. He'd always been handsome, smart, and kind. Now, as the elderly patriarch of a great family, he was also dignified and wise. "Rose, we're overjoyed to welcome you into our family as we did your two big brothers, Jean-Claude and Guillaume. We can tell already that you're a person of great spirit who'll bring joy to us all. To Rose. To the next generation," Marc concluded, his voice ringing out strong and clear.

Celeste lifted her glass, a happy tear sparkling in her eye. "To the next generation," she echoed.

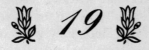

19

1880.

"Don't you just love summer?" fifteen-year-old Rose de Bocage sang out. "Isn't it the most delicious season?" Not waiting for an answer from her best friend, Pierre Oiseleur, she tossed her long, plentiful auburn hair and spurred her horse to a canter.

Pierre kicked his gray gelding, Ambler, hurrying after Rose. When he caught up to her, they galloped their horses down the dirt lane that ran alongside Pierre's family's vineyards. At the end of the road Rose's horse, Lucky, was ahead by a stride. "I won!" she cheered, waving her crop.

Cutting through a gate to an open pasture, they slowed to a walk, letting the horses rest. "I do like summer," Pierre said, finally getting a chance to

159

respond. "I like being in the country." He shot a fast glance at Rose. "And being with you."

Rose inhaled deeply, relishing the green, spicy scent of alfalfa and timothy baking in the sun. "We've always had good times, haven't we?" she agreed cheerfully. Since they were small, she and Pierre had spent every summer visiting their grand-parents, whose estates were next door to each other. After Solange Oiseleur's death the uncle who'd inherited the Oiseleur estate had continued to invite Pierre for the long summer holiday.

Now Rose grinned wickedly at Pierre. "Remember the time with the rabbits?"

Pierre groaned. "How could I forget?"

"We were ten," Rose recalled, smiling impishly, "and I talked you into helping me free the bunnies kept in a cage outside *Grandmaman* Celeste's kitchen."

"Why did you want to do that anyway?" Pierre scratched his head in pretend puzzlement.

"To save the sweet things from becoming stew, that's why!" Rose cried. "It was one of my best schemes. Remember? I plotted it all out perfectly. Oh, I'll never forget the sight of those happy rabbits hopping off into the bushes!"

"*I'll* never forget the sight of your grand-mother's cook waving her rolling pin at me when she discovered the empty cage," Pierre said dryly.

Rose burst into peals of merry laughter. "It's your own fault. You should have run off faster."

"It was always like that, wasn't it?" Pierre remarked, smiling. "You masterminded our escapades and I got the spankings."

"A fair division of labor, I'd say. Come on." She yanked Lucky's nose out of the clover. "Let's race some more."

Obligingly Pierre cantered after her. As they neared the end of the field Rose gestured ahead. "Dare you to take that fence!" she shouted.

"You know Ambler's no jumper!" Pierre shouted back.

"Ambler jumps just fine. *You're* the one with no guts!" Rose taunted. She tapped Lucky's flank with her crop. At the same time she gathered her reins so that he was collected beneath her. Without hesitation she pointed the horse at the tall, wide stone wall. Lucky bunched his muscles and launched into the air. Rose leaned forward in the saddle. They cleared the wall cleanly.

She circled, looking back. Even from a distance she could see Pierre clench his jaw. *He doesn't want to do it, but he will because he knows he won't hear the end of it otherwise,* she thought gleefully. "Hurry up!" she called.

Pierre spurred Ambler forward. The horse zigzagged, clearly not wanting to make the jump. Pierre shook the reins and kicked like crazy. They flew crookedly over the wall, Pierre sitting up too straight, his arms and legs flapping. He nearly fell off when Ambler hit the dirt on the other side but managed to cling to the saddle. Rose cheered. "Hooray! What form. Where do you want to go now? I know—let's raid your uncle's berry patch!"

They trotted on across the countryside, whiling away the long summer afternoon. Finally the sun began to sink. Tying their horses to a tree, Pierre and Rose sat by the edge of a creek, dangling their bare feet in the cool water. "I love summer," Rose mused, returning to her earlier theme, "because the days seem to last forever. When it's this green and leafy, I can't believe it was ever winter or will ever be winter again."

Pierre clasped his arms around his knees. "But in one month summer will be over," he pointed out. "You'll return to your home in Paris, and I . . . I'm going away to school this year."

"What are you talking about?"

"Boarding school. To prepare me for university."

"You mean I won't see you in Paris this winter?" Rose cried. "At *all*?"

Pierre shook his head. "I suppose I'll go home for holidays, but the rest of the time my schedule will be very strict."

Rose picked up a clump of moss and threw it into the bubbling creek. "But we've *always* spent so much time together," she pouted, surprised by the surge of emotion she felt at the prospect of being separated from Pierre. "What will I do to amuse myself?"

"You'll continue being tutored at home," he

surmised. "And you're old enough to start going to parties." He looked at her sideways. "Meeting boys," he added, his voice gruff.

"Hmpf." Lacing her boots back on, Rose hopped to her feet and brushed off her hands on the skirt of her riding habit. "Well, I'll miss you." She brushed his cheek with a quick, thoughtless kiss. "Come on. It must be nearly dinnertime."

Pierre chased her through the trees, back to the horses. "Rose," he panted, "when I'm away at school, may I write to you?"

Rose didn't hear him. Already mounted, she was trotting off down the lane. "Hurry up," she cried over her shoulder. "I'm ravenous." Her lavender eyes crinkled in a smile. "I just hope Cook isn't making rabbit stew!"

"What's this?" asked Anne, pouncing on the sheet of paper that lay on Rose's desk. "Ooh, a letter," she squealed. "From a *boy!*"

Rose and her friends Anne and Marie-Claire had spent the gray February afternoon bundled in fur and strolling along the Seine. Now, having warmed themselves up with hot tea, they lounged in Rose's bedroom, idly paging through a ladies' magazine.

Rose glanced at the letter Anne was waving. "It's just from my friend, Pierre," she said dismissively. "He *is* a boy, but no one special."

"Let *me* be the judge of that," said Anne. "Ahem." She cleared her throat theatrically, then

163

began to read the letter out loud. 'My dearest Rose.' Did you hear that, Marie-Claire? He calls her his dearest!"

"Oh, please," scoffed Rose, rolling her eyes. "We grew up together. He thinks of me as a sister."

"'I'm working hard this term, studying mathematics, science, and history, as well as Latin and Greek. We also have athletics every day.'" Anne skimmed the letter. "There must be something juicier . . . ah. Listen. 'When I get lonely, I remember this past Christmas holiday and how nice it was seeing you. I try not to think about how long it is until summer.'"

"Rose," Marie-Claire teased. "You two are in love!"

"We are no such thing!" Rose protested.

"Then why are you turning red?" Anne asked.

Rose put her hands to her cheeks. Her face *was* hot. "Because I can't believe what ninnies you are," she declared.

"Well, maybe you're not in love with *him,* but he's in love with *you,*" Anne said. "Listen to this: 'Please write as soon as you get this. I treasure your letters.'"

"Are you finished?" Rose asked, snatching back Pierre's letter.

"Rose has a beau," Marie-Claire said with an envious sigh. "I wish *I* had a beau!"

"I wish you had a brain," Rose rejoined. "Such a fuss about a silly letter!"

"Pierre is handsome, isn't he?" Marie-Claire asked Anne.

"Very handsome, I believe," Anne replied.

Rose grabbed a pillow off her bed and threw it at her friends, laughing. "Can we change the subject, please?" she begged. "You two may think about nothing but men and romance, but I have more important things on my mind."

"Such as?" said Anne.

"Such as stopping by the bookseller's. I've been reading about the women's suffrage movement." She checked the watch pinned to her blouse. "The store should be open for another quarter hour."

"A bookstore?" Anne groaned. "Well, all right. As long as we go to the dress shop too. I've heard the bustle is going out of style—I'd like to see the new narrow skirts."

"It's a deal," Rose agreed. She smiled mischievously. "Narrow skirts sound like an improvement, but I'd still rather we all wore knickers like Mrs. Bloomer!"

Later Rose sat at her desk, gazing out the window at the rainy night, a contemplative expression on her face. *The days are getting longer, but the sun still sets much too soon,* she thought, dipping her pen in the inkwell and putting it to a blank sheet of stationery. *Pierre's right—summer is a long way off.*

She began her letter as she always did: *Salut, cher ami.* She frowned down at the words, remembering Anne and Marie-Claire's merciless teasing.

"Well, he *is* my dear friend," she said out loud in self-defense. "We've been pals since childhood. Of course we address each other with affection. It would be unnatural otherwise!"

She thought about what to write next, then put down the pen. Chin in hand, she stared again at the dark, rain-streaked panes of glass. All at once a nameless longing swept over her. She fingered the delicate gold bracelet she wore around her wrist. It had been a sixteenth-birthday present from Pierre. *It doesn't mean anything special,* she told herself. *He had to give me something. Or maybe . . .*

Like any girl her age, Rose liked to read novels. She traded volumes back and forth with Marie-Claire and Anne. Stories of romance were her friends' favorites. *In novels when a woman is in love, she has palpitations and swooning fits,* Rose mused. She put a hand to her chest, checking her heartbeat. It seemed a little fast. *Does thinking about Pierre make me flushed and feverish? Have I lost my appetite—do I lie awake at night?*

She laughed out loud. No, she wasn't in love with Pierre Oiseleur—she was pretty sure of that. What a ridiculous notion! But something was bothering her. Again she felt it—a restlessness. She wanted something . . . but what?

"I know why Pierre's letters affect me this way," Rose declared suddenly. Of course it wasn't Pierre himself she longed for, though she did miss his companionship, particularly since the alternative was the insipid, girlish conversation of Anne and Marie-Claire. She longed for the freedom Pierre was experiencing. He got to go off to school, be out in the world, while she was stuck at home being educated in the "ladylike" arts: music, drawing, a taste of literature and language. It was too boring, especially since she was a good student, already outstripping her governess. *While Pierre prepares for university, I'm learning how to be domestic and decorative. Ugh!*

She cherished a secret dream of joining Pierre at university. She was confident she could do as well as any man. *Grandmaman* Celeste would take her side, Rose knew. If only her own parents weren't so conservative!

She picked up her pen. Dipping it in ink, she began writing, her script a loopy, careless scrawl. "'Pierre, you must tell me what you're reading at school and save all your books so I can borrow them this summer. Oh, I had the funniest adventure recently at the Louvre. I was standing in front of a painting when a stout lady with an umbrella came along and . . .'"

She filled three sheets with sisterly chat. The letter wasn't in the least romantic—she wished she could show it to Anne and Marie-Claire as proof. At the bottom she signed her name with a flourish, leaving out the customary "Love" just to be on the safe side.

❦ 20 ❦

When Rose arrived at Winterthorn for her annual summer holiday, she greeted her grandmother with a bear hug. *"Grandmaman,* it's so wonderful to see you!" she cried.

Celeste laughed. "Careful, child. I'm an old woman. You'll break me in two."

Rose smiled down at her grandmother's sweet, wrinkled face. "I don't think of you as old, *Grandmaman,"* she said fondly. "You're so young at heart." Arm in arm they strolled out to the veranda. "The rosebushes look splendid this summer," Rose observed, breathing deeply. "The fragrance is divine."

"I make sure the gardener takes extra special care of them," Celeste explained, hugging her granddaughter's slender waist, "because they're *your* flowers."

They sat side by side on a wrought-iron bench overlooking the lush gardens. "I suppose this summer will be different," Rose reflected sadly. "Without grandfather."

Marc de Bocage had died just a few months earlier, and the family was still in mourning. Celeste patted Rose's hand, a tear glittering in her eye. "I miss him more than I can say," she said. "But he had a long, wonderful life. And now that you are here, the château won't seem so empty."

"I wish . . ." Rose sighed, then laughed. "I wish I was a little girl again. Isn't that silly? But then grandfather would still be here, and Pierre. Do you know that awful school is only giving him a fortnight's vacation? Just two weeks, when we used to have two whole months!"

Celeste studied her granddaughter. "You miss him, do you?"

"Well, yes," Rose admitted. "A little. Why shouldn't I?" she added somewhat defensively. "He's been my best friend forever. After putting up with Marie-Claire and Anne all winter, it will be nice to talk about something besides the latest fashions. To have *intellectual* discussions."

Celeste smiled. "Ah. I see."

For some reason her grandmother's penetrating gaze made Rose feel like wriggling. She jumped to her feet. "I think I'll cut a huge bouquet of flowers for your room, *Grandmaman*, and another for mine. May I?"

Celeste nodded. "Of course, *ma chérie*."

Grabbing some clippers that were lying on top of the low wall, Rose began vigorously cutting roses. *Really*, she thought. *Must everyone, even Grandmaman, make a fuss about my friendship with Pierre, insinuating that it's something it's not? Wait till I tell him what people are hinting about us. How he'll laugh!*

Pierre looked out the window of the train speeding away from Paris. As the familiar, beloved landscape of the Loire Valley unfolded he felt a lump in his throat. *Home*, he thought. Everything looked the same—trees, fields, the river, church steeples, factories, châteaux. Pierre fingered the brim of the hat resting on his knee. *But I've changed.* He smiled, anticipating Rose's reaction. *I'm inches taller. She'll hardly know me!*

The physical changes weren't the only ones. His year at school had matured Pierre in many ways. He'd grown intellectually and emotionally. He wasn't a boy anymore: He carried himself with a man's sense of purpose and self-confidence. In one way, though, he hadn't changed a bit. A half smile flitted across Pierre's handsome face as he imagined the lively, laughing eyes of a beautiful red-haired girl. He was still madly in love with Rose de Bocage, as he'd been for as long as he could remember.

He'd thought perhaps the year apart would

170

dim his feelings, loosen the hold she had over him. Instead, if anything, his affection was more firmly rooted. Not a day passed that he didn't think of her. He'd read and reread each letter she sent until the paper was wilted and smudged. Always he was searching for meaning between the lines—for some sign that she too cared for him as more than a friend.

Pierre raked a hand through his thick, dark hair. What of Rose? Would she still be a wild, harum-scarum tomboy who wanted only to romp barefoot through the meadows and argue about books? Or would he find that she too had grown up?

Don't hope for too much, Pierre counseled himself. He couldn't help it, though. Rose had been immensely pleased to see him over the winter holiday. Of course, none of their conversations had been particularly serious—they'd joked and kidded each other as of old. Pierre's brown eyes glowed with expectant fervor. Maybe this summer would be different.

Wearing a high-necked white blouse and long, tailored skirt, Rose stood on the platform, waving her arms excitedly even though the train was still a long way off. It roared closer, smoke belching from the stacks, then screeched to a stop at the station. Rose held her breath, scanning the faces of the disembarking passengers. Then there he was: his unruly black hair sweeping back from his high forehead, his skin slightly tanned, his eyes twinkling with pleasure at the sight of her, and . . .

"A mustache!" squealed Rose, throwing her arms around Pierre and nearly knocking him off his feet. "Pierre, what a big boy you are!"

She tickled his ribs and he swatted her playfully with his hat. "And you're a big girl," he teased, taking in her appearance from head to toe.

Rose pirouetted so he could admire her figure from all angles. "I'm rounder than I used to be," she acknowledged, "but a summer of healthy outdoor exercise should make me lean again."

"You wouldn't want to be *too* lean," Pierre said.

Rose laughed. "Not to worry. The curves are here to stay. It's my destiny."

Arm in arm they strolled down to the road. "Just one bag?" Rose observed.

"I've only got two weeks," Pierre reminded her.

"Well, let's send it on with the driver and you and I go on foot. Aren't you just dying to greet all our old favorite spots?"

Pierre tossed his suitcase in the waiting carriage and said a few words to the driver. On the other side of the road Rose gathered up her skirt, preparing to scramble over the fence. "I'm not really dressed for cross-country rambles," Pierre said, indicating his own neatly creased trousers and polished shoes.

Rose threw up her hands. "If you're going to put fashion before fun, I might as well have stayed in Paris with my giggling girlfriends!"

Pierre took off his jacket and rolled up his shirt-sleeves, grinning. "There's a challenge if ever I heard one."

They followed a path through a wooded copse and emerged near Pierre's uncle's vineyards. At the creek they took off their shoes and waded. They ended up at last in an orchard on the old de Beautemps property. Rose sampled an unripe cherry. "Yuck," she announced, pursing her lips. "Green."

As they walked among the antique fruit trees Rose took Pierre's hand and swung it lightly. "It's good to have you home," she told him. "It's too quiet when I'm here by myself."

"Your cousins will all be here soon."

"It's not the same. They don't like the same things as I like."

"And I do?"

"Of course!" She squeezed his hand, then dropped it. "I can talk about serious things with you, politics and literature. What do you think about the modern poets? About socialism? About women's rights and suffrage?"

"Well, I haven't really—" Pierre began.

"Because *I* feel that women should be educated just the same as men," Rose declared, "and should be treated as men's equals in all ways, socially, intellectually, *and* politically."

"We aren't equal, though," Pierre protested.

"Or what I mean is, we're not the same. We're different and always will be. I'm not against women having the vote and participating to a degree in public affairs, mind you. But it's natural for women to contribute more in the private sphere. Since you're the ones who bear children—"

"Ha!" Rose blurted. "Simply because I'm capable of having a baby and you're not, you think I should be restricted to a domestic role?"

A spirited debate ensued, with Rose finally persuading Pierre that while the sexes had a long way to go before they'd be equal, better education for women would start the transformation. Pierre conceded that Rose was as smart as any of his male schoolmates. He was happy to grant the point because he wanted to steer the conversation in a more personal direction. Stopping beside a gnarled pear tree, Pierre broke off a small branch and handed it to Rose. "Do you know, I asked your grandmother once about the gold brooch she often wears," he said. "The one with the pear blossom. Did she ever tell you the story behind it?"

"I don't recall."

"It turns out she first saw your grandfather in an orchard, on the grounds of his family's home near Paris. They had to meet in secret because she was a servant and he was the lord of the manor. They met under a pear tree."

"I think I have heard the story," Rose said, yawning.

"And don't you think it's very romantic?" Pierre stepped closer to her. He wanted more than anything in the world to kiss her.

Rose shrugged. "Nothing could interest me less."

Pierre put a hand on her arm. "Nothing?"

They were face-to-face. A bird chirped in the pear tree, the notes of its song lilting and musical. A warm breeze stirred the branches, making the pattern of sun and shadow ripple like water. Rose seemed momentarily affected by the sensuous beauty of the scene. "Well," she said, her voice softer, "maybe not *nothing*."

She was looking up at him expectantly. Pierre felt himself drowning in the beauty of her lavender eyes. He pulled her toward him. Just as he was about to bring his mouth to hers, Rose jumped away, laughing nervously. "Why, Pierre, I just had the funniest sensation!" she cried, walking off at a brisk pace. "I thought for a second you were going to kiss me. Can you imagine anything more ridiculous?"

Pierre chased after her. "People kiss sometimes," he said. "It can be pleasurable. Have you ever been kissed?"

"Just once, after a party last spring, and I didn't like it much," Rose answered.

"But if you were kissed by someone you cared about—"

"Oh, stop!" Rose begged. "Pierre, you must

175

promise not to talk of these things. I have no patience for it. My female friends think of nothing but beaux and parties, and soon it will be engagements and weddings, and then husbands and babies. But not for me." She stomped her foot for emphasis.

"Not for you?"

"I despise romance and I loathe domesticity," Rose declared, her eyes flashing. "As soon as I'm old enough, I'm escaping my parents' house and their old-fashioned expectations. I'll live on my own."

"You should have a chance to do that," Pierre agreed. "It's only fair. But when the time comes to marry and have children—"

"But that's just my point!" Rose cried. "I'll never marry and never have children. If I do, I'll be trapped, lost forever."

"Lost forever," Pierre repeated, the eager light in his eyes slowly fading.

They left the shady orchard, entering a sunny lane. Rose went on about her theories. "I'll never settle down because I'd have to give up too much. My husband would expect me to stay home and raise children, a dozen children probably, while he conducted business and participated in local politics or what have you. I'd never fulfill my own dream of becoming a writer."

Pierre walked by her side, his fists in his pockets and his chin on his chest. He listened without commenting because he didn't trust himself to speak. Every one of her words was like an arrow piercing his heart. They'd been so close to something back in the orchard. But the magic, the moment, had escaped.

Without intending to, he voiced his sole remaining hope aloud. "You're only sixteen. You'll change your mind."

Rose frowned. "Change my mind about what? Oh, *that*." She laughed cheerfully. "Check with me again in five years, or better yet ten. We'll see."

Five years or ten, Pierre thought as they turned their footsteps back toward Winterthorn. Would he really have to wait that long?

"It seems as if you just got here," Rose said to Pierre two weeks later.

He'd come by her grandmother's to say goodbye before heading to the train station. Rose had suggested a turn in the gardens. "The vacation flew by," he agreed as they wound their way through a maze of tall hedges. "We were busy every minute."

There was nothing accusing in his tone, but Rose knew that he thought her behavior strange. She bit her lip. *I did avoid being alone with him after that uncomfortable talk we had in the orchard,* she realized. *I made sure we were always surrounded by at least a half dozen other people. Why?* "Well, I wanted you to be amused," she said after an awkward silence. "You study so hard at school with no time for fun. Weren't you glad to go to a lot of parties and always be part of a merry, lighthearted crowd?"

"I wasn't complaining." He shot a glance at her. "It's just that . . ."

Rose's heart began to beat faster. *Is he going to try to kiss me again?* she wondered breathlessly. And what would she do if he did?

Just then they heard a train whistle in the distance. Pierre bent down, brushing Rose's cheek with a fast, cousinly kiss. "That sounds only a few miles off. I'd better run. Write to me, OK?"

He dashed off, disappearing around the bend in the hedge. "*Au revoir,* Pierre!" she called after him.

"*Au revoir,* Rose," his voice drifted back.

She stood alone in the middle of the maze, her arms hanging limply at her sides, weighed down by disappointment. *Why do I feel this way?* she wondered, walking back out of the maze with slow, dispirited footsteps. She never liked saying goodbye to Pierre, but this sudden depression caught her off guard. What had she been expecting from his visit?

21

1885. Paris.

Rose sauntered along the riverfront, swinging her leather book bag by the strap and whistling a cheerful tune. Her hair was pinned up in the fashion of the time, but loosely—many auburn strands had escaped and blew about in the spring breeze. All around her the Left Bank bustled with activity: artists sketching the Seine, students arguing politics at riverfront cafés, tourists and shoppers, the wealthy, the bourgeois, the working class. *Paris,* Rose thought, breathing deeply of the city's ripe, tangy scents. *To think I lived here all my life but never knew it was so vibrant and exciting!*

After badgering her parents for years, when she turned twenty they'd finally relented and allowed her to register for classes at the Sorbonne and take a room at a boardinghouse near the university. The unaccustomed freedom was like intoxicating wine, and Rose was drunk on it. She'd made dozens of interesting new acquaintances, intense, unconventional people she knew her parents would never approve of: artists and writers and radicals. "Bohemians," Pierre called them, lifting his lip in that ironic half smile of his.

It was Pierre she'd come to meet this afternoon, and now she spotted him, waiting for her on Pont St. Michel overlooking l'Île de la Cité. "Pierre!" she called, waving a hand in greeting.

He turned to watch her approach. Rose knew she looked a bit of a sight, wearing a bicycling costume of knickers, a blouse, and jacket. Her hair was tousled, and she had no gloves or hat. "Don't say it," she warned him, laughing. "'If your poor mother could see you . . .'"

Pierre chuckled. "I was only going to say, if you're taking to wearing men's clothing, you may help yourself to the contents of my closet anytime."

"What a generous offer!"

They strolled down from the bridge arm in arm, then took seats at a sidewalk café. "I only have time for a quick cup of coffee," Pierre told her, "but I really needed to see you today."

"What is it?" Rose asked. "You look very serious."

Pierre put his elbows on the table and gazed at her over his tented fingers. "I don't know how to begin," he confessed. "I shouldn't stick my nose into your business."

"Are you worried about me staying out late at the cabarets?" Rose teased. "Worried that my wild friends are a bad influence?"

"As a matter of fact . . ." Pierre cleared his throat. "Rose," he said, trying again, "since we started at the Sorbonne last fall, we've grown closer than ever, but we move in different social circles. I know you think my friends and I are stodgy and dull. But some of the people you've become associated with recently . . ."

Rose narrowed her eyes. "Is there someone in particular of whom you disapprove?"

Pierre turned faintly red. "I've noticed that you're spending time with Leo Rivière," he burst out.

"Don't tell me you're jealous." Rose grinned wickedly.

Pierre's flush deepened. "Not at all. But his reputation—"

"Yes, I can imagine in your crowd a man like Leo is considered quite unsavory," Rose said tartly. "Just because he doesn't want to be restricted by old-fashioned values."

"From what I've heard, he has no values at all."

Rose raised her eyebrows. "I didn't realize you listened to idle gossip, Pierre," she remarked somewhat disdainfully.

"Oh, Rose." He grasped her hand, looking

straight into her eyes. "I went about this all wrong. I didn't mean to sound like I was judging you or your friends. But I know for a fact that Rivière has been in many . . ." He searched for the right word, not wanting to be indelicate. "Shall we say, *intimate* relationships with women. And he's broken more than a few hearts. I just don't want you to be hurt."

Rose's expression softened. "You keep an eye out for me, don't you?"

"It's all you'll let me do," he replied, half under his breath.

"Well, I appreciate your concern." She sipped her steaming cup of coffee. "I really do. But you shouldn't waste your time worrying about any trouble I might get into. *I'm* not worried. If I take a lover, so what? If he breaks my heart, so what?"

"Rose!" exclaimed Pierre.

Her eyes twinkled merrily. "It's worth misbehaving just to see that scandalized look on your face," she teased. "Truly, Pierre. I can handle whatever the world sends my way. It's all grist for the mill since I want to be a writer."

Pierre sighed. "Then there's no chance I'll be able to talk you out of seeing Rivière."

"No chance at all." Rose put a hand to her forehead, shading her eyes. "Look, Pierre. Isn't that your lady friend, Angelique?"

A fair-haired young woman in a plain blue dress was walking in their direction. Pierre pushed back his chair. "We're going to a poetry reading. Would you care to join us?"

"No, thanks. I have a date too."

"It's not a date," Pierre said.

"Don't be so defensive. I think she looks perfectly sweet." Rose pinched his arm playfully. "You have my blessing."

They parted as they always did, pressing their cheeks together first on one side, then the other. Rose swung her satchel over her shoulder and sauntered off. Glancing back, she watched Pierre offer his arm to Angelique. *Good old Pierre,* thought Rose with a fond smile. *He takes such good care of everybody! He'll make some girl a wonderful husband one day.*

On a rainy summer night three months later, Pierre was startled from his studying by a loud knocking on the door of his rented town house. He closed his book and hurried to the front of the apartment. "Who's there?" he called.

"Pierre, it's me," a female voice cried. "Please let me in!"

He opened the door quickly. Rose stood outside, bareheaded as usual and without a coat of any kind, soaked to the skin. As soon as she saw him she flung herself into his arms, sobbing.

Pierre drew her inside, closing the door behind them. "Rose, what is it?" he asked. "What's happened?"

She was crying too hard to speak. After sitting her down on the sofa, he ran for a blanket, which he wrapped around her heaving shoulders. "Rose, pull yourself together," he begged. "Tell me what's the matter. Is it about . . ."

"Yes, it's Leo," she sobbed, clutching the handkerchief he offered her. "Oh, Pierre, I've been such a fool! I opened myself up to him—I trusted him. And the whole time he was seeing not one but *two* other women behind my back!"

"The scoundrel! To take advantage of an innocent girl . . ." Pierre clenched his teeth. He couldn't say he'd warned her—she needed comfort, not criticism. "Rose. He didn't—you're not . . ."

"I'm not pregnant, if that's what you're asking. But I cared about him. And I thought he . . ." Her face crumpled again. "Oh, Pierre. Hold me."

Pierre put his arms around her, holding her tight. "There, there," he murmured, stroking her wet hair. "Everything will be all right."

Gradually Rose stopped shaking and crying. Pulling away from his embrace, she gazed up at Pierre with wide, red-rimmed eyes. "I *do* feel better," she said, sniffling. "I knew I would if I came to you."

Pierre felt a spark of hope ignite in his heart. For a year now, since they'd been at the Sorbonne, he'd been wooing other girls without much interest, all the while continuing to love Rose from a distance. *She's learned the hard way about men*

184

like Leo, Pierre thought. *Will it change her feelings toward me?* "Then you must always come to me," he replied, keeping his tone light.

He went to the kitchen, returning a few minutes later with a cup of coffee, pale and sweet with cream and sugar. Rose sipped it gratefully. "Better?" Pierre asked.

"Better," she said.

"I hate to see you sad." He sat next to her on the sofa, his arm around her shoulders. He'd intended to keep his opinion to himself, but suddenly he couldn't help venting it. "You should have known better than to trust your heart to someone like that," he declared. "You deserve a man who'll cherish and protect you, put you on a pedestal, not drag you down into the dirt."

Rose shrugged off his arm and placed her cup on the end table. "That's where you're wrong," she replied, her voice crisp and strong again. "What I've learned from Leo isn't that I need a *nicer* man, but that I don't need a man at all."

Why did I goad her? Pierre thought, wanting to kick himself. "You've always said that, but you can't really believe it, deep in your heart."

"My heart doesn't make my decisions," Rose rejoined. "My mind does, my intellect and common sense."

Standing up, she handed back the damp blanket. "Sorry to barge in here and make a mess of your life as well my own."

"I'll always be here for you," Pierre assured her.

A minute later she forged back into the rainy night, taking his umbrella with her. His umbrella and, as always, his heart.

One autumn night Pierre and a friend stopped by a cabaret on the way home from the library. "Are you sure you want to go in here?" Pierre asked Louis skeptically. It was a smoky, rowdy place with dancing girls and freely flowing liquor. "We won't be able to hear ourselves think."

"That's all I've been doing all day—listening to myself think," Louis rejoined. "I need a change. Come on!"

Chuckling, Pierre followed Louis through the door. The cabaret was packed. As they searched for an empty table Pierre noticed an especially lively group near the bar. A man standing in the center of the group with his back to Pierre said something, gesturing with his cigar. The others doubled over, howling with laughter. "That fellow must be telling a top-notch joke," Pierre remarked.

"An off-color one, I daresay," said Louis.

Pierre was about to turn away. Then he took another look, narrowing his eyes. *It can't be,* he thought. As he watched, the "fellow" removed his hat, revealing a large knot of lustrous auburn hair. Pierre caught a glimpse of a strikingly beautiful— and feminine—profile. He smiled, stifling a sigh. *I should have known.*

Rose spotted him at the same time. "Pierre, over here!" she cried, beckoning.

Pierre elbowed his way through the crowd. Rose sucked on her cigar, then gestured to her companions. "Introductions aren't necessary—you know this motley crew, right?"

Pierre nodded to the men lounging against the bar, trying not to notice the insolent, openly admiring way they looked at Rose. *If she doesn't mind,* he told himself, *I shouldn't mind.*

Rose hooked her arm through his. "You showed up just in time," she announced. "I was about to leave. There's another party across town. Will you come with me?"

Pierre was only too happy to escape and take Rose with him. "At your service, ma'am." Out on the sidewalk he cocked one eyebrow at her. "Or maybe I should've said 'sir.'"

Rose grinned. "It was the most liberating day of my life when I traded my burdensome petticoats for an honest pair of men's trousers. I can move about with such perfect ease and freedom."

"I won't pretend I approve," Pierre said. "From an aesthetic standpoint anyway. A beauty like you shouldn't hide the fact that she's a woman."

"I thought if anything, it was more obvious than ever," kidded Rose.

It was true. Pierre had never fully realized how long and slim Rose's legs were. And her curves were as noticeable as ever. "What I'm saying is, if you don't dress and behave like a lady, you can't expect to be treated like one."

"You've put your finger on it—that's my goal exactly," Rose declared triumphantly. "I don't *want* to be treated like a lady! It's so limiting. Nobody expects ladies to do anything but look pretty and say silly, simpering things, flattering the men around them by mindlessly echoing their opinions. When I'm dressed like this, I can leap right into the fray, say whatever I like, do whatever I like."

At the street corner they waved down a cab. As the carriage bumped along the Paris streets Pierre approached the topic from another direction. "But don't you find that men . . . not me, of course. To me, you are always the epitome of female perfection. But aren't other men"—he indicated the cigar she was still chewing on—"intimidated by this outrageous getup?"

Rose smiled. "As a matter of fact, quite the opposite. I've never had so many suitors."

Pierre shook his head. "My wild, wild Rose," he chided.

"My solid, sensible Pierre," Rose countered. "Such a good citizen."

Pierre looked away from her, not wanting her to read the emotion in his eyes. "Perhaps you're growing tired of me. We seem to have less in common these days, Rose."

"Nonsense." She patted his knee. "I value you more than ever. You *know* me." He faced her again, and their eyes met. Hers were uncharacter-istically somber. "Better than any of the rest ever shall. You know the person beneath the . . . how did you put it? The 'outrageous getup.'"

Pierre grinned wryly. "You *are* a spectacle, Mademoiselle de Bocage."

"*Grandmaman* Celeste would approve," she replied. "She's always been on my side."

The driver stopped at the Right Bank address Rose had given. Rose and Pierre stepped out onto the curb. Pierre offered Rose his arm, and to his surprise, she took it.

He wondered if she could tell how relieved he'd been by her last words. She valued him still—there was still a place for him in her life, as a friend and defender, though they never referred to the Leo episode and, as far as he could tell, she remained romantically aloof from her many would-be suitors.

Yes, I'm still her best friend, thought Pierre. When would that stop being enough?

"In just one week we graduate from university!" Rose declared, throwing her arms around Pierre and squeezing him tight.

It was a Friday night, and she'd dragged him to a round of decadent parties. Rose knew Pierre didn't always feel comfortable around her bohemian friends with their radical opinions and unconventional morals. But as usual he seemed willing to go anyplace just to be with her.

189

They were leaving their third party, which Rose had promised would be the last of the night. Disentangling himself from Rose's exuberant embrace, Pierre helped her on with her coat. "But the celebration's started already," he remarked. "I've never seen people consume so much champagne."

"I only had one glass," Rose said virtuously.

"At *this* party," Pierre pointed out. "What about the other two?"

She giggled. "I *am* a capable adult, Monsieur Oiseleur."

"*That* is open to debate," he grumbled.

"And besides." She flashed him her most irresistible smile. "You'll see me home as you always do. Nothing bad can happen."

On the way back to her flat they stopped at their favorite Latin Quarter brasserie for cups of strong, hot coffee. Rose chatted about the piece she was working on for a radical student newspaper, the last she'd do before graduating. After a few minutes she noticed that Pierre was strangely quiet and subdued. "What's on your mind?" she asked him.

Pierre gazed at her through the steam rising from his cup. "Graduation," he said simply. "All this"—he waved a hand vaguely—"is about to come to an end."

"What do you mean? I plan to go on just as I am now, living in Paris, writing, attending political meetings and rallies."

"But I won't remain in the student milieu," Pierre reminded her. "I'm joining the family business. You and I won't see much of each other."

Rose frowned. "I don't know why you have to take such a gloomy view of things."

"I'm just being realistic," Pierre said. "Thinking about the future. Haven't *you* thought about it at all?"

"Of course," she replied. "I've thought about the fact that with no classes and exams, I'll have more time for what's really important to me."

"And what is that?"

"You know I've always wanted to be a novelist," Rose answered. "I'll keep up my political writing, of course, but I'm also determined to spend at least two hours a day writing poetry and fiction."

"What about your private life? Will there be room for anything besides work?" he pressed. "For love? Marriage and a family?"

Rose sighed in exasperation. "Oh, Pierre. Are we on this subject again?"

"Yes, Rose." Reaching across the table, he took her hand. Rose tried to pull away, but he held fast. "We are."

She couldn't pretend any longer that she didn't know what Pierre was really talking about. A hot flush swept over her face. "Pierre," she said in a small voice, "I'd rather not."

"I've bottled this up for too long," he insisted, his own voice hoarse with urgency. "I knew you weren't interested, weren't ready. But we're not children anymore, Rose. A week from now we'll begin our real, grown-up lives. I think we're old enough to talk openly about this."

"This?" she squeaked.

"Rose, I love you," Pierre declared. "I always have, and you know it. I can't go on like this, though, not knowing your true feelings for me."

Rose stared at Pierre. Deep in her heart she *had* always known that he loved her. She took his devotion completely for granted—it was the rock her life was built on. But she'd always felt safe because they never actually *talked* about their relationship. Pierre respected her need for solitude and independence. *He wants me to say I love him too,* she realized. *He wants me to say that I'll be his wife.* Panic swept over her. "You know I don't like that word—*love,*" she scoffed. "I don't believe in it."

"You mean you don't *want* to believe in it," Pierre countered. "You're scared of it."

"How can I be scared of something that doesn't exist? It's well enough for you, I suppose, but I've never been in love, not once."

"What about Leo?"

"That was an experiment—it wasn't love. I've never been in love and I don't think I ever will be."

"Then where does that leave me? Where does it leave us?" he demanded.

"Do you want me to change?" Rose cried. "Is that it?"

192

"No." Pierre clenched his hands into fists. "Of course I don't want you to change. How could I, when I love you madly? But I've waited too long already. I won't wait forever. Excuse me if I leave you now. As you frequently remind me, you're well able to take care of yourself. Good night, Rose."

He stood up, collecting his coat, hat, and walking stick. As Rose watched him disappear into the night her throat tightened. She came very close to calling after him, *Pierre, wait! I'll think about this, I promise. Just give me a little more time.*

Then she remembered the vow she'd made to herself years ago when she was a girl and then again when she broke up with Leo Rivière. She was a modern woman of the late nineteenth century—she didn't need a man to make her life complete. "I *will* be independent," Rose whispered to herself, angrily dashing the tear from her cheek. "I'll show the world what a woman can do."

🌿 22 🌿

1888.

I must tell Pierre about that funny scene in the editor's office, Rose thought as she trotted up the front steps of her apartment in the Montmartre section of Paris one balmy spring afternoon. *He'll get a good laugh!*

The postman had left a few letters in the box by the door and Rose put them in her pocket without glancing at them. After dropping her narrow-brimmed straw hat on the hall table, she walked back to her library, whistling. Yes, she should invite Pierre over for supper one of these nights. They hadn't gotten together in months.

Two years had passed since graduation, and now that he'd joined his family's business, Pierre was no longer Rose's constant companion. She too was busy, supporting herself by writing articles, short fiction, and poetry for a number of bohemian newspapers. But they were still in close touch, and Rose always saved up her most humorous stories for him. Her life was perpetually full of new acquaintances and experiences, and she never felt satisfied until she'd shared them all with her oldest and most faithful friend.

In the library she took the letters from her pocket. *One from* Maman *and Papa,* she observed, tearing open the envelope. The note inside was brief. "'This weekend . . . a special occasion,'" Rose mumbled, reading out loud. "'All the family will attend . . . the Oiseleurs . . .' Hmmm." The letter was tantalizing, containing few concrete details. *What special occasion?* she wondered. *"You must come home," Maman writes. Not an invitation, an order!*

The weekend was upon her—she'd have to head out to the country that very day. As she began tossing clothes into a valise Rose pondered the mystery. *I'll find out soon enough,* she thought cheerfully.

"Winterthorn looks splendid," Rose told her mother, Lucie de Bocage, on Friday evening. "All the flowers and candles, and the table set for so many guests! It's a large party, then?"

Now that Celeste was so old and frail, her son and daughter-in-law, Rose's parents, lived with her in the château that would someday be theirs. Lucie and Rose were in Rose's bedroom, which was exactly as Rose had left it when she last spent a summer in the country.

"Fifty or so guests, I suppose." Lucie fluttered a slender hand. "Just our closest friends."

"What's the occasion?" asked Rose as she unpacked. "I'm dying to know."

"We're giving the party for Camille and Albert Oiseleur," Lucie explained, frowning at the eccentric articles of clothing that emerged from her daughter's suitcase. "It seems they have big news they want to share with us."

"Big news? What?"

"That I don't know," Lucie replied. "They've been very mysterious. Happy news, of course. Something to celebrate. We've chilled lots of champagne."

"Will Pierre be here tonight?" Rose asked.

"Yes, Camille and Albert made a special point of telling me that Pierre would be with them."

Rose felt a flutter in her rib cage. *Why should my heart race at the thought of seeing Pierre?* she wondered. Out loud she murmured, "Now, what should I wear?"

Lucie pursed her lips as she studied Rose, who was dressed as usual in men's-style trousers, shirt, and jacket. "I do hope you're not planning to go to the party like that. People gossip enough about you and wonder how your father and I ever could have raised such a—"

"Oh, *Maman,* don't worry," Rose broke in, laughing. "I won't embarrass you. There are plenty of dresses in the closet. Help me choose one."

After a few minutes' consideration Lucie and Rose agreed on a pink organdy gown. "Not this year's style," Lucie said with a sigh as she laid the dress on the bed, "but better than pants."

Her mother left her alone. Shedding the clothes she'd traveled in, Rose wrapped herself in a silk robe and sat down at the dressing table. Picking up a silver-backed hairbrush, she began brushing out her long, red hair.

She studied her reflection. She'd belted the robe loosely, and her graceful neck and strong, ivory shoulders were revealed. *My figure is good,* Rose thought, *and my face is pretty—at least, men have always told me so.* She'd never worried much about her appearance, but now she found herself patting her cheeks to make them pinker and considering a change in hairstyle. She wanted to look beautiful, and she thought she knew why.

An hour before the party Rose strolled outside in the gardens. Everywhere she went, something reminded her of the past . . . and of Pierre. *There's the kitchen door, right near where Cook kept the rabbits,* Rose mused. *And there's the tree I dared Pierre to climb.* He'd fallen from one of the highest branches onto a pile of hay, and when she ran up to him, he was lying perfectly still. Her heart had stopped—she'd thought he was dead—and then he'd sat up abruptly, shouting, "Boo!" She'd screeched at the top of her lungs. Rose smiled at the memory. *Served me right, I suppose.*

She wandered through the maze of hedges, recalling that she'd walked there with Pierre many summers ago. There'd been tension between them—what were they talking about? *It must have been one of those conversations we used to have,* she reflected, *when Pierre would drop hints about his feelings for me and I'd dance away from them.* She remembered another encounter, right before graduation, when Pierre confessed his love for her. She'd rebuffed him and for a while he'd been distant, but eventually they were as thick as ever.

A strange feeling of quiet happiness settled over her. She stopped in front of some rosebushes, bending to inhale the heavenly scent. *I must be getting old and sentimental,* she decided as she picked one of the blossoms. Here she was, thinking that if she had that conversation with Pierre today, she'd respond very differently. She wasn't so afraid of losing her independence—she almost liked the idea of settling down. Who said she couldn't have a husband and a writing career too?

Rose turned back to the house. In the distance she heard the sound of wheels and hooves clattering on gravel. A carriage was coming down the drive to the château. *Pierre and his parents,* she thought, her eyes shining with anticipation. Tucking the rose into her hair, she hurried inside. Her parents were in the front hallway, awaiting their guests. Rose joined them just as the butler announced the Oiseleurs.

Lucie de Bocage and Camille Oiseleur greeted each other with kisses. "So wonderful to see you," Lucie said.

As her father shook hands with Albert Oiseleur, Rose looked past them eagerly. Pierre and a few other people had just entered. When Pierre saw Rose, his eyes brightened. "Rose!" he exclaimed.

Warmth flooded her heart. Blushing with pleasure, Rose stepped forward quickly, her hands outstretched. Then she focused on the shyly smiling young woman clinging to Pierre's arm. Rose faltered.

"Rose, I'm so glad you're here." Pierre patted the girl's hand, which rested on his arm in an affectionate, possessive way. "I want you to be the first to meet Christianne. My fiancée."

At the time Rose thought the dinner party on Friday evening was the most excruciating experience of her life. Being forced to pretend she was overjoyed when Pierre's parents formally announced their son's engagement had been horrible: lifting her wineglass through all those interminable toasts to the happy young couple and the sight of Pierre and Christianne gazing at each other with adoration! But it was nothing to the pain she felt now, two days later, sitting in her family's ornately carved pew at the parish church, watching Pierre and Christianne exchange wedding vows.

Her gloved hands clasped tightly, Rose stared

forward with blurry eyes. *I won't cry*, she thought, struggling to maintain her composure. *No one must know that my heart is breaking.*

"Do you, Pierre Oiseleur, take this woman, Christianne Bernard, to be your lawfully wedded wife," the priest intoned, "promising to love, honor, and cherish her . . ."

Rose looked down, unable to bear the sight of Pierre and Christianne at the altar. *It should have been me*, she thought, biting her lip so hard it bled. *Oh, why was I so blind?*

She'd always made fun of her girlhood friends when they fantasized about their weddings: the gown, the flowers, the gifts, the handsome bridegroom, the trousseau and honeymoon. "We shouldn't think only of becoming wives and mothers," she'd lectured them. "We're people, you know, just as men are. We can contribute something besides babies to the world." But she too had cherished an image, deep in her secret heart, although she'd never admitted it to anyone, even to herself. She'd always assumed one day she'd walk down the aisle with her best friend. She and Pierre, inseparable since childhood, would grow old together.

"I now pronounce you man and wife."

Rose forced herself to lift her eyes as the final words of the marriage ceremony echoed through the church. A trumpeter played a joyful fanfare. Pierre and Christianne marched back up the aisle, their faces wreathed in smiles.

"She's a beautiful bride," Rose's mother whispered approvingly in her ear. "Pierre chose well."

Rose nodded wordlessly, choked with bitterness. The de Bocages filed out along with the other friends and relatives of the Oiseleurs. *He did not choose well,* Rose wanted to cry. *He betrayed me! How could he marry another?*

Then Rose remembered what Pierre had said that night on the Rive Gauche. "I love you, but I won't wait for you forever. . . ."

She'd blithely thought that no matter how many times she hurt and rejected him, Pierre would always be there for her. She'd been wrong. He'd given up on her at last and looked elsewhere for happiness. *And the whole time I was in love with him too,* Rose thought. *Why didn't I see it sooner, before it was too late?*

One by one the wedding guests congratulated the bride and groom. Afraid that she might burst into tears, Rose ducked out of the receiving line and stood off to one side. At last Pierre and Christianne started down the church steps to their waiting carriage.

Someone held out a basket of fragrant pink rose petals. Mechanically Rose took a handful and tossed it after the departing couple. People clapped and cheered. Christianne turned to blow a kiss to her parents and Pierre waved a jaunty good-bye.

Rose stared after the departing carriage, the blank expression in her eyes masking a depthless sorrow. Though she was surrounded by a joyful crowd, she'd never felt more alone.

❧ 23 ❧

1893. Paris.

The summer breeze ruffled the curtains of the open window above Rose's desk. Putting down her pen, she gazed out at the cornflower blue sky. Then she looked down at the sheet of paper in front of her and the thick stack of sheets on the corner of her desk: the manuscript of her novel. She *should* write a few more pages before calling it quits for the day.

Rose pushed back her chair. She ran a brush through her thick auburn hair, then twisted it into a knot and secured it with an ebony clip. Buttoning her shoes, she grabbed a hat and headed out into the tree-lined street.

An hour later she was on a train going to the Loire Valley. She hadn't given her family any warning, so there was no one to meet her when she arrived. Unfazed, she set off on foot through the fields as she had often done in the past. *Maman and Papa will be so surprised!* she thought, smiling to herself. She didn't often come home for visits anymore, even short ones. Ever since Pierre's wedding five years ago, she'd found it hard to face the old familiar scenes.

At Winterthorn she greeted the housekeeper with a warm hug. "I know you didn't expect me, Irene, but don't worry. You needn't go to any trouble. I'm not staying the night."

"But your parents aren't here!" Irene informed her, dismayed. "They've gone to the coast for a month, as they always do in the summer."

"That's right. I came on a whim, without even thinking." Something occurred to her. "But do you know what? It's really *Grandmaman* I wanted to talk to. How is she?"

"As well as can be expected for someone who recently celebrated her hundredth birthday. Frail, but up here . . ." Irene tapped her forehead. "Sharp as a tack. She's outside, in the garden."

Rose went out to the garden. Her grandmother was sitting in a chair facing the sun, a blanket wrapped around her shoulders. *She looks so small,* Rose thought, *like a little bird. A hundred years old!* "*Grandmaman,* look who's here to see you," Rose announced, kneeling down in front of Celeste's chair and taking her grandmother's hands.

203

Celeste squeezed Rose's hands, her grip still surprisingly strong. "Welcome, my dear. I was just thinking about you."

"You were?" Rose pulled up a second chair. "And what were you thinking?"

"I was thinking about the story you gave me to read a few months ago, the one about the lovers who met in an orchard. It was very sad."

"I'm afraid I don't know how to write a love story with a happy ending."

"Your stories used to be quite lighthearted," Celeste noted.

"When I was young," said Rose with a smile. "I'm twenty-eight now. My writing comes from a deeper, more complicated place."

They sat for a minute in companionable silence, basking in the warm sun. Then Celeste said suddenly, "There's a new man in your life, isn't there?"

Her grandmother's perception always took Rose by surprise. "How did you know?"

Celeste didn't explain. "Tell me about him."

"His name is Robert Eastman. He's an American," Rose said. "We met at a political meeting. He's a writer, like me. He's traveled all over the world—he speaks a dozen languages."

"Are you in love with him?" Celeste asked.

"I don't know," Rose said softly after a moment's careful thought. "I care for him, certainly, and I admire him. I like being with him. But it's not . . . it's not the same feeling I had when I was young, when I was in love with . . ."

"I remember that feeling," Celeste said, a whisper of a smile flitting across her wrinkled face.

"Was Grandpa your first love?" asked Rose.

"My first and only."

"Do you think . . ." Rose sat forward, her fingers gripping the arms of her chair. "Do you think, for each person, there can be only one true love in a lifetime? And if that person chooses someone else . . ."

"For me, there was only Marc," Celeste replied. "We faced many obstacles, but at last we were able to wed. But if Marc had married another, though I would have mourned my loss, I believe I would have kept my heart open, hoping for it to heal so someday I could love again."

Tears brimmed in Rose's eyes. "It's so hard," she whispered.

Celeste reached out for Rose's hand. "I know, my child. But do you want to be alone forever?"

"I haven't done so badly on my own," Rose said. "My first novel will be published next month and I've already started another. I'm successful."

"Yes, but are you happy?"

Rose didn't answer. She sat with her grandmother in the garden until the sun sank behind the château. After supper she took the train back to the city, not sure if the trip to Winterthorn had helped her understand her feelings more clearly or if her emotions were even muddier than before.

"I'm so proud of you, Rosie," Robert Eastman said, a slight American accent lending Yankee color to his fluent French. "It's a wonderful novel." His eyes crinkled in a merry smile. "I'm sure it will sell like hotcakes and bring you everlasting fame and fortune."

Rose lifted a copy of her novel from the box her publisher had sent over and stroked the cover reverently. "I can't get over it," she admitted, a wide smile on her face. "I mean, I've seen my name in print before, countless times. But those were just newspaper stories. This—this is a *book!*"

"We have to celebrate," Robert declared. He went to the kitchen, returning with two glasses of champagne. He gave one to Rose, then took her other hand. "Come here," he said, leading her out to the terrace.

The sun was just sinking in the western sky, bathing the city with warm, golden light. Robert's chestnut hair gleamed like burnished copper and his blue eyes were brighter than Rose had ever seen them. "To Rose de Bocage," he said, lifting his glass. "The most beautiful, talented woman in the city of Paris. No, make that in the entire world."

Rose smiled. "I can't drink to that, silly."

"OK, how about this." His expression grew

more serious. "To Rose. The woman I love. The woman I want to marry."

Rose's smile faded. "Oh, Robert. I wish you hadn't."

"I'm sorry. Did I spoil the moment?" He placed both their glasses on the balustrade and took Rose's hands in his own. "It seemed like as good a time as any. You know my feelings. I've wanted this for a long time. I thought you did too."

She looked away, her eyes roving over the darkening Paris skyline. "I may . . . and I may not."

He squeezed her hands. "We'll have a fantastic life together, Rosie. We'll travel all over the world, anywhere and anytime you please. And you know I support your writing career wholeheartedly. Oh, and I worship the ground you walk on, if that counts for anything."

She smiled crookedly. "Of course it does. I didn't mean to sound ungrateful. I just . . . I need a few more days."

"Take as much time as you like," Robert urged her.

Two days later Rose was still considering Robert's marriage proposal, struggling to understand her heart. *I think I love him,* she mused, looking out the window at the soft summer rain. *No, I do love him—I do. So why does part of me still hold back?*

The rain let up late in the morning. The sky was still low and gray, but Rose was eager to escape the house. Taking an umbrella just in case, she walked to the Left Bank to browse the book stalls. She spent half an hour poring over volumes, finally deciding on a copy of Montaigne's essays. Her purchase tucked under her arm, she strolled on. As she ducked between two stalls she nearly bumped into a tall man in a gray overcoat. *"Pardonnez-moi,"* she murmured, not glancing at his face.

He stepped aside to let her pass. Then he spoke. "Rose?"

Rose blinked up at him. Color flooded her face. It was Pierre. She hadn't seen him since his wedding day, and her tongue was completely tied. Pierre too appeared flustered, but after clearing his throat a few times, he managed to say calmly, "You remember my wife, Christianne?"

The two women shook hands. "It's nice to see you again," Rose murmured.

"And my sons." Pierre indicated the little blond boys clinging shyly to his trouser legs. "David and Edouard. They're twins."

"They look like angels," Rose said with a tremulous smile.

They stood in awkward silence. Just then the little boys decided to toddle off toward the river's edge. Christianne hurried after them. "So," said Pierre. "I hear from my parents that you'll soon have a novel published."

"It's out now, actually."

"I'd like to read it."

"I'll send you a copy," she offered.

"That would be nice."

"And your business, it's going well?"

"Quite well."

Rose looked after Christianne and the boys. "What a lovely family."

"I feel very fortunate," Pierre said.

Christianne returned, holding a child by each hand. "I think it's time to visit the patisserie," she told her husband, flashing a smile at Rose. "We promised them something sweet."

"Well." Pierre held out his hand. "Rose. I hope . . . it was pleasant. . . . Congratulations," he finished clumsily.

They gazed at each other, their eyes full of the feelings it was no longer appropriate for them to express. Rose looked away first. "Good-bye, Pierre."

Pierre and his family disappeared among the stalls. As soon as she was alone Rose sank down on a nearby park bench, her shoulders racked with silent sobs. After a few minutes she took a handkerchief from her pocket and dried her tears. She continued to sit on the bench, watching the passing scene. Overhead the clouds parted—a ray of sun streamed down, warming her.

All of a sudden Rose realized that she felt lighter, as if a weight had lifted from her, a weight she'd carried for a long time. *Pierre has his own life, his own family,* she thought calmly. Meanwhile, at long last, she'd been presented with a chance at happiness herself. Perhaps it wasn't the life she'd imagined, but it could be—and perhaps would be—a good one.

She jumped to her feet and headed quickly toward home. She couldn't wait to see Robert.

"This was the hardest thing I ever did," Rose told her husband, Robert Eastman.

Five years had passed; it was May 1898. "Harder than writing a novel?" Robert teased, pulling his chair closer to his wife's bed.

Rose looked down at the swaddled baby lying in her arms. "But worth it," she said. "So, so worth it."

The new parents gazed for a long time at their daughter, their eyes glowing with love and awe. "Look at her eyelashes and those perfect, tiny ears," gushed Robert. "She's a little princess."

"What kind of person do you suppose she'll be?" wondered Rose, lightly stroking the baby's cheek.

"A holy terror, I imagine," said Robert with a laugh, "because I plan to spoil her rotten."

Rose smiled at her husband. "She's a miracle, isn't she?"

"A miracle," Robert agreed. He took his wife's hand and kissed it. "The second one of my life. The first was finding you."

A feeling of deep contentment filled Rose's weary, aching body. "I'm so lucky," she said, tears sparkling in her eyes. "A week ago we celebrated our fifth wedding anniversary, and on the same day my second novel was published. Today we have a child. And did you know this would have been my grandmother's birthday?"

Robert shook his head. "I wish Celeste were still alive to meet the little one. But what a good coincidence, eh?"

"There's never been a woman as strong and kind as Celeste de Bocage," Rose agreed. "I hope she *does* take after *Grandmaman.*"

"Which leads us back to who 'she' is," said Robert. "What do you want to name her?"

Rose peered into the baby's sleeping face, searching for clues. "I don't know. Something . . . poetic."

"Something regal."

Inspiration struck. "Isabelle," Rose suggested.

"Yes, that's it!" Robert took the baby, cradling the small bundle in his burly arms. "Welcome, Isabelle Eastman," he declared, his voice gruff with emotion. "We have great plans for you."

"And high hopes," added Rose.

Robert gazed into his wife's eyes. "And boundless love."

Rose smiled. "And boundless love," she echoed.

🌿 *24* 🌿

1914. Paris.

Sixteen-year-old Isabelle Eastman floated around her bedroom in her cotton chemise and petticoat, giddy with the excitement of dressing for her first dance. She slipped the pale green organdy dress over her head and shook out the skirt's soft folds of ruffled fabric, then fussed for a few minutes, trying to tie the darker green sash in a perfect bow. "*Maman,*" she called down the hall. "Come help me with my buttons!"

Rose Eastman appeared at her daughter's door. "Look at you," she exclaimed. "Pretty as a picture."

Isabelle twirled so that her ankle-length skirt billowed around her like a cloud. "I love this dress," she exclaimed. "It feels like springtime."

Though her abundant red hair was streaked with gray, at almost fifty Rose was still a strikingly beautiful woman, and never more so than when her lavender eyes twinkled with laughter as they did now. "Come here, Springtime. The back of your dress is gaping open and your petticoat is showing."

Isabelle stood patiently while her mother-buttoned the back of her dress and adjusted her sash. "There." Rose patted Isabelle's shoulders. "All set."

Isabelle ran to the mirror and studied her reflection. "Earrings," she remembered. "Should I wear my pearls? No. The little gold stars?"

Rose stepped forward, taking something from her pocket. "Perhaps you'd like to wear these. They belonged to my grandmother, Celeste. She had green eyes like yours."

Isabelle held out her hand and Rose placed something that glittered in her palm. "Oh, *Maman*," Isabelle cried. "Emeralds!"

"Try them on," Rose urged.

Isabelle slipped on the earrings and shook her head to make them jingle. "They're exquisite," she gushed. "They make me feel like a queen! I never want to give them back."

Isabelle had inherited her mother's intelligence and self-confidence, but she was also given to extravagant flights of fancy. "I intended for them to be yours eventually," Rose said with an indulgent smile. "I suppose . . ."

Isabelle hugged her mother impulsively. "Thank you, *Maman!*"

Rose extricated herself from her daughter's embrace. "Your hair is all in a tangle," she observed. "Let me help you with it."

Isabelle sat in front of the mirror as her mother brushed her lush, dark brown hair until it was as glossy as satin. "My first dance, *Maman*. I feel like I'm about to walk through a magical door into a whole new world. I'm finally a woman."

"Don't be in *too* much of a hurry to grow up, *ma petite*."

"I can't help it. I want to see what's on the other side of that door. Maybe I'll meet someone tonight," Isabelle conjectured, her eyes dreamy, "and fall in love."

But you're still so young, Rose started to say. She bit her tongue. *When I was a young girl, I thought love was silly and useless. Perhaps it's better to have some romance in your soul.* Rose pulled back a section of her daughter's hair and secured it with a gold filigree barrette. "Maybe you will," she agreed with a soft smile.

The parish hall was lively that June night with the strains of dance music and the babble of young voices. Isabelle had just arrived with her friends Jeanette and Madeleine and their chaperone, Jeanette's aunt Dorothea.

As soon as they could the three girls sneaked away from Aunt Dorothea. "That's better!" Jeanette declared as they helped themselves to cups of punch at the refreshment table. "We'd have no fun at all with

Auntie chiding us about our manners and breathing down our necks as we try to talk to young men!"

"Do you think we will?" asked Isabelle. "Talk to young men, I mean."

"Of course!" Jeanette tossed her head in the fashion of a silent movie star. "And see how many handsome ones there are to choose from!"

Isabelle nodded, suddenly feeling incredibly shy. The room *was* filled with young men, some in civilian clothes and others in military uniform. "But we can't just march up to them," she murmured. "We have to wait for them to approach us."

"That's true," said Madeleine, "but I'm sure we won't wait long."

Isabelle peeked around her punch glass, still scanning the crowd. A young man on the other side of the room caught her eye. The air left her lungs and she found herself suddenly breathless. *Oh, my,* she thought. He was tall, with broad shoulders, black hair, piercing light eyes, and a magnetic smile. "And how dashing he looks in that blue officer's uniform," she whispered.

"Who looks dashing?" Jeanette wanted to know.

"We have to walk that way," Isabelle responded, trying to maneuver her friends in the young officer's direction. "I *must* dance with him. But try not to draw attention to yourselves. I don't want it to be too obvious."

The girls sidled a few paces, then paused, then strolled a little more. Isabelle risked another glance at the young man and caught him looking their way.

Is he interested? she wondered. *Am I having the same effect on him as he has on me?* She lost sight of him. When the crowd parted again, a young man in uniform appeared. "Is that the one?" Madeleine whispered, jabbing Isabelle with her elbow.

Isabelle shook her head. "No."

"Well, whoever he is, he's coming this way," hissed Jeanette. "And he's looking at you!"

The young man, who was tall and sandy haired with brown eyes, stopped in front of them. Cap in hand, he bowed politely. "Good evening, ladies," he said, his voice pleasant. "My name is Charles Doret."

Jeanette introduced herself and her friends. "I wonder," said the officer, "if Mademoiselle Eastman would care to dance?"

Isabelle blushed profusely. "Um . . ."

Madeleine gave Isabelle a shove. "She'd *love* to," Jeanette declared on Isabelle's behalf.

Before she could gather her wits, Isabelle found herself moving about the dance floor in Charles Doret's arms. "I'm sorry if I took you by surprise," he apologized.

She laughed. "Oh, no, *I'm* sorry. I hardly know how to behave. It's my first dance."

"That explains it. I was wondering why I hadn't noticed you before."

Isabelle looked over Charles's shoulder and glimpsed the black-haired young officer watching them. "There are quite a few men in uniform here tonight," she observed.

"My regiment is billeted just a mile away," Charles replied. "It's nice for us to mingle in elegant company. Soon enough we'll have no time for parties."

"Do you think we'll be at war?" asked Isabelle, trying to spot the dark-haired man again.

"Within months, if not weeks," Charles said with certainty. "The German army is mobilizing."

Isabelle's father, a journalist, had just published a story about the assassination of Austro-Hungarian Archduke Ferdinand and the unstable European political climate. She knew enough to converse intelligently on the subject, but at the moment it didn't interest her in the least. *I must find out the dark-haired officer's name,* she thought. "Military life must make you very close to your fellow officers," Isabelle remarked casually.

"They're my best friends," Charles confirmed.

"Did you know any of them before you joined up?"

"Only Jacques Oiseleur," said Charles. "The tall fellow over there, with the black hair. We've been pals since boyhood."

Isabelle's heart pounded. The tall fellow with the black hair . . . *Yes, it's him! Maybe Charles will introduce me.* Just then the music stopped. Isabelle stepped away from Charles. "Thank you for the dance," she said.

"My pleasure," he responded, his brown eyes warm. "I hope we'll be partners again soon."

As he escorted her off the dance floor Isabelle's eyes raked the room. But though many soldiers were still there, the one she was looking for had gone. All that remained was her memory of his face and his name. *Jacques Oiseleur*.

Isabelle's eyes blinked open. Morning sun streamed through her curtains, making the daffodil yellow walls of her bedroom glow. She stretched languorously, a sleepy smile on her face. *What a dream I had last night!* She pulled the crisp white cotton sheet up to her chin, giggling as she remembered the details. She'd never been kissed before, but she'd dreamed about kissing. About kissing the handsome officer from the dance, Jacques Oiseleur!

Isabelle splashed her face with cool water from the basin on her dresser and ran a brush through her hair. Dressing quickly, she ran downstairs. A hot breakfast waited for her in chafing dishes on the dining-room sideboard, but instead she grabbed an apple and ran outside.

It was a gorgeous late spring morning. The sky was as blue as a robin's egg and the breeze carried the delicious scent of damp earth and new green plants. Isabelle curled up in the swing her father had hung for her from the thick gnarled branch of an old tree. She crunched her teeth into her apple.

She couldn't stop thinking about Jacques Oiseleur. *What's happened to me?* she wondered as she hopped down from the swing to put her apple core in the hutch for the rabbit. Her heart was bouncing in her chest like a red rubber ball. She put her hands to her cheeks—her face was flushed and warm. She was awake, but she still had the airy, intoxicated feeling of a dream. *Have I fallen in love with him even though we didn't speak a word?*

Isabelle paced the garden, her footsteps as erratic as her tumbling thoughts. If only Jacques had asked her to dance instead of Charles! Had he wanted to—was he just shy? Or did he have a girl-friend? What if she never saw him again? As she strolled near the house she heard a window opening. Rose leaned out from her first-floor study. "Darling, you'll be late for school."

"Yes, *Maman.*" Isabelle waved a hand. "I'm on my way."

Back inside she wrapped her lunch of bread, cheese, and fruit in a cloth napkin. Then she gathered her books and fastened them with a leather strap. Swinging the strap over her shoulder, she headed out to the street.

At the sidewalk she turned slowly to look back at the house. Maman *can't see me—her study's in the back. And Papa's out of town.* She faced the street again. To the right it was a half-mile walk to school and to the left, a mile or so down the road. . . her eyes sparkled mischievously. *I can't leave it to chance,* she decided, turning left toward the outskirts of Paris—and the barracks where Jacques Oiseleur and his troop were billeted. She sprinted, her books bouncing and her hair flying, hurrying so her truancy wouldn't be discovered.

        ✳   ✳   ✳

"I'm here to visit my brother," Isabelle told the guard at the entrance to the barracks.

"I see," he said, winking at her. "Go ahead, mademoiselle."

Blushing, Isabelle hurried through the gate. *Now what?* she wondered, looking around her. The barracks was a maze of dirt roads and low, plain buildings that all looked alike. Suddenly her scheme seemed foolish. *I can't just march up to him in the mess hall, in front of everybody!*

She was about to turn on her heel and make her escape when she glimpsed a group of officers approaching. From a distance one of them looked like Charles Doret. *Oh, dear,* Isabelle thought, panicking. *I can't let him see me.*

There was a door open in a building just a few yards away. Isabelle dove through it, praying the officers hadn't spotted her.

She found herself in a barn that smelled of hay and horses. Isabelle exhaled a sigh of relief. She leaned against one of the stalls. "I'll just hide in here with you for a minute," she told the bay gelding within, whose coat was groomed to a high gloss, "and then as soon as the coast is clear—*oh!*"

A man stepped from the shadows in the corner of the stall. Isabelle jumped. When she saw who it was, she nearly fainted. Jacques Oiseleur!

"I thought I was—I didn't see . . . ," she babbled,

220

blushing with mortification. "You're probably wondering how—why—".

"I'm sorry if I startled you," he said.

"It's my fault. I shouldn't be in here." Isabelle took a deep breath, steadying herself. She'd been about to flee, but now she realized that she couldn't have stumbled on a better opportunity. *I must look like an idiot, but I'm talking to him! And we're all alone. Except for the horse, of course!*

"Were you looking for someone? Can I help you?" he offered, emerging from the stall to stand beside her.

"Actually . . ." She mustered all her nerve. "I know you'll think me outrageously bold, but . . . I saw you at the dance last night."

"I saw you too," he said, looking down at the floor, a faint pink color rising up under his suntan.

Isabelle felt encouraged. "It was a nice party, wasn't it?"

"Sure. I enjoyed the music."

"But you don't care for dancing?" she guessed.

He shrugged. "Not much."

"Well, I love dancing. But I like other things too," she added. "Would you . . . it's a lovely day. Would you—if you're not too busy—like to take a walk?"

"Shouldn't you be in school?" he asked, his eyebrows lifting.

"It's a holiday," Isabelle fibbed. "The . . . headmistress's birthday."

"Ah."

She gestured at the horse. "But if you're working . . ."

"I'm done for now. Just cleaning him up after our morning drills," said Jacques.

"It's a beautiful horse."

"He's a good mount."

They stood awkwardly. Then Jacques cleared his throat. "I should've said this sooner. My name's Jacques Oiseleur."

"I'm Isabelle Eastman."

They shook hands. "Isabelle." He repeated the name shyly. "I'd like to take a walk, but . . . when I saw you just now, I assumed you were looking for Charles."

"For Charles? Goodness, no," Isabelle exclaimed.

"You mean, you're not Charles's girl?"

"We met for the first time last night and had a very pleasant conversation. But there's no relationship like that between us."

"Oh." Slowly a smile spread across his face. "Well, good."

The smile melted Isabelle's bones like butter. An attack of shyness overwhelmed her. "You probably have a lot of things to do. I'm just in the way. I'll—"

She started to turn away. "No, wait," said Jacques, touching her arm. "I have time for a short walk. Come on."

He led her to a door at the other end of the barn. They ducked between a few buildings and found themselves in a tree-lined lane. "No one will see us here," Jacques told her. He gestured at the fields. "Just the cows."

Isabelle laughed. "I don't want to get you in trouble."

"Don't worry," he assured her. "The army's not so strict. We spend most of our time grooming our horses and polishing our bayonets and waiting for something to happen."

"You must be very brave," she remarked admiringly.

"We'll see. I haven't been tested yet." He gazed down at her, his eyes twinkling. "You're the brave one. Coming to the barracks all by yourself!"

Isabelle grimaced. "Do you have the worst impression of my character?"

"Not at all. I think you're . . . refreshing."

They walked down the lane, chatting and laughing. Isabelle floated on the perfumed spring air, not even feeling the earth beneath her shoes. She hadn't really known what she was looking for when she sneaked into the barracks, but now that she'd found it—found *him*—it seemed so inevitable. *Destiny*, she thought.

They reached the end of the lane and turned around reluctantly. "I'm usually tongue-tied around girls," Jacques confessed, "especially pretty ones. But somehow with you, Isabelle, it's different. I feel I've known you a lifetime. Does that sound strange?" Tentatively he reached for her hand.

"Not at all," Isabelle said, her eyes shining. "That sounds exactly right."

25

"You didn't have to wait up for me," Isabelle playfully chided her parents one July night a few weeks later. It was ten o'clock, and she'd just come in from a walk with Jacques. "Look at the two of you. You can hardly keep your eyes open."

Robert Eastman chuckled. "Now that you're home safe, I can crawl into bed."

"Sweet dreams, Papa," Isabelle said.

Rose remained on the parlor couch, her sewing on her lap. "Sit with me," she invited, patting the cushion beside her.

Isabelle joined her mother. "You really don't have to worry when I'm out with Jacques," she said. "He's the most honorable man alive, a complete gentleman."

"I take your word for that, darling," Rose assured her. "I trust your judgment. Still . . ." She smiled wryly. "I'm a mother, first and foremost. And mothers worry about their daughters."

"But when their daughters are old enough to take care of themselves—"

"You're only sixteen," Rose reminded her.

"I may be only sixteen, but I'm not a child."

Rose took a few stitches on the blouse she was mending, wondering how to voice her concerns without inflaming her daughter's volatile emotions. "I don't want you to think I disapprove of your friendship with Jacques," she began carefully. "He sounds like a fine young man—and I am quite well acquainted with the Oiseleur family. I grew up with a second cousin of Jacques's." Rose's voice trembled a moment with emotion, but she quickly regained control. "But that's a very different story," she continued. "I want you to remember that Jacques is a soldier. When war is declared—and it will be, soon—he'll be sent to the front. I don't want you to lose your heart to someone who might . . . get hurt."

"It's too late for that," declared Isabelle passionately. "He already has my heart. We're in love, *Maman.*"

Rose stared at her daughter. "Oh, Isabelle."

"*Maman,* why do you look sad when something so wonderful has happened to me?" Isabelle cried.

"I'm not sad; I'm just . . . worried."

"Don't be, *Maman.* I know there are risks, but I'm not afraid." Isabelle clasped her mother's hand.

225

"Nothing's more important than love, *Maman*. Would you have me turn away from my chance at happiness?"

Rose gazed into her daughter's wide, innocent eyes. She remembered her own first love, Pierre Oiseleur. How many chances had he given her? And she'd thrown them all away, building a hard, independent shell around her fragile heart. "No," Rose whispered at last. "Of course I wouldn't, darling."

On every street corner newspaper headlines screamed the story. France was at war with Germany!

The Eastman household was in a flurry as Rose and Robert excitedly discussed the news with friends and relatives, neighbors and colleagues. Isabelle only had one thought, however. An icy-cold knot of fear formed in her stomach. *Jacques.*

She ran all the way to the barracks, the heat of the early August day pressing down on her like a stone. By the time she reached the gate, she was panting and drenched in sweat. The guard, who knew her by now, just waved her through, sympathy flickering in his somber eyes.

The first familiar face she spotted was Charles Doret's. "Charles!" Isabelle cried, waving frantically.

Charles said a few words to his companions, then hurried over to her. "Isabelle," he said, seizing her hand.

When she first started seeing Jacques, Isabelle felt a little uncomfortable around Charles. Though he never said anything, she'd sensed he was disappointed that she hadn't been interested in him. He was too unselfish and good-natured not to be happy for his best friend, however.

"It's so awful," she said now, clutching Charles's sleeve. "Will you go to the front soon?"

"Within the week," he answered grimly.

"I must find Jacques. Where is he?"

"The officers have been in meetings all day," Charles replied. "Jacques may still be tied up."

Isabelle bit her lip, disappointed. "When you see him, will you tell him I was looking for him?"

"I'm sure he'll come by your house tonight if he can get away," Charles assured her. "You'll be uppermost on his mind."

The barracks were humming with activity, and Charles couldn't spare any more time. *I might as well go home and wait there,* Isabelle thought unhappily, turning back to the gate. But she found her footsteps taking her instead to the stables. At the stall where Jacques kept his bay horse, Saber, Isabelle burst into tears. "I can't bear it," she sobbed. "Oh, Saber, take care of him, won't you? Don't let him be wounded or . . . or . . ."

"Isabelle, is that you?"

She whirled around. "I saw Charles and he told me you'd been here," Jacques said hoarsely. "I was about to follow you home but thought I'd

227

look in here first. I just had a hunch . . ."

They ran into each other's arms and hugged as tightly as they could. "Please don't go," Isabelle whispered.

"You know I have to," Jacques murmured, stroking her hair. "But I'll miss you terribly. Come on, let's get out of this stuffy old barn."

Hand in hand, they ran to the winding lane where they'd walked the first day they met. As soon as they were out of sight of the barracks they scrambled over a fence into a field and fell, embracing, onto the soft green grass under a tree. "Oh, Isabelle," said Jacques, his voice cracking with emotion. "You mean so much to me. How can I leave you?"

"I'll go to the front with you," she declared tearfully. "I'll be a nurse."

"They won't let women go where there's danger. You'll be able to help here at home."

"But if something should happen to you!" She buried her face against his neck.

"I'll be fine," he promised. "When the war's over, I'll come back to you, Isabelle."

Thunder rumbled in the distance and a hot breeze stirred the leaves of the trees. "When the war is over," Isabelle repeated, shivering despite the oppressive warmth of the day. "We don't know when that will be. The war could last for years!"

"There will be furloughs. If you'll wait for me, Isabelle—"

"I don't want to wait," she declared fiercely.

Jacques's face fell. "Of course. It's a lot to ask of you," he said, choking out the words. "I'd hoped that someday, we might . . . we might be married. But I understand if—"

"I don't want to wait," Isabelle said again, her voice vibrating with meaning.

Jacques stared into her eyes. "Isabelle, what are you saying?"

In answer she wrapped her arms around his neck and kissed him full on the lips. "When we say good-bye a week from now, I want to be saying good-bye to my husband," she whispered.

"Are you sure this is what you want?" Jacques asked Isabelle, taking both her hands in his.

It was the night before his regiment was to leave for Verdun, on the river Meuse northeast of Paris, where the Allies were fighting to repel the invading German forces. Isabelle had sneaked out of her parents' house and come to the barracks, wearing a plain white dress with a pale blue sash. Looking up into Jacques's eyes, she nodded. "I've never been more sure of anything in my life."

"Do you know how much I love you, Isabelle Eastman?"

She stood on tiptoes so they could kiss. "As much as I love you, Jacques Oiseleur."

The army chaplain was waiting for them in his makeshift sanctuary. Charles Doret accompanied them to serve as Jacques's best man. Waving Charles ahead, Jacques hung back for a moment longer. "It's what I want too, but maybe it's wrong," he said, nervously crumpling his cap in his hands. "Marrying in secret. We should have told your parents. I'd like their blessing."

She'd thought long and hard about confiding in her mother and father but decided not to. She knew they wouldn't approve—they'd worry and criticize or forbid the match outright. "When the war's over, we'll have a real wedding," Isabelle promised. "My parents will absolutely adore you as a son-in-law."

Finally, Jacques smiled. He held out his hand to show her it was shaking. "So much for soldierly courage!"

They entered the sanctuary. The chaplain greeted them with a benevolent smile. "You're not the first young couple I've wed these past few days," he told them. "The human heart is a funny thing. In the midst of darkest danger, we affirm love and life. Come here, my children."

Isabelle and Jacques stood before him, their hands joined. Charles stood to the side, two wedding rings in his coat pocket.

Isabelle turned her head to look at Jacques. She didn't have a proper wedding dress, or flowers, or bridesmaids. There'd be no cake or party or dancing, no honeymoon, no new home. She'd be a wife, but she'd be alone, and she knew her heart would break in two when she kissed Jacques good-bye and sent him to the front. *But I don't care,* she thought, her eyes starry with love. *I'll be married to the kindest, handsomest, most wonderful man in the whole world. We won't have to be parted for long. And then we'll have the rest of our lives to be together, to have the life we dream of.*

When the chaplain asked her if she would take Jacques to be her husband "till death do you part," Isabelle answered without hesitation. "I do," she said clearly.

❧ 26 ❧

Six months later France was a nation under siege. Isabelle's father was often gone from home, reporting on the fighting from the front lines. Her mother had put aside her current novel-in-progress to write political pieces, attend meetings and rallies, and volunteer at a local hospital. Isabelle too went to the hospital nearly every day after school. There were other war brides working there, and though Isabelle couldn't reveal her secret, she felt a deep kinship with them.

Any one of these men might be my own dear Jacques, Isabelle thought one February afternoon as she bathed a wounded soldier's feverish brow with a cool, damp cloth. After changing his bandages she rose to her feet. "Mademoiselle, I wonder if you could help me," a soft voice requested.

Isabelle turned. A soldier a few beds down lay

propped on one elbow. She saw, with a mixture of pity and horror, that his other arm had been amputated. "What can I do for you?" she asked gently.

"If you'd write a short letter for me," he said. "To my wife."

"Of course." She hurried off in search of paper and pen. When she returned, she pulled a chair close to the soldier's bed. "Go ahead."

"Dear Lisa." He stopped, lowering his eyes self-consciously.

"Don't be shy," begged Isabelle. She glanced over her shoulder to make sure no one else was within earshot. "I have a husband at the front," she told the soldier, "and I *live* for his letters. Don't mind me. Just pretend you're talking directly to her."

The soldier smiled gratefully. "All right, then. Dear Lisa. I know you heard I was shot. I'm in the hospital and they're taking good care of me. Lost the arm, though, so I'll be no good back on the front line. I'll be home soon, my darling."

The soldier dictated a few more sentences. Isabelle copied them faithfully, all the while fighting back tears. This man had suffered a terrible injury, but he'd survived, and soon he and his wife would be reunited. *When will I see Jacques?* she wondered. *And what awful things will he have to endure in the meantime?*

It was dark as Isabelle hurried home through the snowy streets of Paris, a thick scarf wrapped around her head and throat to ward off the chill winter wind. In the front hall she shed her heavy wool coat and kicked off her overshoes, then sorted rapidly through the day's mail. *Two letters for me!* she saw, her blood quickening with excitement. *From Jacques and from Charles too!*

The precious letters clutched in her hand, she hurried into the parlor, where a fire crackled on the hearth. Curling up in a chair in front of the fire, she opened Charles's letter first.

Dear Isabelle,

I know Jacques writes to you frequently, but I thought you might like a secondhand report on the state of his health and spirits. I'm glad to say he continues to be physically well and strong. It's good to be together. When things get rough, we can lean on each other. I promise I'll get him back to you in one piece, safe and sound.

Tears sparkled in Isabelle's eyes. "Good, dear Charles." She sniffled. "What a true friend you are to both of us."

She skimmed the rest of his note, then put it aside. For a minute she sat with Jacques's letter unopened on her lap. She'd saved the best for last, and she wanted to draw out the pleasure for as long as possible.

Finally she opened the envelope. At the sight of Jacques's familiar script her throat tightened. A tear splashed onto the page. "Dearest Isabelle," Jacques began.

It's been a long, brutal winter. Right now we're camped just a mile from the Germans near the town of Saint-Mihiel. The foot soldiers dig themselves trenches that quickly fill with mud and ice—I almost feel guilty that we officers stay relatively dry, though never warm. I'm only warm when I think about you, which I try to do as much as possible. It's all that keeps me going, Isabelle—the knowledge that someday I'll see you again. Talk to you again, hold you again . . .

Isabelle closed her eyes, pressing the letter to her breast. When she and Jacques married on the eve of the war, it had seemed romantic, impulsive. She loved him passionately, but she didn't yet know the pain of separation, the anguish of living in fear and uncertainty. She'd been a child then. Now she was a woman, with a woman's deep feelings. Tears streamed down her face. "Someday," she whispered with firm conviction. "Someday."

"You want to go *where?*" Rose asked.

"To Rheims," Isabelle repeated. "They need nurses in the hospital."

"That's right on the western front," her father said grimly. "There's been some mighty fierce fighting there lately."

"It's too dangerous," Rose declared.

"I'm going anyway," argued Isabelle. A whole year had passed and still the war—and her separation from Jacques—dragged on. "I want to be closer to Jacques. In case . . . in case . . ."

Rose slipped an arm around her daughter's shoulders. "Of course you're worried about him. But I'm sure he'd want you to stay where it's safe."

"A hospital on the front lines is no place for you, Izzy," her father agreed.

"You don't understand," Isabelle cried. "Jacques is . . . he's . . ." She swallowed. After all this time, she couldn't bring herself to tell her parents that Jacques was in fact her husband. *I don't want them to find out this way, when things are so tense. I want us all to be happy about it.* "He's the most important person in the world to me," she finished quietly, regaining her self-control. "No matter what you say, I *am* going to do this."

"Oh, Isabelle." Rose's face crumpled. She held open her arms and Isabelle stepped into them, burying her face in her mother's hair. "Of course you should do what you feel you must."

"Thank you, *Maman*," Isabelle whispered.

A fortnight later she was settled in a boarding-house in Rheims. Every day and long into the night she tended the sick and wounded at the nearby hospital. It was grueling work. These soldiers, brought straight from the battlefield, were more horribly injured than those she'd tended in Paris. Many died right in front of her. As soon as a bed was empty another maimed and battered body came to fill it. It was often midnight before Isabelle collapsed on her own bed, where she'd lie awake for hours, the gruesome scenes of the operating room flashing before her eyes. She'd be up again at dawn, trudging back to work.

One September morning she stopped on her way to the hospital to watch a shower of yellow leaves flutter from a tree along the roadside. The sky was deep cobalt blue, the breeze fresh with the first crisp edge of autumn. She breathed deeply, filling her lungs with cool, clean air. *How beautiful the scene would be,* she thought, *if it weren't for the distant rumbling of guns.*

But it was hard to feel gloomy when the sun was so bright. She walked briskly, a healthy glow in her cheeks. Every day, when the new wounded came in, she looked at the faces and said a silent prayer of thanks that her husband wasn't among them. Jacques was due for a furlough soon. *Our luck just has to hold out for a few more weeks,* Isabelle thought.

At the hospital she donned a clean cap and apron and quickly set to work. The morning flew by. She was about to duck outside for a short lunch break when a tall, sandy-haired soldier entered the ward, leaning on one crutch. Isabelle glanced at him briefly, then looked again, recognition dawning. "Charles!" she cried.

Racing over, she was about to fling herself into his arms when she checked herself. "It's OK," Charles said, smiling. "I'm just a little bruised. I'll survive a hug."

They embraced gingerly. "I'm so glad to see you," Isabelle exclaimed. "And you're not badly wounded—what a relief."

"It's my ears, mostly. Came a little too close to an exploding shell. I may lose the hearing on one side." His expression grew somber. "I got off easy."

Isabelle stepped back, searching his face with her eyes. "Charles, how is Jacques?" When he didn't answer immediately, her mouth went dry. "Charles," she repeated, her voice a hoarse croak and her eyes dark pools of fear. "How is . . ." She couldn't finish the question. Charles just gazed at her, his own eyes wet with emotion. "No," Isabelle whispered.

He reached out, gripping her arm with a steadying hand. She knew what was coming—the words she'd dreaded hearing all these long, difficult months. "Isabelle, Jacques is dead."

"No." Her voice became a keening wail. "No!" Her knees buckled. The last thing she was aware of was Charles reaching out to catch her as she fell.

❧ 27 ❧

Isabelle lay in bed, the blanket pulled up to her neck. The winter sun was high—she should have been up hours ago. But for some reason she couldn't seem to find the strength to move her arms and legs. Slowly she sat up, pushing aside the covers. In a trancelike state she moved across the room and washed her face, then dressed in a plain navy blue dress and matching wool stockings. She brushed her hair mechanically, staring into the mirror without focusing on her reflection.

Three months had passed since that nightmarish day in Rheims when Charles broke the news of Jacques's death. When Isabelle's parents came to take their daughter home, they'd assured her that with time her loss would grow easier to bear. They'd been wrong. If anything, her pain seemed fresher, sharper.

Isabelle buttoned up her leather shoes. She walked downstairs, her hand on the banister, pausing on each step. As she went to the dining room she passed the open door of her mother's study. Rose glanced out at her. "Good morning, dear."

Isabelle replied in a monotone. "Good morning, *Maman.*"

In the dining room she filled a plate with eggs and toast, then sat down in a chair facing the window. Outside, the December sky was pale and lemony. *It looks like snow,* Isabelle thought without interest. She took a bite of food, chewing and swallowing though it had no taste. She buttered a piece of toast, then dropped it uneaten on the plate. Shoving back her chair, she left the table.

At her parents' encouragement she'd registered for a class at the Sorbonne. Studying gave her something to do since she couldn't bring herself to return to nursing at the hospital. But there were still too many empty hours in the day.

She wandered into the parlor. Looking out the window, she saw the garden swing where she'd sat that long-ago spring morning before going to the barracks and meeting Jacques. A wave of helpless grief washed over her. Down the hall she could hear the muted clatter of her mother's typewriter. More than anything Isabelle wanted to run and bury her head in her mother's lap. *If only I'd told her the truth before,* she thought, her eyes blurring with tears. Rose and Robert seemed to think

240

Isabelle would recover more quickly if they never spoke of Jacques. *They don't know I've lost a husband. I'll never get over this. Never.*

The doorbell rang precisely at three o'clock that afternoon. Isabelle opened the door, smiling. "I could set my watch by you," she told Charles. "You're never a minute late."

He stamped his shoes on the mat, shaking off the snow. "I look forward to our walks," he said.

The war was far from over, but Charles was living in Paris, having been discharged from the service because of his hearing impairment. Every day he came to take Isabelle for a walk around the block. At first she hadn't wanted to go, even though she knew the fresh air and exercise was good for her. She didn't want to see anybody—even Charles. Now the outings were the brightest spot in her otherwise gray days. Charles was the only person who knew her secret, the only person with whom she could talk freely about Jacques.

Isabelle put on a coat and hat and joined Charles outside. He offered her his arm and they began their stroll. A light snow was falling—flakes clustered on Isabelle's dark eyelashes. For a few minutes they didn't speak. It was a companionable silence. *He understands my moods,* Isabelle thought gratefully. *He understands because he loved Jacques almost as much as I did.*

Charles walked between Isabelle and the street,

shielding her from being sprayed with water by motorcars driving through mud puddles. At the corner they waited for a trolley to pass, then crossed the street and entered the park. They sat on a bench overlooking a frozen duck pond. Isabelle took a deep breath, then turned to Charles. "Tell me again," she said softly, "about the day he died."

Charles's jaw tightened. "It won't bring him back, Isabelle. The wounds will never heal if—"

"You were the last person to see him alive," she cut in, her eyes pleading. "I need to hear about it. I didn't . . ." Her voice dropped to a ragged whisper. "I didn't get to say good-bye."

Charles was silent for a minute. Then he began reciting the facts, his tone expressionless. "We were charging across a field near Rheims. It was slow going—the field was tangled with barbed wire and pitted with trenches—and the German fire was heavy. His horse was shot out from under him, but he kept going on foot. I was a few paces behind when the artillery shell exploded."

Struggling to contain his emotions, Charles ended the story there. Isabelle clasped her hands together tightly, then asked the question she'd asked countless times before. "Are you sure there's no chance he survived? You were injured—unconscious. Are you *sure*?"

Charles looked at her with indescribable sorrow. "Our losses were heavy that day. Many of the bodies couldn't even be identified. But his name was on the list of the dead. That shell landed right on him. I'm sorry, Isabelle."

Isabelle looked away, biting her lip. "Come on," Charles said gently. "I'll take you home."

"We're walking to the Lamartines's for dinner," Rose said to Isabelle one summer evening many months later. "Would you like to join us?"

Isabelle looked up from the book she was reading. Her parents stood together in the hall, hopeful smiles on their faces. "No, thank you," she said politely.

"Come with us, Izzy," Robert urged. "The weather couldn't be finer—it'll do you good to get out of the house."

"I'm happy here with my book, Papa," she replied.

Rose and Robert exchanged a glance. "You go ahead," Rose told her husband. "I'll be right there." As Robert left the house Rose stepped into the parlor. "Isabelle, darling. Can we talk?"

"Of course, *Maman*." Isabelle put her book aside and folded her hands in her lap. "What about?"

Rose sat next to her daughter on the couch. "I think you know what about," she said gently. Isabelle's lips tightened, but she didn't speak. Rose took one of her daughter's cool, pale hands. "You know I hate to see you like this, still so sad and solitary after all these months."

"I can't help the way I feel," Isabelle said defensively.

"I know you can't." Rose squeezed Isabelle's hand. "I know your heart was broken. But at some point you'll have grieved enough. It will be time to go on with your life."

"You don't know what it's like," Isabelle cried, snatching her hand away. "You don't know what I suffer."

Rose sighed heavily. "It's true, I was never in exactly the same position. But when I was young, I lost someone I loved in a different way. The second cousin of Jacques's—I'm sure I've mentioned him before."

Isabelle sniffled. "You did?" she said, curious in spite of herself.

Rose nodded. "He was my best friend. We were as close as sister and brother. When we were teenagers, I discovered he was in love with me, but I didn't take his feelings seriously. I was so busy being independent! By the time I realized I loved him too, it was too late. He married another woman."

"How terrible!" Isabelle exclaimed.

"I was sure I'd never get over him," Rose admitted. "I was in complete despair. But one day I woke up and realized I was still happy to be alive. I still had love to give."

"And then you met Papa?"

"Yes."

Isabelle knew her mother was trying to make

her feel better, so she smiled. "Thanks, *Maman.*"

"Will you come with us?"

"Not this time. Maybe another day."

Rose bent forward to kiss Isabelle on the cheek, then left the room. Isabelle heard the front door click shut. Around her the house fell silent.

Too distracted to return to her reading, Isabelle wandered upstairs to her bedroom. Sitting at her desk, she opened the top drawer. A bundle of letters was tied with blue satin ribbon. Undoing the bow, Isabelle slipped one of the letters from its envelope. They were all from Jacques, the last postmarked the day before he was killed. "My dearest Isabelle," he'd written.

The kaiser's army is stronger than we thought. At night I'm so weary, but I can't sleep knowing that in the morning we'll send thousands more of our men to brutal deaths. Sometimes I fear none of us will make it home. Then I picture your face and hope returns. Do you know how much I love you, Isabelle Oiseleur?

Tears spilled down Isabelle's face, splashing onto the page. Maybe her mother had settled for someone else, but her devotion couldn't have been as deep as Isabelle's to Jacques. "I'll never forget you, my sweet husband," Isabelle promised, kissing the letter. "You'll always be the only one."

Summer passed, and fall and winter. Late one sunny spring afternoon in 1917, Charles Doret came by the Eastmans's house. Though they no longer met every day because she was a full-time university student and he had a desk job with the army, their walks were still important to Isabelle. Charles had become her best friend.

When she answered the door, he presented her with a single red rose. Isabelle sniffed it, smiling. "What's this for?"

"Don't be coy," he replied with a grin. "It's your birthday."

"Oh, birthdays. I'm too old for that sort of thing."

Charles laughed. "Yes, you're all of nineteen, right?"

"I lost count. Besides, you're not supposed to ask a lady her age!"

Arm in arm they strolled down the sidewalk. "I thought we'd watch the sunset from the Eiffel Tower," Charles suggested, "then go for a picnic by the Seine."

"That sounds nice." Isabelle smiled up at him. "I guess I don't mind birthdays after all."

On their way to the Eiffel Tower they chatted about work and school. Soon, as always, the conversation turned to the latest developments in the war. "It won't last much longer now that America has finally joined the Allies," Charles predicted. "The Germans will be begging for an armistice."

"Peace," reflected Isabelle sadly. "I wonder what it will be like? I feel as if I've always lived in a world at war."

At the Eiffel Tower they rode the elevator to the first observation deck. Joining a handful of tourists at the rail, they looked out over the sprawling Parisian metropolis. "We'll never take it for granted again, that's for sure," said Charles. "Peace, I mean. Not when it's cost us so much."

Charles didn't mention anyone's name, but Isabelle knew they were both thinking about Jacques. She nodded without speaking, her eyes on the horizon. When she turned back to Charles, he was taking something from his jacket pocket. "I have a birthday present for you," he said, handing her a small velvet jewelry box.

"You shouldn't have."

"Open it," he urged.

Carefully Isabelle lifted the lid of the box. When she saw what lay inside, the color drained from her face. "Oh, Charles," she whispered.

Charles took the box from her and removed the diamond ring. "May I?" he asked.

She didn't protest as he slipped the ring onto her finger. "It—it fits," she stammered.

"Isabelle, I've wanted to ask you this for a long time," Charles began, taking her hand and looking straight into her eyes. "Will you marry me?"

She looked away, biting her lip.

"I know our relationship is . . . different." He cleared his throat. "Different than what you shared with—with your first husband. But am I wrong in thinking that you care about me?"

"Oh, no. I do care about you, very much," she assured him. "But I don't know if . . ." He waited patiently for her to continue, his eyes bright with hope. Isabelle searched her heart, wanting to be honest with him and with herself. "I don't know if I can be a good wife to you. I'm just not sure I . . ." She couldn't bring herself to say words that she knew would wound him. *I'm not sure I love you.*

"It'll take time, I know," Charles said quickly, "but someday you'll grow to love me. I love you enough for both of us. We could make it work, Isabelle."

She looked down at the ring on her finger, struggling to sift through her mixed emotions. Was Charles right? Could she marry him without loving him and trust that love would come in its own time? What *did* she feel for him, exactly? *Gratitude,* she thought, remembering how he'd cared for her after Jacques's death. *And friendship.* Charles believed it was enough. Was it?

I should say no, Isabelle decided. *It's not fair when my heart will always belong to another.* But Jacques was dead. Did she really want to live alone, with nothing but his memory for companionship, for the rest of her life?

She *did* care for Charles, and he'd make a good husband. Life wouldn't offer her a better chance at happiness. Isabelle took a deep breath. "Yes, Charles," she said. "I'll marry you."

28

1918. Paris.

On November 11 the thankful cry was on every Parisian's lips: "The war is over!" The city celebrated the armistice with solemn processions and singing of the "Marseillaise." Isabelle and her husband, Charles, gathered with others at her parents' house to drink champagne and share remembrances. Every man and woman in France had lost a loved one—a son, a brother, a father, a husband. Even as they toasted the victory over Germany, they were telling stories of friends lost in battle.

Isabelle kept her own tears bottled tightly inside. She stayed on the fringes of the party, her arm around Charles's waist, listening to the others without participating in the conversation. At one point Charles steered her into the hallway. "Are you OK?" he asked.

"Of course." She forced herself to smile brightly. "Just a little tired."

"Peace at last. We're all going to make a fresh start." Charles hugged her to him. "Let's put the past behind us."

She knew he was referring to Jacques. She also knew that even though her marriage to Charles was a happy one, she would never stop thinking of Jacques and what might have been. *If only he'd lived to see this day.* "Yes, Charles," she agreed. "Let's look to the future."

A few weeks later Isabelle was working in the front yard of the house outside of Paris where she and Charles lived. After an hour of raking leaves she sat down on the porch steps to rest.

It was a gray November day—there was a nip of winter in the air, the smell of coming snow. Isabelle was warm from her exertion, though. She lifted an arm to blot her forehead on the sleeve of her jacket. When she dropped her arm again, she noticed something, or rather someone. A few minutes earlier the country road had been empty, but now a man appeared in the distance, his footsteps raising dust.

She watched him approach, wondering who he was and where he was heading. As he drew nearer, limping, she saw he was dressed in a faded, patched French officer's uniform. *A soldier,* she thought. *Coming home from the war. On foot, the poor man, and carrying that heavy duffel bag. I should offer him something to eat and drink.*

She stood to go into the house for a glass of water. Then she looked again at the man in the road. He'd almost reached her house, and now she could distinguish his features. He was gaunt and tall. From a distance she'd thought he was older—his hair looked gray. Now she realized he was a young man, his dark hair flecked with dust from the road. His jaw was square, his cheekbones prominent, his eyes light.

The soldier stopped at the gate and looked up at her. Isabelle stared into his burning, bright eyes. Her knees buckled and a mist swept before her gaze—she knew she was about to faint.

It was Jacques.

Jacques ran up the path, reaching Isabelle's side just in time to catch her before she crumpled to the ground. "Isabelle." He patted her cheek gently, repeating her name in a voice ragged with emotion. "Isabelle!"

She blinked, her eyes wide with disbelief and her whole body shaking. "Jacques, is it really you? But you can't be alive! I thought—we thought—"

"As soon as they released me from the German prison camp I went directly to your parents' house," Jacques told her, "but no one was there. I headed here, figuring Charles could tell me where to find you. I didn't expect you to be—"

Just then Charles appeared in the doorway. When he saw Isabelle and Jacques, he started forward, then stopped in confusion. "Jacques?" he croaked, his face ashen. Isabelle threw a desperate glance over her shoulder at Charles. Jacques expected his friend to rush forward and embrace him, but instead Charles hurried to Isabelle's side, wrapping his arms around her protectively.

Jacques took a step backward, his own bewilderment increasing. This wasn't the welcome he'd anticipated. He knew Isabelle and Charles would be shocked to learn he was alive. But this was something else. As he stared at them comprehension slowly dawned. "No," he said hoarsely, looking from Isabelle to Charles and back again. "Isabelle, you didn't—you're not—"

"I thought you were dead," Isabelle cried, burying her face in her hands and bursting into tears.

Jacques saw the diamond glinting on her finger. Charles too wore a gold wedding band. A fiery anguish sliced through Jacques's heart, the pain sharper than a bayonet thrust. *My wife and my best friend, together. They betrayed me.* "How could you?" he choked out.

"I saw the shell explode," said Charles. "You couldn't have survived!"

"But I did." Jacques clenched his teeth. "How

long did you wait until you stole her away from me? One month? Two?"

"Jacques!" Isabelle cried.

"That's not how it happened," Charles protested. "Jacques, you have to believe us. We didn't—"

Jacques shook his head fiercely. "While I was rotting in that prison, the two of you were—" He couldn't utter the loathsome words. Spinning, he grabbed his duffel bag and limped away from the house as fast as he could.

"Wait!" Isabelle begged. "Please. We can explain!" Jacques broke into an awkward run, the duffel bag slamming painfully against his bad leg. Charles shouted after him, but Jacques didn't look back.

His war injuries, the horror of the prison camp, were nothing compared to this. The only thing that sustained him as a prisoner of war was knowing that Isabelle was waiting for him and that someday he'd be liberated and they'd be together again. Now he'd found out he'd been living for a lie. Isabelle had forgotten him and given her heart to another—to his own best friend.

Tears spilled from his eyes, mingling with the dust on his pale face. *They say they believed I'd been killed—well, I wish I had been,* Jacques thought. *Why didn't I die on that battlefield?*

The next day, after a sleepless night, Charles was up at dawn. "I'm going after him," he told

Isabelle, who was sitting in a rocking chair by the bedroom window, wrapped in a quilt. She'd never come to bed. "And I'll go to the war office and find out how this monstrous error could have occurred." He waited for her to look at him. Isabelle remained still as a statue, her face turned away, her nod barely perceptible.

Charles spent a long, frustrating day talking to unhelpful bureaucrats and chasing down dead-end leads. At dusk he returned home, footsore and discouraged. Isabelle was sitting in the kitchen, a cold cup of tea on the table in front of her. When he entered, she stood up quickly. "Well?" she said, her voice vibrating with urgency. "Did you find him?"

He shook his head, drooping against the kitchen counter. "No one's seen him. He's disappeared without a trace."

Isabelle sank back into her chair. "I can't bear it," she cried. "After all he suffered. How he must hate us!"

"We had no idea," Charles reminded her. "There were so many casualties at Rheims. All they could tell me at the war office was that the government didn't know Jacques had survived until Germany surrendered. Somehow his name never made it onto any of the prisoner lists."

Isabelle raked her hands through her tangled hair, her green eyes wild. "We should have known he couldn't be dead. We should have tried harder to find out what happened to him."

Charles grasped her shoulders and shook her. "Isabelle, listen to me. *We didn't know.* They told us he was dead—we had no reason to doubt that. We haven't done anything we should be ashamed of."

"But we're not really married," she sobbed. "You're not really my husband."

Charles dropped his hands. Her words cut him like a knife. He wanted to deny them, but he couldn't. "Isabelle," he said hoarsely. "You know I love you. I'd do anything for you. Even if . . . even if it means losing you. I'll find him for you, and I'll make him understand how this happened. Is that what you want?"

She hid her face in her hands. "I don't know," she whispered.

He'd hoped she'd say no, insist that she loved him too, better than she'd loved Jacques. Gritting his teeth, Charles turned and left the room. It would be the hardest thing he'd ever done, but he'd keep his word. He'd find Jacques.

To the east the dark sky was streaked with pale pink and green. Sunrise was still an hour away. Jacques stood on the dock at the coastal city of Calais, his battered duffel bag at his feet and his collar turned up against the cold dawn mist.

The sea was calm and the docked ship rested low and steady in the water. Despite the early hour, though, there was a lot of activity on board. Sailors shouted and hauled on ropes. Passengers straggled on, lugging heavy trunks and suitcases.

The sun was just edging up over the horizon when the ship's whistle blew. Bending, Jacques grabbed the duffel and flung it over his shoulder. As he put his foot on the gangway he hesitated. *Isabelle,* he thought, a new pain torturing his sore and broken heart. *I'll never see you again.* It was so ironic, after all he'd been through. When he'd gone into battle and later as he languished in the prison camp, when hope seemed most irrational, he'd always been sustained by the faith that he'd be reunited with her. Now he was turning his back on her intentionally, about to put thousands and thousands of miles between them. *She deserted me first,* Jacques reminded himself. Anger surged through his veins and his eyes clouded with hurt. He couldn't stay another day in France, knowing that she was living as another man's wife.

He strode up the gangway, his face a mask of stony determination. "Papers," the porter requested.

Jacques fumbled in his trouser pocket. "I bought a one-way passage," he said.

The porter checked the ticket, then nodded. "On board with you."

Jacques walked around the ship's deck, finding a corner upwind from the smokestacks. Sitting down, he wrapped his arms around his knees. The sun was now hanging in the morning sky, low and round and blindingly bright. The horn sounded again and the ship lurched mightily. Jacques leaned back and closed his eyes. As the ship pulled away from the dock he didn't look back.

When he opened his eyes again, the coast had receded and they were on the open sea. Jacques took a deep breath of salty ocean air. He was headed for India, an exotic new land. It would be a new start. Maybe he'd find fame and fortune, maybe not. One thing was for sure: he'd never again set foot on his native soil. He'd never go back to the country he'd risked his life fighting for . . . and where he'd lost the only woman he'd ever love.

The months passed, and Isabelle sank deeper and deeper into a depression. It was like plunging from a cliff—she was powerless to help herself, to stop the free fall. Every morning when Charles left for work, she vowed to do something productive with the day. Clean the house, read, write letters, visit her parents or her friends. Instead at day's end he usually found her where he'd left her, sitting in the kitchen in the dark, staring blankly into space.

One night when Charles came in, she looked up at him but didn't greet him. In silence he moved around the kitchen, lighting a fire in the wood-stove, putting water on to boil, gathering the ingredients for dinner. As Isabelle watched with listless, disinterested eyes she suddenly glimpsed their future. An endless stream of meaningless days just like this one, with her and Charles just going through the motions, pretending they had a

257

normal life when really it was hollow and empty. A couple, together, but somehow each painfully alone. *I hate this house,* Isabelle thought abruptly. *I hate this life!* "We have to get out of here," she burst out.

He turned to her, surprised. "What do you mean?"

She gripped the edge of the table so fiercely her knuckles whitened. "We can't go on living here. Charles, let's move away." A new, pleading note entered her voice. "Someplace where we won't always be reminded of . . ."

He frowned. "Do you really think we can escape it?"

"We have to try," she cried. "What choice do we have? If we stay in Paris, we'll always be haunted."

Crossing the kitchen, Charles dropped to one knee in front of Isabelle. He seized her hands, squeezing them tightly. "Isabelle, if I thought it would make a difference, I'd go to the other side of the world with you. If I thought you'd be happy—if I thought someday you might love me as much as you loved Jacques. I know you don't think of me as your true husband, but—"

"You *are* my true husband." Isabelle gazed into his tortured eyes. Charles had searched high and low for Jacques. Isabelle had given up hope of ever finding him. If she was going to have a future at all, it was with Charles. *But I won't make a promise I can't keep. I don't know if I'll ever love Charles that way*. "We have to try," she repeated. "It's all that's left to do."

The next day when Charles came home, he presented Isabelle with a fat envelope. "I spent all our savings," he announced simply.

She opened the envelope. "Boat passage. Two one-way tickets." She lifted her eyes to her husband's face. "America!"

"I thought since it was your father's native land, it wouldn't seem like such a strange place," he explained. "It's a good country for making a new start."

Isabelle held the tickets reverently, as if they were something magical, with the power to change lives. "America," she said again. For the first time in months a smile dawned on her face.

❧ 29 ❧

1924. Sweet Valley, California.

Isabelle Doret stepped out of her back door in
Sweet Valley, California, one summer morning.
Before visiting the chicken coop in search of fresh
eggs for breakfast, she stood for a minute on the
porch steps, soaking in the warm rays of sunlight.
Later in the day it would be hot and dusty, but at
this early hour the air was still fragrant and cool.

A breeze stirred the leaves of the trees in her
backyard: lemon, peach, walnut. *It's like the Garden
of Eden,* Isabelle thought. *I live in paradise.*
Barefoot, she cut across the grass to the chicken
coop. Clucking softly to the hens, she nudged them
from their nests, then filled her apron with eggs.

Back inside the house she put a kettle of water
on the stove for coffee and began to heat up a

heavy cast-iron skillet. Her husband entered the kitchen just as she was cracking eggs into the pan. "Do I smell fresh bread?" Charles asked, kissing his wife on the cheek.

"Wheat and honey," she told him.

"My favorite. But you know . . ." He tickled her waist—or rather, the place where her waist used to be. She was five months pregnant. "You shouldn't be working so hard. We can afford to hire a maid and a cook. You should be taking it easy."

"But this isn't work." Isabelle sprinkled some fresh herbs on top of the bubbling eggs. "I love my garden and my fruit trees and my chickens. This"— she gestured around the airy kitchen, decorated with bright-colored Mexican tiles—"makes me happy."

Charles smiled. "In that case let's try some of that bread."

When breakfast was ready, they sat across from each other at the table. Charles blew on his coffee. "I still think we should get a girl to come in a few mornings a week to clean for you," he told Isabelle. "You'll need the help more than ever after the baby comes."

Isabelle thought for a minute, then nodded. She valued her independence, but Charles was right. "And I suppose now that you're mayor of Sweet Valley," she said, her eyes twinkling, "people expect us to keep a more elegant establishment."

"I'm sure the gray-haired ladies would raise their eyebrows if they knew my wife was running around barefoot," Charles agreed with a grin, "but I think

261

Mr. and Mrs. Mayor should please themselves."

When Charles headed into town for the day—his office was on Main Street, just a five-minute walk from their house—Isabelle left the dishes in the sink and went back out to the porch. Charles had built a glider bench for her, and she curled up in it, one of her calico cats on her lap.

She'd been telling the truth when she said her house and garden made her happy. Five years ago she wouldn't have imagined such contentment was possible. But coming to the United States was the smartest thing she and Charles could have done. Isabelle loved Sweet Valley. It was a new land, full of wide-open spaces: rolling golden hills, lush green valleys, bordered on one side by the endless blue of the Pacific Ocean. The people who lived there were open and friendly—no one seemed troubled by history. It was the perfect place for a new beginning.

Isabelle stopped petting the cat, Patches, and rested her hand on her own gently rounded abdomen. This was the best part: after years of hoping, she and Charles were finally expecting their first child. *A baby is all we need,* Isabelle thought. *Then we'll really and truly feel like a family.*

She sat on the porch until the sun was high in the blue sky. She hadn't forgotten the past—she'd never forget it. But at last she'd found peace.

Sweet Valley had been settled in the 1860s. More than half a century later, Main Street was a bustling stretch of shops and offices. The architecture had a distinctly Spanish look, and the buildings were punctuated by plots of green parkland. Isabelle strolled along the sidewalk, a woven basket hooked over her arm. She'd already been to the dry goods store and was heading for the butcher's. She took her time, enjoying the sunshine and occasionally greeting a neighbor. It was a small town, and everyone knew everyone else.

But here comes a stranger, Isabelle thought, seeing a ruggedly handsome man approaching her. He looked like a California native, though—a real American cowboy in leather chaps and boots, denim pants and work shirt, and a broad-brimmed hat. She smiled, appreciating the cowboy's picturesque appearance. Then he drew closer and she got a better look at him. The man was tall and broad shouldered, with black hair, a tanned, weather-beaten complexion, and blazing light blue eyes. She stopped in her tracks, the breath leaving her lungs in a gasp. It was Jacques Oiseleur.

He walked right up to her, and then he too paused. For a few long moments he gazed at her steadily, his blue eyes showing absolutely no emotion. Then, without speaking, he continued on his way.

Isabelle felt the blood rush from her head. She stumbled to a nearby bench and collapsed on it. A thin woman with carrot orange hair and glasses rushed over to her. *Oh, no,* Isabelle thought with a silent groan. Positively the last person she wanted to talk to—Evelyn Pearce, the town gossip.

"Mrs. Doret, do you *know* that man?" Evelyn demanded, vigorously fanning Isabelle with her pocketbook. "Look at you, practically fainting on the public sidewalk. You shouldn't be out in this heat, in your condition."

"Oh, well . . . ," Isabelle murmured weakly.

Evelyn craned her neck, peering after Jacques. "Jack Fowler's his name, or so I've heard. They say he's lived all over the world—an utter vagabond."

"Jack Fowler," Isabelle repeated.

"He bought the old Rancho Arroyo Seco on the other side of the hills west of town, and as you can see he's as poor and rough as can be. He didn't even tip his hat to you!" Isabelle didn't respond. "Mrs. Doret, you really must get out of the sun," Evelyn advised.

"Yes." Isabelle got slowly to her feet and fumbled for her basket. "I think I will go home."

"I'll walk with you," Evelyn offered. "You may still be feeling woozy."

"No, thank you," Isabelle said quickly. "I'm fine, really. And it's just a few blocks. Good-bye, Evelyn. I'll see you soon."

Evelyn looked disappointed that she wouldn't have the chance to gossip further with the mayor's wife, but fortunately she didn't insist on escorting Isabelle home. Isabelle walked away from the other woman as fast as she was able. She turned off Main Street onto a side street but didn't head directly home. Instead she kept walking, block after block, without paying attention to where she was going.

Her head was in a whirl. *Jacques*, she thought, her heart racing. What a strange, terrible, wonderful coincidence! Years later to find themselves in the same place, so many thousands of miles from Paris! He'd recognized her too, but it had been impossible to tell what he felt. She stopped for a moment near a grassy pasture to catch her breath.

"Jack Fowler." Isabelle whispered the name out loud. He'd walked back into her life, and instantly she'd realized one essential thing. It didn't matter that she was Charles's wife or that she was carrying Charles's child. It didn't matter that Jacques believed terrible things about her and probably hated her. Her heart had a will of its own, and it still belonged to the first man she'd ever loved.

That night Isabelle held back for as long as she could—all through dinner, and during the hour when she and Charles listened to the radio and read their books. Finally, as they were getting ready for bed, she couldn't contain her curiosity any longer.

"Charles, did you know . . ." She paused, her fingers trembling as she buttoned the neck of her cotton nightgown. "Did you realize that someone named Jack Fowler lives on a ranch outside of town? And that Jack Fowler is . . ."

Her husband stared across the bedroom at her,

a mix of emotions flickering across his face. "Yes," he said curtly. "I knew."

"I saw him in town today," she explained. "I couldn't help wondering . . . have you . . . have you met him? Talked to him?"

Charles loosened his necktie with a violent flick of his wrist. "Yes," he said again. "When I learned he was in the area a few months back, I went out to the ranch to see him, to welcome him to Sweet Valley and offer my hand in friendship."

"And?" Isabelle prompted eagerly.

"And he cut me dead," Charles related, his expression grim. "I tried to explain, one more time. I begged his forgiveness. But he accused me of purposefully misleading you." He could barely choke out the words. "Of knowing the truth and hiding it to get you to marry me."

"Oh, Charles," Isabelle said sorrowfully.

"I was ready to be his friend again," Charles declared, his jaw tightening. "I could help him get a start in this town. But not after that."

They finished undressing in silence, then turned off the light and climbed into bed. Isabelle lay in the dark with her back to Charles, her eyes wide open. She couldn't help thinking about Jack, perhaps at that very same moment lying down on his own bed just a few miles away. *But there might as well still be a whole continent and an entire ocean between us*, she thought bitterly.

❖   ❖   ❖

266

For a half hour Isabelle tossed and turned restlessly. Finally Charles heard her breathing grow quiet and steady. Propping himself up on his elbow, he gazed down at her sleeping face. *She still loves him,* he realized, anger surging through him. Despite it all: the passage of time, the way things ended with Jacques back in France, and how hard Charles had always worked to give her everything she wanted. *She still loves him—she can't hide it.*

Carefully, so as not to wake his wife, Charles climbed out of bed. Standing at the window, he pushed aside the gingham curtain. The summer night was peaceful. Crickets chirped in the grass, a faint breeze stirred the leaves in the trees, a crescent moon hung low in the black sky. But Charles was blind to the beauty of the scene. Tears stung his eyes. *How dare he come to Sweet Valley and try to ruin all of this for me,* he thought, clenching his fists. When he'd gone to Jack's ranch a few months before, Charles had been saddened and frustrated by the fact that Jack still refused to believe the truth, that Charles and Isabelle hadn't knowingly betrayed him. Tonight, seeing that his wife still had feelings for the other man—passionate feelings, deeper than any she'd ever had for him—Charles felt his sorrow and anger slowly harden into hatred.

I know what you're up to, Jack Fowler. You think I stole Isabelle from you, and now you're here to steal her back. "Over my dead body," Charles whispered to the night sky.

"I won't be home till late," Charles told Isabelle one August morning. "I'm driving to Fort Carroll for a meeting with some other town mayors to talk about water rights."

"That sounds interesting," Isabelle fibbed.

"Will you be OK?" He circled his arms around her. "If you need anything, you can call Bert and Felicia next door."

"I'll be fine," she assured him, presenting her cheek for a kiss. "See you tonight."

From the living-room window she watched Charles drive off in their new Buick sedan. The moment he'd announced that he'd be out of town all day, a feeling of dangerous excitement had started to simmer inside her. Now her pulse raced and her face grew hot. *I can't,* she thought, putting a hand to her heart. *I shouldn't.*

She hurried out into the hallway to examine herself in the mirror. She fluffed her hair with her fingers, then frowned. She was wearing her prettiest maternity dress, but nothing could disguise the fact that she was nearly seven months pregnant. "I'm as big as a house," she moaned. Well, it wasn't going to be news to him—it had been obvious the day he'd seen her in town. *Am I doing this or not?* Isabelle asked herself silently.

She ran out the back door. The pickup truck was parked next to the barn. Clambering up into the driver's seat, she gunned the engine. On the street she turned left, heading away from the center of town. Soon the paved road ended and she was bumping along a rough dirt track.

A few other times in the past month she'd come this far, then turned back. Today she kept going. She had to see him. She'd take the road to where it ended . . . at the old Rancho Arroyo Seco, now known as Fowler's Ranch.

Jack Fowler had just finished his morning chores when he saw the cloud of dust far down the road. He put a hand to his forehead, shielding his eyes from the sun. *Yellow pickup truck,* he observed. *A woman driving.*

He wasn't surprised. He'd known she would come sooner or later. Taking a bandanna from his back pocket, he wiped the sweat from his forehead. With long, unhurried strides he started down the drive to meet her.

She parked on the grass a hundred yards from his unpainted, one-story house. He watched her get out of the truck, graceful despite her advanced state of pregnancy. They walked toward each other, both stopping while there was still some distance between them. "Hello, Isabelle," he said.

"I know you don't want to see me—I shouldn't have come without an invitation," she began. "But I needed to talk to you. You have to let me tell my side of the story."

"I'm listening."

"Jacques—Jack." She clasped her hands. Her eyes were as brilliant as emeralds, her complexion clear and glowing. He was sure she'd never been more vibrantly beautiful. "When Charles broke the news that you'd been killed, I wanted to die too. You don't know how deeply I grieved. Charles and I grew close because he was the only person I could talk to about you. When he asked me to marry him . . . I guess there wasn't any reason to say no. I didn't love him, but I liked and respected him. I didn't love him," she repeated, "and I don't love him now."

"I believe you," Jack said. "I believe all of it."

"You do?" She took a step forward, her eyes wide with hope. "Then you'll forgive Charles and me?"

"I forgive you." Jack scowled. "But not Doret. He was there with me on the battlefield, Isabelle. He saw me get hit. He should've questioned the casualty report. But he always wanted you and he saw his chance to take you."

"No." Isabelle shook her head. "It didn't happen that way."

"He let you believe a lie," Jack insisted. "Anyway, it's done. Over and done."

For a long minute they stood facing each other, separated by an unbridgeable chasm. Isabelle lifted a hand, reaching out to him across the distance. "Over and done?" she echoed.

There was a question in her voice . . . and an invitation. The air between them crackled with emotional intensity. Jack hesitated, torn between conflicting impulses. Then the mood was shattered. "Jack, I've got your lunch," someone called.

Jack and Isabelle both turned. Behind them, at the door of the house, stood a lovely young woman with smooth brown skin and cascading raven black hair—the daughter of one of Jack's cowhands. He lifted a hand in acknowledgment. "Be right there, Anita." He turned back to Isabelle, his resolution now firm. "Yes, over and done."

"But I still love you!" Isabelle cried, years of suppressed longing bursting forth.

"I'm sorry for that," Jack said honestly. "I can't say the same."

Isabelle flinched as if he'd struck her. He gestured to her rounded figure. "Go home to your husband, Isabelle," he added, more gently.

Without a word Isabelle whirled and ran back to the truck. The engine roared. He saw her yank sharply on the steering wheel. The tires dug deep ruts in the grass. Back on the road she sped off in a cloud of dust. Jack watched until the yellow pickup truck disappeared behind a stand of oaks, then he turned to look around at his house, his land. The ranch was his future—Isabelle was the past. It hadn't really been that hard a choice.

🌾 *30* 🌾

1952. Sweet Valley.

"It was a lovely luncheon," Emily Barr Doret told her father-in-law, Charles. "Everything was perfectly elegant."

"It's not every day a man celebrates the christening of his first grandchild," replied Charles, beaming at the baby cradled in Emily's arms. Two-month-old Grace Isabelle Doret was tiny, fair haired, and delicate, nearly lost in her white lace christening gown. "Nothing but the best for this little lady."

In honor of Grace's christening Charles and Isabelle had hosted a luncheon at the Sweet Valley Country Club, of which Charles was a charter member. Over the course of years the Dorets had become the most prominent family in Sweet Valley. Charles was still the town's mayor and he also owned a profitable manufacturing company, now managed by the elder of his two sons, baby Grace's father, Alan. Most of the guests had departed, leaving only the family. Silver-haired Charles surveyed his brood proudly. Alan and Paul were fine sons— smart, successful young men who'd chosen well in both their careers and their personal lives. Emily and Laura were well bred and educated—they'd be good wives, mothers, and partners. In her fifties his own wife, Isabelle, was still the most strikingly beautiful woman in Sweet Valley. Her dark and wavy brown hair didn't have a streak of gray, and she'd maintained her splendid figure. She'd decorated their hilltop mansion with taste and flair and lately developed an interest in collecting European art, particularly the nineteenth-century impressionist painters of their native France. In his business and as the town's mayor he entertained frequently, and Isabelle was the perfect hostess.

Alan approached his father, seeming to read his mind. "It's a pretty good life, eh, Dad?" he said.

"Yes." Charles smiled. "A pretty good life."

Charles walked over to his wife. Isabelle stood at the picture window, looking out at the golf course. They'd been so busy tending to their guests, they hadn't exchanged a word during the entire luncheon. "The party went off pretty well, wouldn't you say?" Charles remarked.

Isabelle nodded. "The filet mignon was a bit overdone, but otherwise the meal was nicely prepared and served. They always do a good job here at the club."

"She's a fine baby, isn't she?"

"A beautiful baby," Isabelle agreed.

They stood for a few minutes in silence. Outwardly they appeared relaxed, but Charles sensed tension in his wife's posture. He waited for her to broach the subject, his own shoulders rigidly squared. "I was talking with Peter Morrow," she began at last, "about the proposed zoning change."

Charles narrowed his eyes. "What about it?"

"The board approved it with a unanimous vote." Isabelle looked her husband straight in the eye. "You used your mayoral powers to block it."

"That's my prerogative," Charles reminded her coolly. "The board can make any recommendations they like, but I decide what's best for this town."

They strolled across the room so the others couldn't overhear them. "You're just trying to prevent Jack Fowler from selling his land to developers and making a fortune," Isabelle declared.

The bitterness between husband and wife, never far beneath the surface, now boiled forth. Charles had achieved all his ambitions in life, but there was one thing he hadn't been able to control. His wife had always been secretly in love with another man. Charles hated Jack Fowler with every fiber of his being. "I did what's best for Sweet Valley," he said, clenching his teeth. "If Jack Fowler rots out on that ranch of his, so much the better."

Isabelle's green eyes flashed. "So you don't deny it's

vengeance, and not honest politics, that drove this deal!"

"Think what you like," he snapped.

Isabelle lowered her voice. "Jack has next to nothing, Charles. You won me years ago. When will that be enough for you?"

He looked into her face, his eyes hard. "When I can be sure you aren't thinking of another man every time I take you in my arms. When I know that you don't wish that I had been the one taken prisoner during the war or killed."

Isabelle looked away, biting her lip. Just then Emily called out to them. "Mom and Dad, come see! Grace is making the cutest faces."

False smiles in place, Isabelle and Charles rejoined the family.

A year later Jack Fowler stood gazing out at his ruined fields. For days a torrential rain had pounded the southern California coast. After two years of drought the land had been baked hard as rock and couldn't soak up the much needed rain. With nowhere to go, the water raged through the valley, tearing the vulnerable plants up by their roots, wrecking fences, even threatening the ranch house and barns.

Jack felt a hand on his arm. "Come inside," his wife, Anita, begged. "There's nothing you can do out here."

He shook off her hand. "Let me be," he ordered roughly.

She stood beside him for a moment, her yellow

rain slicker flapping in the wind. Though she didn't say anything more, he knew her heart was breaking too. She had just as much of her lifeblood invested in the ranch—this was as hard on her as it was on him. Finally, shaking her head at his stubbornness, she retreated to the shelter of the house.

Jack leaned against the fence, rain running cold down the collar of his oilcloth coat. *My land,* he thought mournfully. Just a few years ago he'd owned the most successful ranch in the valley. He'd expanded it over the decades, diversifying his crops and livestock holdings. His three children had their homes there, and they all made a living from its bounty. His eight-year-old grandson, George, his pride and joy, had the run of the place and was growing into a strong, sturdy, quick-witted lad.

But bad luck must have been biding its time, waiting until it had a fat, prosperous target to pounce on. First disease ravaged the cattle herds. Then came the drought, and now the floods. Jack and Anita were in the process of losing everything. *And I know who to blame,* Jack thought, overcome with bitterness. He'd have sold the land a year ago and made millions if the mayor hadn't blocked the zoning changes. "Doret." Jack spat the name into the muddied earth. He hated Charles even more than Charles hated him. "Right now you're up and I'm down, but someday the tables will turn," he vowed. "The bad blood between us will never die."

❦ *31* ❦

1960.

Isabelle sat on a blanket in the shade at Secca Lake with her eight-year-old granddaughter, Grace. "Why are we having this party again, Grandma?" Grace asked, leaning forward to stick her finger in the whipped-cream frosting of a cake displayed on top of a picnic basket.

Isabelle gave Grace's hand a light, playful slap. "It's your granddad's and my wedding anniversary."

"You've been married a long time, huh?" said Grace, licking the frosting from her finger.

"Let's see. Ten, twenty, thirty . . . more than forty years."

"Forty years!" Grace's gray eyes were wide. "Wow."

Isabelle laughed. "Yes, that about says it."

Charles and some of the others had been playing croquet on the lawn. The game was over, and they dropped their mallets. "Time for cake," Alan declared. "And some of that lemonade, Mom."

Isabelle poured glasses of fresh-squeezed lemonade. The family lounged on beach blankets, basking in the sun. It was an idyllic scene. *More than forty years,* Isabelle mused. She couldn't pretend all of them had been happy, but she wouldn't trade her family for the world. Her two sons were devoted, she truly liked her daughters-in-law, and her five rambunctious grandchildren were a joy. *We're healthy and wealthy,* she thought, a wry smile on her lips, *if not always wise.*

Charles came to sit next to her. Slipping an arm around her waist, he dropped a light kiss on her cheek. "The cake looks fabulous," he said. "I hate to cut into it."

"But you have to, Granddad," insisted Grace's six-year-old brother, Robert. "And give me the biggest piece!"

Everybody laughed. Isabelle watched contentedly as Charles offered around thick slices of lemon-filled coconut cake on paper plates. Then, in the middle of cutting a piece of cake, she saw her husband freeze. His eyes were fixed on the lakeshore just fifty yards from their grassy picnic site. Though it was a sunny, pleasant day, they'd pretty much had the town park to themselves. Another group had arrived. When she realized who it was, Isabelle's heart momentarily stopped beating.

Jack Fowler, one of his grown sons, and a handful of grandchildren had swum across from the other side of Secca Lake. Now Jack stood on the beach, gazing up at them with cool, appraising eyes. Water dripped from his body, which was still muscular and lean though he was well into his sixties.

"What are *they* doing here?" Isabelle's younger son, Paul, wondered disdainfully.

"It's a public park," Paul's wife, Laura, pointed out.

"I knew we should have had this party at the country club," Paul grumbled. "We wouldn't have been bothered by riffraff there."

Charles got slowly to his feet and started to walk toward the water. "Charles, don't," Isabelle said in a low voice. He didn't heed her. Marching purposefully to the lake's edge, he stood directly in front of Jack.

Isabelle was too far away to hear what the men were saying or even to be able to tell who'd spoken first. Their expressions and gestures came across loud and clear, however. Charles's face was a mask of belligerent pride; Jack's whole body was coiled taut and dangerous as a panther's.

They exchanged inaudible remarks, and then Jack raised his voice. "You may be king of Sweet Valley, Doret, but you don't own this beach," he declared. "The Fowlers are poor as dirt, thanks to you, but we can swim anywhere we please."

"If you're a failure, it's your own damn fault," Charles retorted.

Suddenly chaos broke loose. Jack stepped forward, a fist raised. His son Joshua grasped his arm, but Jack struggled free. Alan and Paul raced down to restrain Charles, whose own fists were doubled up.

The sons dragged the two old men apart before either could land a blow. Isabelle and the rest of her family watched in dismay. "Let's get out of here, Mom," said Emily, quickly sweeping the picnic things back into the hampers.

Wordlessly Isabelle helped gather up their belongings. "What's wrong?" asked Grace, looking from her grandmother's face to the scene at the beach and back again. "Why do we have to leave?"

"We just do," Isabelle said grimly.

Grace started to cry. "But we didn't even get to eat the cake. And I wanted to swim."

"Come, child." Isabelle grabbed Grace's hand.

Laura and Emily hoisted the picnic hampers while Isabelle herded the grandchildren toward the parked cars. The men followed, still arguing. "You shouldn't have butted in," Charles said angrily.

"Dad, you were making a fool of yourself and of all of us," Paul rejoined. "Stooping to Fowler's level."

Grace was wailing in earnest now. As Isabelle bent and scooped her slender granddaughter up into her arms to carry her the rest of the way, she shot a glance at her husband. Charles was red under his suntan, his handsome features twisted with fury.

It was so long ago, she thought, tears scratching her throat. *World War I, the devastation it wrought in our lives.* Another world war had come and gone. Now their adopted country was waging a cold war, but for the most part the 1950s had been a prosperous, peaceful decade. *For the nation, but not for us,* Isabelle reflected sadly. She remembered a spring evening, more than forty-five years ago. She'd worn a green chiffon dress to a dance where she'd met two handsome young officers who happened to be best friends. She'd fallen in love with one of them . . . but ended up spending the rest of her life with the other. *How did love and friendship turn into such fierce hatred?* she wondered. And when, if ever, would it end?

Sixteen-year-old George Fowler stood at the edge of Secca Lake, up to his tanned ankles in the cool water, and watched his father, Joshua, argue with his grandfather. "Do you want to run after their car, Dad?" Joshua asked testily. "And drag the mayor of Sweet Valley out onto the pavement and beat him up?"

"We were just having a discussion," Jack insisted, his jaw set in stubborn lines.

"Ha," grunted Joshua. "Well, you chased them out of here—you made your point."

"I thought it was neat, Grandpa," piped up George's ten-year-old brother, Brad. "I'm glad you didn't let that rich man push you around."

Jack tousled Brad's dark hair, flashing a triumphant look at Joshua. "I want my boys to know they're as good as anybody," Jack said. "That's all I want."

George slunk down the beach, his shoulders slouched. A few other people at the park had witnessed the fight between his grandfather and Mayor Doret and he could see them, their heads close together, gossiping. He could imagine what they were saying. "Those rough, ill-mannered Fowlers . . ."

Grandpa started it, George thought, shame tinting his cheeks red under the suntan. *A discussion—yeah, right. He doesn't know how to talk to anybody without yelling.*

There was a roar of engines in the parking lot and George turned his head. The Dorets were driving off in their fancy cars. *Must be nice to be rich,* thought George, envy simmering in his angry young heart. It wasn't just money. Rich people like the Dorets seemed different in so many ways. They were educated and well mannered. Even when they were on a picnic, they had an air of elegance about them. "I want to be like that," George whispered.

"Hey, George, come on," he heard his father shout. "We've got to get back to the shop."

George kicked a pebble with his bare foot, then turned and headed back toward the others.

Fowler's Ranch was failing. There had been ups and downs over the years, but these were the tightest times the family had ever known. Joshua was working at a local butcher shop, a job he detested, in order to bring in some extra money. Even George had an after-school job, making deliveries for the butcher. Still they could barely afford to keep food in their own cupboards. "Coming, Dad," George hollered back.

After drying off on threadbare towels, the Fowlers crammed into the rusty pickup truck. George rode in the back. As they bounced out of the parking lot and picked up speed on the open road, George savored the cleansing feeling of the wind raking his near-naked body.

The sky was blue and the world was green with the promise of summer. *But we have to go back to the crummy ranch*, George thought bitterly. He pictured the Dorets's opulent hilltop mansion, and suddenly a resolution was born in him. Maybe a failing ranch and a menial butcher shop job were good enough for his dad and grandfather, but they weren't good enough for him. *I'm going to make a success out of my life*, George vowed, his jaw square with determination. *I'll be more rich and powerful even than Mayor Doret*. It would be an uphill battle—he was starting at the bottom of the heap—but he'd fight his way to the top. He'd never let anything, or anyone, get in his way.

32

1971. Sweet Valley.

"Don't tell me you're taking a day off," joked George Fowler's assistant, Dave.

It was a Saturday in late June. They were at the tiny office they shared in the renovated warehouse on the outskirts of Sweet Valley, which housed George's fledgling computer business. As he slipped his arms into the sleeves of his windbreaker George grinned. "Just the rest of the morning," he assured Dave. Since he started the company, George had been logging eighty-hour work weeks and this one wasn't going to be any different. "I just need to think about this business plan I'm working on to attract new investors. I'll be back after lunch." He pointed a finger at Dave. "And you'd better have those figures ready for me by then."

Dave saluted. "Aye, aye, captain."

George pointed his car toward the coast. It was a gorgeous day—sunny, mild, with a fresh breeze off the ocean. The beauty of his surroundings wasn't entirely lost on George. He registered it mentally, filing it away under its appropriate practical category. *Good weather for walking on the beach and brainstorming,* he decided. *Get the ol' juices flowing. I need some fresh ideas, and fast.*

George noted with surprise that the parking lot at the beach was nearly full. Then he laughed at himself. Of course—most people weren't stuck in offices on the weekend like he was. But then, most people were content to be ordinary, to follow a slow, steady path to their life's goals. Not George Fowler.

He'd always been fiercely ambitious. At Sweet Valley High he'd studied tirelessly to earn a scholarship to an Ivy League university. He'd worked two jobs to put himself through college. Now he was twenty-seven, and after a few years at a big computer company on the East Coast, he was his own boss. Starting a new business was difficult and risky, but George knew the payoff could be tremendous, and he felt in his bones that computers were the future. Someday, when people in Sweet Valley—in all of California—spoke the name Fowler, they'd think of him, high tech and high class, not of an eccentric family living on a run-down old ranch.

George kicked off his tennis shoes and rolled up the cuffs of his khaki trousers. He walked along the sand, not paying any attention to the bikini-clad girls sunbathing and frolicking in the surf. At the far end of the beach he sat down on a driftwood log, facing the sapphire blue Pacific.

There was only one other person this far from the parking lot—a girl in very short white cutoffs and a hot pink tank top, flying a kite. He watched her run along the sand, her pale blond hair flying out behind her. The kite soared high above, then dipped on a current of air. All at once it spiraled, nose-diving into the sand just a few yards from George.

The girl jogged up to him. "Sorry," she said with a disarming smile. "I wasn't aiming for you, I promise."

"My whole life flashed before my eyes," he kidded. "I even saw the headlines in tomorrow's *Sweet Valley News.* 'Killer Kite Claims Another Victim!'"

She laughed. "Want to try it?" she asked, holding out the kite.

"No, thanks."

She studied him, her gaze appraising but uncritical. "Yeah, I guess you're not exactly dressed for beach sports."

George looked down at his khakis, short-sleeved seersucker shirt, and tie. "Nope."

"Just taking a break, huh?"

"Yep."

"Well . . ." She gave him a little wave. "Nice talking to you."

She started off, the kite in her hand. "Wait a minute," George called after her, rising to his feet.

She turned back. "Yeah?"

The breeze ruffled her fine-spun hair. George found himself staring at her. She was medium height and slender, with a perfect figure. Her eyes were clear and gray, the features of her face delicate. Without a doubt she was the most beautiful girl he'd ever seen in his life. "Would you . . . I was wondering," he began awkwardly. "I have to go back to the office now, but maybe later—if you don't have anything better to do, that is . . . I'd like to see you again," he finally managed to declare. "Would you have dinner with me tonight?"

She dropped her gaze. "Well, um, actually . . . I sort of have . . ." She looked at him again, straight in the eyes. She smiled, blushing slightly. "Yeah, OK. Sure."

"Do you know the clam bar at Marpa Heights?"

She nodded. "I'll meet you there at seven. Bye!"

She ran off down the beach, the kite bobbing in the breeze behind her. George followed her with his eyes, smiling wryly to himself. *Wow. How did that happen?* He hardly ever went out on dates— he didn't have time for a social life. Now on an impulse, he'd asked out a total stranger.

He realized there was something he'd forgotten to find out. "Hey, what's your name?" he shouted.

She whirled, her hair flying. "Grace," she shouted back.

He had gotten so caught up working on the business plan with Dave that George had lost track of the time. He was twenty minutes late getting to Marpa Heights. As he strode into the restaurant his heart was in his throat. *What if she didn't stick around?* he thought. He gave himself a mental shake. *Man, get a grip. Why would it matter? You don't even know her.* But it did matter. He *wanted* to know her.

The clam bar had outdoor tables. A girl in a batik T-shirt and bell-bottom jeans was sitting alone at a table by the railing, looking out at the pounding surf. She had her back to him, but he recognized the shimmering hair. "Grace," George said.

She swiveled, greeting him with a warm smile. "Hey. I thought you weren't going to show."

He pulled out a chair and sat down next to her. "I'm sorry. Things were kind of crazy at the office."

"At seven on a Saturday night?"

"If I hadn't made these plans with you, I'd have probably been there till midnight."

"Wow. What do you do for a living that's so intense?"

"I have my own computer company. There's a lot at stake right now—it's the make-or-break phase."

She sipped her drink, looking suitably impressed. Then she laughed. "Before I ask for the rest of your life story, maybe we should go back to the beginning for a minute. There's something you forgot to tell me."

He cocked his head. "There is?"

She laughed again. "Your name, silly."

He grinned. "Right." He held out a hand. "George Fowler, at your service."

Her eyes widened. She hesitated for a moment before taking his hand. "Well, you already know me," she mumbled. "Grace."

"Grace what?"

"Grace, um . . . Doret."

George stared at her. "As in Charles Doret, who was mayor of Sweet Valley for just about forever?"

She nodded apologetically. "And you're a Fowler as in Jack and Joshua Fowler?"

"My grandfather and my dad," George confirmed.

For a minute they just looked at each other in befuddled silence. Then Grace smiled faintly. "Maybe you don't want to have dinner with me after all."

George thought he hated all the Dorets, but that was before he met *this* Doret. "Are you kidding? The stuff between our families is ancient history."

"Not *that* ancient. My grandfather still practically

has heart failure when anyone mentions your grandfather's name!"

"Mine's the same way," George admitted. "He says Charles Doret ruined his life."

"Well, Charles Doret says Jack Fowler ruined *his* life!"

They both laughed. "Let's not talk about them," George suggested.

"Fine by me," Grace agreed.

They ordered a big basket of fried clams and a couple of sodas. Over the ocean the sun was setting. As the fading light bathed Grace in a golden glow, her beauty took George's breath away. "Tell me about you," he said, leaning forward with his elbows on the table. "What do you do?"

"I'm a student," she replied.

"A graduate student?"

"No way." She laughed. "I'm a sophomore at Sweet Valley University."

George sat back in his chair. "So you must be, like, nineteen?"

"Yep." She munched a fried clam. "How about you?"

"Twenty-seven," he told her.

She blinked. "Wow."

George laughed. "Too old?"

She shook her head. "No. I'd say . . . just right."

They talked for hours. When they couldn't think of an excuse to linger any longer at the clam bar—they'd ordered just about everything on the menu—they headed down to the beach for a moonlit stroll. It was nearly midnight when George walked Grace back to her car. *I shouldn't get involved with her,* he told himself. *I don't have time for a girlfriend. And of all the girls I could pick, this girl—a Doret!*

She opened the driver's-side door and looked up at him expectantly. George bent his head, planning to kiss her cheek. Instead his mouth found her lips. *This girl. This incredible girl.*

It was impossible. She was totally wrong for him. Their families were archenemies. She was so much younger than he was—just a college kid. But none of that mattered. For the first time in his life George was falling in love.

Grace drove home in a happy daze. She hadn't had a drop of alcohol, but she felt a little bit drunk. *Wow, what a kiss,* she thought, touching her lips lightly with her fingertips.

She was living at home for the summer, and when she reached her parents' mansion on Country Club Drive, she sneaked inside quietly, hoping her mother and father weren't still awake. Luckily the house was dark and silent. Upstairs she collapsed on her bed, her head spinning.

What a night, she thought, hugging herself. *I can't believe I did that! Am I crazy? Yes, I'm definitely crazy.* She counted up the reasons why she shouldn't get involved with George Fowler. *He's way too old for me and way too serious. He's a workaholic!* Actually, on second thought, she decided that she liked those things. They were part of what made him so incredibly attractive. The real problem was that he was a Fowler. The blood feud between their families wasn't a joke. *Mom and Dad would kill me if they ever found out,* Grace thought with a heavy sigh.

And that wasn't the only reason her parents would be furious if they knew she'd had a date with George Fowler. Grace sat up. Clasping her arms around her knees, she stared into the shadowy darkness of her room. Dimly, she could see a framed photograph on her desk. *I shouldn't have gone to the restaurant in the first place,* she berated herself. *Even* before *I knew his name.*

When she and George were getting acquainted, there was one thing she'd neglected to mention about herself. It just so happened that the photo was of her fiancé. She was engaged to be married to another man.

For two weeks Grace and George met every single night, careful to pick places where they wouldn't be spotted by anyone they knew. Grace was hoping her interest in George would fade, but instead she liked him more and more. Finally she summoned all her courage and confessed the whole story of her engagement to Everett Garrison III. "I didn't tell you sooner because . . . oh, I don't know why," she burst out. "I'm just so confused. I've been dating Everett forever, but there's never been any spark. I wasn't in a hurry to get married, to him or anybody, but our families really pushed it."

"Everett Garrison." George's expression was grim. "His dad was mayor after your grandfather, right?"

Grace nodded. "The Garrisons are incredibly rich and important, and it was really all our parents' idea. Well, maybe not all. Everett's always been nuts about me."

"Do you care for him?" George asked point-blank.

"I'm fond of him," Grace admitted. "I used to think I was in love with him, but then . . . then I met you." She gazed up at George, her eyes glowing. "And I realized what love really felt like."

They were parked at Miller's Point in George's car. George made an abrupt movement, as if he were about to take Grace in his arms, then pulled back. "We shouldn't get together anymore," he said gruffly.

Grace started to cry. "But I can't bear not to see you," she said tearfully. "I'll break it off with Everett."

"What about your parents?" George asked. "Do you really think they'd ever accept the idea of you and me together?"

She couldn't lie. If and when she told her parents she was dumping Everett Garrison III for the grandson of Jack Fowler, they'd hit the roof. "I don't know," she said honestly. "I'll have to go

293

about this carefully. Ease into it. But I'd like to give them the benefit of the doubt. They're not bad people, just kind of . . . set in their ways." She smiled, her face full of youthful hope. "I'm sure if they could get to know you, they'd adore you."

George was still facing forward, his hands on the steering wheel, his posture stiff and hurt. She stroked his arm gently. "For now," she added, "is it enough that *I* adore you?"

Turning, he folded her in his arms, showering kisses on her hair. "More than enough," he said, his voice brimming with emotion. "More than I ever dreamed of."

The summer flew by for George. His new business was taking off. A successful public stock offering had boosted the company's value, and suddenly he found himself on the verge of great wealth. Then there was his personal life. Two months after their first encounter on the beach, he and Grace saw each other whenever they could. She still hadn't told her parents about him, though, and she was still officially engaged to Everett Garrison III.

"I hate thinking about the two of you together," George confessed one night as they cuddled on a blanket at the beach.

"We don't *do* anything." Grace tickled his ribs. "Everett is very proper. I mean, he hardly ever even kisses me."

"Then he doesn't know what he's missing."

George pulled Grace to him. The kiss was deep and passionate. When they separated, he gazed intently into her eyes. "How much longer can we go on like this, Grace? It's almost September. You'll be starting school again. And your parents are planning a fall engagement party, and then in December . . . the wedding."

"I'll say something to them soon," she promised.

He didn't push her—he was too afraid of losing her. "It's getting late. I'd better take you home."

After two months they were still cautious about being seen together, but sometimes they took a risk. That evening he'd picked her up in downtown Sweet Valley. For the first time George was driving Grace back to her parents' house. As they entered her neighborhood he flashed her a grin. "I always wanted to live in this part of town. Someday I'll build a house right across the street from your folks."

Grace grinned back. "Well, I always wanted to go out with a cowboy. Too bad you switched to computers."

"Ranching isn't romantic," George told her. "It was a tough life for a kid. I couldn't clear out of there fast enough."

"But you came back to Sweet Valley," she pointed out.

"Yes. Guess I felt I had something to prove to my hometown."

When he reached the Dorets' driveway, he drove

another fifty yards, then pulled onto the shoulder beyond a dense clump of shrubbery. "Sorry to make you walk," he said.

She grabbed his hand playfully. "Come with me. I want you to see my bedroom."

George laughed. "Are you crazy?"

"Yes . . . about you. We can sneak around to the backyard," she pressed. "No one will see us."

Pocketing his car keys, George let Grace pull him from the car. Hand in hand, they ran across the lawn, staying close to a shadowy line of trees. George looked up at the spacious house, built in the style of a French country villa.

There was a pool in the backyard. The underwater lights were on, and it glowed in the night like a jewel. "How does a skinny-dip sound?" Grace whispered, slipping her arms around his waist.

George kissed her on the lips. "Delicious. But dangerous."

"OK, how about the cabana, then?" She pointed to the pool house, which George couldn't help noting was about the same size as the ranch where his grandparents still lived. "There's a pull-out couch in there. . . ."

He looked over his shoulder, his nerves jumping. "I don't know, Grace. Maybe this isn't too smart. Obviously I'd love to stay with you, but what if we get caught?"

"My parents have been in bed for hours," she assured him. "Their room is on the other side of the house. Unless the groundskeeper is here doing a little midnight gardening . . ."

They didn't make it to the cabana without stopping for another kiss. Grace twined her arms around George's neck, her body melting and pliant. George felt the desire surge in his blood. "We're out of our minds," he murmured, laughing under his breath.

"I know," Grace breathed. "Isn't it wonderful?"

He ran his hands up and down her back under her flimsy gauze shirt, his lips hungrily devouring hers. His mind went blank—he wasn't aware of anything but Grace, the taste of her, the feel of her.

They were so lost in each other, they didn't hear the car coasting down the driveway toward the garage. Suddenly headlights sliced into the darkness that had protected them. Standing between the pool and the cabana, they were caught in the beams with no place to hide. They jumped apart, but it was too late for George to run. Grace clung to his hand. "Oh, no," she gasped in horror.

The car engine died, but the headlights stayed on. George lifted a hand to shield his eyes. A middle-aged man and woman, dressed for a party, stepped from the car. George had never met them, but he recognized them immediately, and from the expressions on their shocked faces, he knew they recognized him too.

It was Grace's parents, Alan and Emily Doret.

❧ 33 ❧

Later, Grace couldn't remember how or even if she tried to explain George's presence to her parents. Did her father say something to George—did George himself speak? All she knew was that suddenly George was gone, and she was alone with her parents. In her entire life she'd never seen them so angry. "What on earth do you think you're doing, Grace?" her mother cried.

"I was just—we were only—"

"Do you know who that young man is, Grace Isabelle Doret?" her father roared.

Grace couldn't help laughing. "Of course, Daddy. Do you think I'd kiss a perfect stranger?"

"Grace, this is not funny!" her mother shrieked.

"How long has this been going on?" Mr. Doret demanded.

"Just a couple of months," said Grace, clasping

her hands. "Please. I know you're mad, but—"

"Mad. Mad! 'Mad' doesn't begin to say it," Mrs. Doret snapped. "What about poor Everett?"

Grace bit her lip. "I don't love him. I won't marry him."

Her parents stared at her. An ominous silence fell over them. Then it broke with a thunderclap. "*What* did you say?" Mr. Doret asked.

"I won't marry him," Grace repeated, her voice a frightened squeak. "You can't make me!"

"You *will* marry him," Mrs. Doret declared, her own voice icy. "And you will never see George Fowler again."

"Fowler." Mr. Doret spat out the name. "Of all people, somebody from that despicable family. Our enemies! How could you, Grace?"

"Dad, he's not the enemy," she protested. "He's a good man. He loves me, and—"

"Stop!" Mr. Doret commanded. "I don't want to hear any more of this foolishness. You'll marry Everett and you'll never see George Fowler again."

Grace folded her arms across her chest, her gray eyes flashing with rebellious fire. "And what if I don't do what you want me to?"

"Then you'll no longer be a Doret," her mother answered. "You won't be our daughter, and you won't live in our house. Do you understand, Grace?"

Grace's jaw dropped. Her parents couldn't be serious. "You'd really throw me out of the house? You'd *disown* me?" she cried.

"We mean what we say. Don't put us to the test," her father warned harshly.

Her parents went into the house, leaving her standing in the driveway. As the reality sank in, Grace dropped to the pavement, her whole body racked with sobs.

It was a horrible, impossible choice, but she knew what she was going to have to do. "And we didn't even get to say good-bye, George," she whispered, the tears streaming down her face.

The exclusive Sweet Valley Country Club was the perfect lush setting for the social event of the season. Hundreds of guests in tuxedos and full-length formal gowns danced under the autumn moon on the terrace or mingled in the dining room, nibbling on hors d'oeuvres and sipping champagne. Anyone who was anyone in Sweet Valley was there, and Grace Doret was the star of the evening.

She'd never been more miserable in her entire life.

"I can't believe you're getting *married!*" shrieked Lydia Pearce, flinging her arms around Grace. "And to the richest, cutest boy in town. You are the luckiest girl on the *planet!*"

Grace disentangled herself from Lydia's smothering embrace. "Thanks, Lyd," she muttered.

Marian Hanlon descended on Grace next. "The first of us to tie the knot," Marian remarked, her envy palpable. "You're leaving us all so far behind, Gracie!"

Grace winced. She hated being called by her

childhood nickname, especially by someone as smirkingly sophisticated as Marian. "I'll still be at SVU," Grace responded. *Though I wouldn't mind dropping out if it meant I didn't have to see you!*

"I can't believe you're going to bother finishing your degree," commented Lydia. "I'd quit in a minute if I was about to become Mrs. Everett Garrison the Third."

"Well, you're not," Grace pointed out. "I have to mingle, ladies. Ta-ta."

She hadn't taken more than a step when she bumped into her parents. "Oh, honey." Emily Doret beamed at Grace, then burst into tears. "This is the happiest night of my life."

"And this is just the engagement party. How are you going to hold yourself together at the wedding?" Mr. Doret teased his wife.

Grace forced herself to smile. "It's a great party, Mom and Dad. Thanks."

"Don't forget to thank the Garrisons too," her mother prompted her. "They've been looking all over for you."

"Don't worry, Mom," Grace promised. "I'll do the right thing."

"You always do, honey," her mother said proudly.

Do I? Grace wondered bitterly as she wandered through the party, flashing false smiles at everyone she met and making meaningless small talk. *Yes, I guess I do. I broke up with George, didn't I? Just to please Mom and Dad.* She saw her fiancé, Everett, making his way toward her. A lump formed in her throat. *And just because it's the "right" thing to do, in two months I'm going to walk down the aisle with a man I don't love.*

"We haven't danced yet," Everett said to Grace, his tone reproachful. He slipped an arm around her waist. "Come on."

Suddenly Grace felt as if she couldn't breathe. *If I stay in this room one second longer, I'll die.* "Everett, I—I have to go to the bathroom," she fibbed. "Be right back."

Desperate to escape, she dashed off toward the terrace. Outside, she sucked in a deep breath of cool night air. Then she spotted an elderly woman in an elegant black sequined gown, sitting alone at a table at the edge of the lawn. "Grandma," Grace said. "Are you having a nice time?"

Isabelle gestured to the other chair. "Sit with me for a while, dear," she invited. Grace did, and Isabelle took her hand. "The question is, are *you* having a nice time."

Her grandmother had always had an uncanny insight into Grace's soul. *She's the only one I can talk to,* Grace realized. "No, I'm not," she confessed, dashing a tear from her eye. "I feel like I'm on a runaway train—this is all happening so quickly. And marriage means forever. What if I'm making a mistake?"

"It's not unusual to have cold feet at a time like this," observed Isabelle. "But if you truly love the boy, it will all work out fine." She narrowed her green eyes, her gaze penetrating like an arrow straight to Grace's heart. "*Do* you love him?"

Grace bowed her head. Her parents had forbidden her to tell anyone, even her grandmother, about the episode with George. "I . . . I'm not sure," she whispered.

"Well, it's a good match. Like ours, his family is powerful and affluent. Everett will be a successful, important man—as his wife, you'll have a prominent position in Sweet Valley society."

"But I don't care about those things!" Grace burst out.

An approving smile flickered across Isabelle's face. "Then marry the one you love," she urged. "It's the only route to happiness. Believe me," she added, her voice fading to a whisper, "I know."

George stayed late at the office, even though it was a Saturday night. He'd been working around the clock for days to finalize a big deal. Finally, at nine P.M., the call came that he'd been waiting for, the one on which it all hinged.

When he hung up the phone, a triumphant smile spread across his tired face. "I did it," he said out loud to the empty office. "I really did it."

He slid open his top desk drawer. Taking out a small box, he stuck it in his jacket pocket. Then he switched off the lights and headed outside, locking the office behind him.

As he drove fast through the streets of Sweet Valley he remembered the humiliation of being run off the family property by Grace's parents as if he were some kind of thief. And then the pain of losing her, the only girl he'd ever loved. He knew she was trapped, and it hadn't been in his power then to fight for her. *But now the stage is set,* George thought. For generations the Dorets had trampled on the Fowlers. Now he was about to turn the tables.

George checked the clock on the dashboard, then stepped on the accelerator. The car's engine roared.

He had a party to crash.

After her conversation with her grandmother, Grace couldn't bring herself to go back inside to Everett, her parents, Mr. and Mrs. Garrison, and all the hundreds of people who wanted to toast her future marital bliss. *"Marry the one you love, marry the one you love. . . ."* The words seemed to echo in the night breeze that whispered through the leaves. *It's too late,* Grace thought with a sniffle, ducking behind a tree and dropping forlornly onto a secluded bench. She'd sent George away—she'd hurt him terribly. She might as well marry Everett. What difference did it make?

"Oh, George. I miss you so much!" Tears had been tickling the back of Grace's throat all evening. Now they spilled forth. "Shoot," she muttered, taking a tissue from her beaded evening bag and dabbing at her face. Her mascara was running all over the place—her blush and eye shadow were probably ruined too. Grace started crying harder.

Just then she glimpsed a movement out of the corner of her eye. A tall figure approached through the trees. *It's probably Everett.* Grace jumped up, ready to run. She couldn't let her fiancé see she'd been bawling. Then the man drew closer. It wasn't Everett at all. It was George Fowler.

Grace stopped, her eyes wide with astonishment. "George, what—"

Without a word he strode up to her and dropped down to one knee. He took a box from his pocket and opened it. In the moonlight a large diamond glittered. George took Grace's hand. Removing the engagement ring Everett had given her, he slipped the other ring in its place. "Marry me, Grace Doret," he said simply.

For a moment Grace was too astonished to speak. She stood very still, her pale blue chiffon dress billowing gently in the breeze. George gazed up at her, his eyes full of love and hope. *It's like a fairy tale,* Grace thought. She'd been under a spell, but the handsome prince had broken it. Now she was free to go after what her heart desired most. "I will," she said with a smile of pure joy. "I *will* marry you, George Fowler."

He stood up and wrapped his arms around her. "You've made me the happiest man on earth," he declared, his voice rough with emotion.

The strains of dance music wafted through the trees. Still holding each other close, Grace and George began to sway. Grace could hardly feel the grass under her feet—she felt closer to the stars twinkling overhead. "This was turning into the worst night of my life," she told George, smiling into his warm brown eyes, "but now things are looking up."

George bent his head to kiss her. "I guess there's an engagement to celebrate after all," he agreed.

❧ 34 ❧

Grace slept late the next morning. It was almost noon when she heard somebody shouting. Throwing on her bathrobe, she padded downstairs to see what was going on. She met her mother at the door to her father's study. They arrived just in time to see Mr. Doret slam down the telephone, his face red with fury. "My goodness!" Mrs. Doret exclaimed. "Darling, what's the matter?"

"That was my chief financial officer," Mr. Doret explained, fuming. "You won't believe what's just taken place. Some upstart computer company has leveraged Doret Manufacturing! They're buying out all our stockholders, every last one of them, and planning to update our machinery to make computers!" Just then the telephone rang again. He grabbed it, barking into the receiver, "Hello?"

Grace watched in fascination as her father

listened to whoever was on the other end of the line. Mr. Doret's face grew pale and then an instant later turned absolutely purple. This time when he slammed down the phone, she felt the floor shake.

For a solid minute he was too enraged to speak. "Tell us what's going on," Mrs. Doret pleaded.

"I just found out who's behind all this," Mr. Doret choked out. His furious gaze settled on Grace. "George Fowler!"

"You should have seen his face," Grace said to George on Sunday evening as she buckled her seat belt. "He was livid. I have to admit, I was pretty surprised too!"

George grinned. "Sorry I didn't say anything last night, but I was too busy kissing you." He gestured around the first-class cabin of the jet airplane. "Are you sure about all this, Grace?"

"Absolutely," she replied.

They'd arranged it all at the country club the previous night. They didn't say anything to anyone—Grace pretended she was still happily engaged to Everett. But on Saturday she secretly packed her bags. On the way to the airport they'd stopped at the town hall to be married by the justice of the peace. Now, before their families even realized they were missing, they were on a flight to Paris for their honeymoon.

As the plane taxied down the runway George

squeezed Grace's hand. "Wait till you see the romantic little hotel I've picked out. You'll love it."

"I'm sure I will, as long as I'm with you." They kissed tenderly. Grace rested her head on George's shoulder. "You're really stuck with me," she told him. "My family will never have me back after a stunt like this."

"Fine with me. I've wanted you more than anything for the longest time."

"Even more than you wanted to take over my father's manufacturing company?"

"That was just business. It was nothing personal. Well . . . OK," George admitted. "It was a little bit personal. But it's a good deal all around. We're all richer for it."

"My dad still won't ever forgive you, though," she predicted.

"No," George agreed. "I doubt he will."

The plane took off. "I feel like a bird that's just been freed from its cage," Grace said to her new husband.

"You can do whatever you want now," George promised, "be whoever you want. We'll be even richer than your parents."

"But I married you for love, not money," said Grace.

George wrapped his arms around her. "And we'll be in love forever, won't we?"

"Forever," she agreed, lifting her face for a kiss.

The sun was sinking in the west as they unpacked in their hotel room. Grace stepped out onto the balcony to admire the fiery sky. "Paris," she breathed. "I can't believe I'm here."

George came up behind her and wrapped his arms around her, resting his chin on top of her head. "Tomorrow I'm going to take you to the finest couturier in Paris to buy you a wedding dress. We'll get married all over again."

Grace sighed deeply, contentment filling her soul. "Doesn't France feel like home?"

George laughed into her hair. "Maybe, just for the vacation, I should change my name back to Oiseleur."

She turned to face him. "By now everyone back in Sweet Valley knows we eloped. What do you suppose they're thinking?"

"Let me see . . ." George grinned. "It's a good bet the male members of both clans have been using a lot of four-letter words."

Grace wrinkled her forehead thoughtfully. "You know what, though? I think there's one person who won't be surprised. She might even pleased. My grandmother, Isabelle."

"She didn't like ol' Everett?"

"She didn't like the idea of me marrying someone I didn't love. I bet she'll be happy for us, even though it was her husband who started the Doret-Fowler feud."

"I've always wondered about that," George

commented. "I feel like I don't know the whole story."

"It doesn't matter now, does it?" Grace smiled up at him. "The feud's history. From now on, the Dorets and Fowlers are one."

He pulled her closer. "For richer or for poorer, but hopefully always richer," he teased.

"In sickness and in health."

"Till death do us part." He bent his head to kiss her. "I love you, Grace Doret Fowler. And I always will."

🌿 *35* 🌿

A Number of Years Later. Sweet Valley.

Her driver dropped Isabelle Doret off at the main entrance to the hospital. A widow in her seventies with snow white hair, she was still strikingly beautiful. Her delicate facial features had grown even more refined with age; her posture was still straight, her footstep light and graceful. She entered the lobby and walked quickly to the information desk. "I'm here to visit my granddaughter," she announced. "Grace Fowler. She had a baby yesterday afternoon."

"The maternity ward is on the second floor, wing B," the receptionist replied.

Isabelle rode the elevator to the second floor. The head maternity nurse checked her clipboard. "Room eleven," she said.

The door to the room was ajar. When Isabelle peeked in, she was greeted by a sight that brought tears to her eyes. George Fowler was bent over the bed where Grace was reclining. A tiny baby with a shock of black hair lay snuggled in Grace's arms. Husband and wife gazed at their new daughter with adoration.

Isabelle knocked lightly on the door. "May I come in and meet my new great-grandchild?"

"Oh, Grandma!" exclaimed Grace. "Of course!"

Isabelle crossed to the bed. "Look at her. What an angel!"

"You're the first person in the family to meet her," Grace said.

"What did you name her?"

"Lila."

Isabelle reached out her arms. "May I?"

She settled into an armchair next to Grace's bed. George laid the infant in Isabelle's arms. "I'm so glad you're here, Grandma," said Grace. "No one else will come. Mom and Dad have never forgiven us, and George's parents are just as stubborn."

"Maybe they'll relent now that Lila's here," Isabelle remarked, looking down at the baby's enchanting face. "Lila, are you the prettiest little baby in the world?" she cooed.

The baby made a gurgling sound. George chuckled, beaming proudly. "I think that was a 'yes.' She already knows how special she is."

Just then there was another knock. They all

looked toward the door. A tall, lean, gray-haired man stood awkwardly in the doorway, a cowboy hat in his hand. Isabelle's heart leaped. "Am I intruding?" Jack Fowler asked.

"Come in, Grandpa," George urged with a welcoming smile. "The Fowlers are underrepresented in here."

Jack dropped a kiss on Grace's cheek. Then he stood in front of Isabelle. She felt her face grow warm. She hadn't been this close to Jack—hadn't talked to him face-to-face—since that dusty summer afternoon almost fifty years ago. "What have you got there, ma'am?" he asked, smiling.

"Our great-granddaughter." Isabelle smiled back. "Would you like to hold her?"

"Oh, no." He shook his head. "She's too small— I'd probably drop her. I just want a look at her." He studied the baby intently. "Those beautiful green eyes," he murmured, glancing at Isabelle. "Wonder where she got those?"

Isabelle blushed. "Why, they're just like yours, Grandma!" Grace declared.

Jack admired Lila for a few more minutes. Then he looked back at Isabelle. "How about we leave these kids to themselves, Mrs. Doret? Let me buy you a cup of coffee."

Isabelle raised her eyebrows. Then she laughed. After so many decades of animosity . . . a cup of coffee! "I'd be delighted," she replied.

When they were sitting next to each other on a

bench in the hospital's outdoor courtyard, Isabelle laughed again. "Look at us," she said. "Too old to fight anymore."

Jack sipped his coffee. "I never wanted to fight with you, Isabelle."

"Nor I with you," she said softly.

"Things seem different now that Charles is gone," he observed, "and since I lost Anita."

"Do they?"

He looked into her eyes. "I always . . . ," he began. "I never . . ."

He didn't finish the sentence. Isabelle turned away, pretending to admire the bright coral blossoms on the geranium growing nearby. "So, what do you think about these two," she said, changing the subject. "About Grace and George? Defying us all to get married."

Jack laughed. "I approved wholeheartedly. The boy has spunk. And he couldn't have picked a brighter, lovelier girl."

"Even though she's a Doret?" Isabelle teased.

"That's what makes it so right, in my eyes," Jack replied. "Doesn't it seem that way to you, Isabelle?"

She nodded. "Things have come full circle."

A thoughtful silence fell over them. Jack was the first to break it. "Isabelle, I often wished I responded differently that day you drove out to the ranch."

She flushed, remembering how she'd thrown herself at him, declaring her love, only to have him send her back to Charles. "Oh, Jack, let's not—"

"No, listen," he insisted. He put down his coffee so he could take her hand. "I thought I'd stopped caring for you. My pride was so deeply wounded. There you stood, pregnant with another man's child! But I never got over you." He took a deep, shaky breath. "There, I said it. It was always you, Isabelle."

Isabelle had long ago come to terms with the emptiness at the center of her life. She'd lost Jacques Oiseleur, her one true love, and though her children and grandchildren were a consolation, her marriage to Charles had been a bitter disappointment. Now a glad lightness entered her heart. Jack was looking at her, the ghost of a smile in his eyes. For a moment she was transported back in time almost sixty years. *He's still the man I fell in love with in 1914,* she thought.

"I guess our love for each other was stronger than we recognized," she said softly. "It never died. Do you know I felt that two years ago when Grace and George eloped? Our love had been reborn in them."

"We have to stand by them," Jack agreed, "especially now that Lila's come into the world."

"We have a family together at last." Isabelle's voice trembled with emotion.

"And a baby to share."

They were still holding hands. Isabelle gazed at Jack, her eyes shining with quiet happiness. "As it was always meant to be."

❧ 36 ❧

1975.

Grace Fowler stood in front of the picture window in the cavernous living room of Fowler Crest, the Spanish-style mansion where she lived with her husband and two-year-old daughter. Outside, night had fallen. A half-empty wineglass was in her hand; in the dining room down the hall a candlelit dinner for two had long since grown cold. Once again Lila had been put to bed without getting to say good night to Daddy.

The phone rang and Grace hurried to pick it up. "Hello?"

"Grace, it's me," her husband announced briskly.

"What's all that noise?" she asked.

"I'm calling from the airport," he explained. "You know the deal we've been working on with that semiconductor company on the East Coast? I need to go out there in person. I'm taking the red-eye. Sorry I didn't have time to stop by the house."

"I'm sorry too," she said, swallowing her disappointment.

"I'll be back late tomorrow night. Kiss Lila for me."

"Will do."

There was a click. Grace replaced the receiver, biting her lip to keep from crying. *Why should I care so much?* she wondered. It wasn't as if this was anything new. George was always hopping on planes without giving her any warning. He'd been a workaholic when she met him, and he'd only gotten worse with time. "It's the cost of doing business," he'd say whenever she complained that she missed him. "I'm doing this for you, Grace."

She wandered aimlessly through room after room. Fowler Crest was opulent and enormous, nearly twice the square footage of the spacious house where she'd grown up. George had wanted to make a statement—he wouldn't be satisfied with anything less than the grandest residence in Sweet Valley.

I live in a castle, Grace thought as she slowly climbed the wide, sweeping staircase to the second floor. *I have servants who do everything for me and more money than I could ever spend. But I'm dying of loneliness. I might as well be a widow, and Lila might as well not have a father.*

"You went *where?*"

George's voice boomed through the echoing

318

spaces of Fowler Crest like a cannon. Grace jumped. "I—I took Lila to see my—my mother," she stammered.

"I thought I made it clear that I never wanted you to set foot in Alan and Emily Doret's house," George declared. "And I don't want Lila having any contact with them either."

It was the following night. George had just returned from the airport, and he and Grace were having a late supper. "Mom and Dad have been trying to patch things up with us ever since Lila was born," Grace said, her tone placating. "They want to put the past behind us and be a family again."

"They should have thought about that before they hit me with all those lawsuits," George stated.

"Well, you were the one who kept the feud going by taking over my father's company," Grace reasoned. "The point is, they're my parents and Lila's grandparents. It doesn't seem fair to—"

George cut her off. "You won't see them again. Do you hear me?"

"But George!"

"They've always treated me and my family like dirt." His voice shook with anger. "When you married me, you stopped being one of them. You're a Fowler now, Grace. Lila and I should be family enough for you."

"And maybe you would be if you were ever around," Grace countered.

"Is that what's at the bottom of all this? I'm not

319

doing enough for you? Maybe you regret marrying me—you wish you'd stayed with Everett Garrison."

"No, of course not," Grace cried. "I'm the one who should be jealous. You love your business more than you love me, and you always have."

"Don't be ridiculous."

"It's true." Grace was sobbing in earnest now. "The company's always come first. Why did you even want a wife? Did you ever care for me at all, or was I just a trophy?"

"Get a hold of yourself, Grace," George said coldly. "This hysterical behavior is very unbecoming . . . and unproductive."

She continued to weep, her face in her hands. George folded his cloth napkin and placed it on the table, then pushed back his chair. "If you feel like being reasonable, I'll be upstairs," he told her. "One thing isn't open to negotiation, however. You will *not* take Lila to see your family ever again, under *any* circumstances."

He left her sitting alone at the long dining-room table. Grace blotted her face with her napkin, but the tears didn't stop flowing. *We used to be so much in love,* she thought forlornly. *How did our marriage get to be like this?*

The phone call came a few weeks later while Grace and George were getting ready for bed. Grace answered it. Curious, George watched his wife's face grow pale as she listened to the person speaking at the other end. "Thanks for calling," Grace said finally. "I'll do my best."

"Who was that?" he asked when she hung up the telephone.

Grace climbed into bed, pulling the covers up to her waist. "It was my mother," she answered. "My grandmother had a stroke. She's in the hospital. They think . . ." Grace's chin quivered. "They think she may not pull through."

"Well, she had a good long life," George commented.

"Is that all you can say?" Grace cried.

"It's hard for me to get sentimental about anything that has to do with the Dorets," he replied, reaching up to turn off the bedside light.

In the dark he heard Grace whisper, "I want to go with my mother to visit Grandma in the hospital."

"No," George said.

"But George! Isabelle's not like the rest of my family. She made peace with Jack Fowler, remember? And she came to us when Lila was born. She loves me and I love her."

"I said no, and that's final."

They lay in the dark, their backs to each other, not touching. She didn't speak again, but he could tell she was crying. An urge swept over him to take her in his arms and comfort her. *Why am I being so rigid?* he wondered. *What am I trying to prove?* But he didn't make a move to touch his wife. His hatred of the Dorets ran deep, and it masked his

321

most secret fear: that maybe he didn't deserve Grace, and never had, and someday he'd be punished for stealing her away.

The phone rang again the next afternoon, when George was at work. Grace and Lila were in the huge recreation room of Fowler Crest, building a tower with brightly painted wooden blocks. Grace leaped for the telephone. "Hello?" she said breathlessly.

It was the news she'd been dreading. "Isabelle died half an hour ago, sweetheart," Emily Doret reported tearfully.

Grace sank onto the leather couch. "Oh, Mom."

She spoke with her mother for a few minutes, learning the details of Isabelle's final hours. When she hung up the phone, she waited for the tears to start. Instead she felt herself growing more and more angry. *He kept me from her—I didn't even get to say good-bye,* she thought. *And he'll probably forbid me from going to her funeral too!*

"Mommy, look!" Lila chirped. Flashing a gleeful smile, she knocked over the blocks. "Boom boom!"

"That's good, honey," Grace said. Suddenly she knew what she was going to do. *I don't have to put up with this. Lila deserves better, and so do I.* "It's time to put the blocks away." Grace scooped up her daughter. "I'm taking you on a trip."

It was raining that night when George's chauffeured car pulled up in front of the home of Alan and

322

Emily Doret. George himself got out to ring the bell.

Grace answered the door. "Get Lila," George commanded sternly. "I'm taking you back to Fowler Crest."

Grace shook her head. "We're staying with my parents for a few days," she said, her voice clear and strong. "At least through the funeral and maybe a little bit longer. You and I need some time to think about what we can do to make this marriage work."

"Our marriage was working fine until you let your family sabotage it," he accused.

"Our marriage is a charade!" Grace retorted. "We've stopped loving each other, George. I don't even think you love Lila."

Her words stung like a slap. "Bring my daughter to me," he ordered. "You can do what you please, but Lila's coming home where she belongs."

"Lila stays with me," Grace insisted. "We'll call you next week."

George stood on the front steps in the rain, his hands balled into fists. He'd never felt such helplessness or such fury. *Because you know Grace is right,* a voice somewhere deep inside him whispered. He stifled the voice. "You'll regret this, Grace," he warned.

"Good-bye, George," she said. The door closed in his face.

Three days later, when the family came home from Isabelle's funeral, there was a strange car parked in the driveway. A subdued Alan Doret, his eyes red rimmed from weeping, went to investigate and returned with an envelope in his hand. "This is for you," he told Grace.

Grace slipped off her black gloves and opened the envelope. As she glanced over the pages the color drained from her face, leaving her complexion white as snow against the somber black of her dress. "It's from George's lawyer," she gasped. "He's filed for divorce and . . . and he's accusing me of desertion and kidnapping." She stared in horror at her parents. "He's suing for sole custody of Lila!"

For Grace the weeks that followed were like a nightmare. She hired a lawyer of her own and pleaded with George in person. He refused to back down. "I'll take you back on my terms," he said coldly.

"Be fair, George," Grace begged. "How can there be any hope of happiness for our family if you insist—"

"On my terms," he repeated.

"It would be like living in a prison!" Grace cried.

"It's your choice, Grace."

Grace's parents tried to talk her out of taking the battle to court. "We'll do our best to help you, honey," Mr. Doret promised, "but George is one of the richest, most powerful men in southern California. He's hired the sharpest team of lawyers in the state."

"The judge won't take Lila away from me," Grace argued. "I'm her mother."

But when she faced George and his attorneys in court, Grace's confidence faltered. Day after day the hearings went on. Grace crumbled before the cruel legal onslaught. At long last the judge made his ruling. George Fowler was granted sole custody of his young daughter. Grace Fowler was denied even visitation rights.

As George hurried from the courtroom with Lila in his arms, Grace tried to run after him. "No! My baby!" she screamed, her heart shattering into a thousand pieces.

"I know this is hard for you to understand," Grace said softly, struggling to keep her voice bright. She brushed the silky dark hair from Lila's smooth forehead. "But Mommy has to go on a trip."

"Mommy go bye-bye?" Lila said.

Tears glimmered in Grace's eyes. "That's right, sweetie."

George had allowed her to come to Fowler Crest one last time to say good-bye. A taxi waited in the drive, loaded up with suitcases. From Fowler Crest, Grace was heading straight to the airport. She'd bought a one-way ticket to France. It was too hard living in Sweet Valley, in the place where she'd once been so deliriously happy as a young wife and mother, the place where it had all gone wrong. *If I can't even see my own beloved Lila . . .*

"When Mommy coming back?" Lila wanted to know.

Grace bit her lip. "I—I don't know. Will you be a good girl?"

"Yes," Lila promised. "Mommy come back soon if I'm good?"

Grace's self-control disintegrated. She threw her arms around Lila, hugging her fiercely. "I love you so much," she sobbed.

"I love you too, Mommy," Lila said, puzzled by her mother's outburst.

Grace continued to hold Lila tight. A figure appeared behind them in the doorway. "You'll miss your flight, Grace," George said, his tone expressionless.

Reluctantly Grace released Lila. The little girl ran back into the house. George and Grace stood face-to-face. "I'll never understand why it had to be this way," Grace told her ex-husband, her gray eyes still swimming with tears.

George lifted a hand, as if about to touch her. Then he let his arm fall to his side. "Good-bye, Grace," he said. She searched his face for sympathy, for some sign that he knew what she was going through. She might as well have been looking at a total stranger.

Grace hurried down the walk to the waiting taxi. She didn't look back as they sped away from Fowler Crest. She wouldn't have seen anything if she did—she was blinded by tears. "Good-bye, my darling Lila," she whispered.

37

Fourteen Years Later

George Fowler had gotten home from the office late, as usual. On the way to the master suite on the second floor of Fowler Crest, he stopped by his daughter's room to say hello. Standing in the hall outside Lila's door, he heard the muffled sound of crying. He hesitated, then knocked. "Li? It's me. Just wanted to let you know I'm home. If you want to talk . . ."

The door remained closed. "I'm OK," Lila said after a moment.

"You sure?"

"Yeah." She sniffled. "I'm sure."

"Well, if you need anything . . ."

"Thanks, Daddy."

George continued down the hall, loosening his tie. *How do you talk to a sixteen-year-old girl?* he wondered. It was completely mystifying and frustrating. She said she was fine, but George knew she wasn't. She needed to talk to someone, but she didn't want to talk to him. It was pretty obvious how she felt, though she was too polite to say it: "You wouldn't understand, Daddy."

It was a cool night, and the maid had started a fire in the fireplace in the master suite. George tossed his suit coat on the bed and sank into a leather easy chair. He gazed into the fire, his brow furrowed. He'd had a good day at the office, and when he had left, he'd felt on top of the world. His business was flourishing. Just that week his picture had been on the cover of the premier finance magazine in the country. At the age of forty-five he was at the pinnacle of his profession. The empire he'd built single-handedly exceeded even his own ambitious expectations. *But then I come home to an unhappy teenager and I'm helpless,* he thought morosely.

A few months earlier Lila had suffered a traumatic experience. A boy she was dating, John Pfeifer, had tried to force her to have sex with him. She'd fought him off, but the emotional damage was serious. Going to a counseling center, Project Youth, seemed to help for a while. But lately Lila, ordinarily one of the most vivacious and popular girls at Sweet Valley High, had become more and more withdrawn. Even her father, who didn't spend that much time with her, couldn't help noticing the dramatic change in her appearance and behavior.

Maybe if she and I were closer, she'd open up to me, George mused. It was too late to change the past, though. The fact was, he didn't know his daughter all that well. Business had always been his top priority. He worked long hours and traveled frequently. He tried to make it up to Lila by showering her with expensive gifts—she had her own sports car and a walletful of charge cards. But George knew deep in his heart that material things couldn't compensate for a parent's attention and affection.

And as long as I'm being honest with myself, he thought, *she's not the only one who's lonely.* He was the richest and most successful man in Sweet Valley—perhaps in all of southern California. But his life was hollow. "Where did I go wrong?" George asked the empty room.

He didn't expect to be so nervous, just making a simple telephone call, but his hand was perspiring as he punched in the digits of the international number.

The phone rang once, twice. George thought about hanging up. Then he remembered Lila, whom he'd caught playing hooky from school that day. He'd offered to take a day off from work to be with her, to take her on a shopping expedition or even whisk her off to New York City for the weekend. Nothing interested her and he had no idea how to reach her. *She needs a mother,* he'd decided. At the moment there was no special woman friend in George's life, no potential stepmother for

Lila. He could only think of one person to turn to.

After four rings someone picked up the phone. "*Allo?*" a woman said in perfectly accented French.

It had been fourteen years since George had heard that voice. He cleared his throat, suddenly feeling as nervous and bashful as a boy. "Grace, it's George," he said at last. "George Fowler. I'm calling about our daughter."

"I can't believe Grace is coming here!" Lila exclaimed. "Do you think she'll like my dress, Dad? Maybe purple is too garish. I should've worn black!"

They were on their way to the Beverly Hills Hotel to meet Grace Doret Fowler Rimaldi for dinner. George's ex-wife had been surprised to hear from him, but when he described Lila's troubles, Grace didn't hesitate. "Let me tie up some loose ends at work," she'd said. "I'll be there as soon as I'm able."

Now George shot a glance at Lila. They were sitting in the back of his limousine, sipping mineral water. "You look lovely," he assured his daughter.

Lila smoothed the short skirt of her close-fitting purple dress, then nervously fingered her pearl necklace. "It's just that she hasn't seen me since I was two," she fretted. "I don't even know her. What if we have nothing to say to each other?"

George felt a pang of guilt. Whose fault was it that mother and daughter had been separated for so long? Who'd chased Grace from Sweet Valley and made it perfectly clear she shouldn't ever bother coming back? "Your mother can't wait to see you," George told Lila. "Don't worry that you won't live up to her expectations."

By the time the limousine pulled up in front of the Beverly Hills Hotel, though, George's own pulse was racing. They stood at the restaurant's entrance, scanning the crowded room. "Daddy, is that her?" Lila squeaked, digging her fingernails into her father's arm.

George's eyes came to rest on an elegant woman in a dusty teal silk dress and jacket. She was sitting alone, looking at a menu. Her pale blond hair fell in a smooth curtain against her cheek. Her complexion was still flawless, and when she looked up and saw them across the restaurant, her eyes lit up like candles.

For an instant George felt as if time were racing backward. He was young man again, in his twenties, standing on a windy beach, gawking at the most beautiful girl in the world. *She hasn't aged a single day,* he thought. "Yes, Lila, that's her," he murmured.

As they made their way toward her Grace rose to her feet, smiling nervously. "Lila, I'd have known you anywhere," she said softly, extending a hand to her daughter.

Lila took her mother's hand. Grace kissed her on both cheeks, continental style. For a minute they just stood smiling shyly at each other. Then, laughing, Grace flung her arms around Lila. "Oh, darling," she whispered. "I can't tell you how good it is to see you. It's been too long."

"I'm happy to see you too, Mom," Lila said, crying softly. George turned his head away to hide the fact that his own eyes glinted with tears.

When the two women stepped apart, Grace looked at her ex-husband. "George, I'm so glad you got in touch. I've wanted this over the years—to see Lila—but I didn't know how . . . or whether . . ."

"I shouldn't have waited so long to call you," he replied.

"Well, we're here now." Grace smiled. "The past is behind us. Let's look to the future."

George felt a surge of unexpected hope in his heart. He'd had no idea seeing Grace again would affect him this way, but he was overwhelmed by her beauty, her charm, her gentleness, just as he'd been that day at the beach so many years ago. *How could I have let her go? What was I thinking, to drive away the only woman I've ever loved?* Was it too late to make amends, to start over? "Grace," he began, reaching out to touch her arm.

Her eyes slid past him and she lifted a hand to beckon to someone. George turned his head. A tall, slender man wearing a flashy European suit approached their table. His long hair was pulled back in a wispy ponytail and one ear was pierced. George cocked an eyebrow.

"George, Lila, I'd like you to meet Pierre Billot," Grace said as the man stepped to her side. "My boyfriend."

38

"We have a lot to catch up on," Grace remarked to George the next afternoon.

The four of them had just finished brunch. Grace was doing her best to smooth things over, but it was obvious that both George and Lila had taken an immediate dislike to Pierre and considered him an intruder. To her relief, right after the meal Pierre declared his intention to return to Beverly Hills to shop and sightsee. Grace had remained in Sweet Valley, and now George was reacquainting her with the grounds of Fowler Crest.

"We do," George agreed. They paused on a high point of ground looking out over the lawn and tennis courts. "How long have you and Pierre been together?"

"Oh, let's see. About a year. But it isn't . . ." Grace blushed. "I know he doesn't seem quite my type. We're probably not a long-term thing. I mean, I don't see us—"

"You don't have to defend him to me," George broke in. "It's certainly nice for you to have a companion on a long trip like this."

Grace blushed even pinker. She couldn't admit to George that in the past twenty-four hours she'd started to view Pierre in a whole new—and not very flattering—light. Back in Paris she'd been relatively content with their relationship. Now, seeing him side by side with George, she was almost embarrassed by him.

"How about you?" she asked quickly. "Are you seeing anyone?"

"Not right now."

"And you never remarried."

George shook his head. "No."

"Too busy for a wife?" Grace ventured.

George glanced at her, a sad shadow in his eyes. "I'm busy, certainly, but that's not the reason. I never met the right woman. There's no one who compares to—" He stopped abruptly. Turning, he gestured back toward the house. "Come on. Let me show you the renovation I'm planning. Remember how you always thought the place needed a solarium? Well . . ."

As Grace followed George, listening to him talk about architects' sketches, she couldn't help wondering about the fact that both she and George remained single. She'd remarried years ago, but it hadn't lasted. *And getting involved with someone like Pierre,* she mused. *It's almost as if I don't want it to work.* Was it just because she'd been hurt so badly by George that she didn't want to risk being hurt again? Or was it something else?

"This is a lovely luncheon," Grace told Lila two weeks later. "I'm touched that you'd go to so much trouble for me."

"Don't be silly." Lila hugged her mother. "It's no trouble at all. I wanted all my friends to meet you and see how great you are." Her lower lip trembled slightly. "Before you have to go back to France."

Lila had invited all her own Sweet Valley High friends, plus many of Grace's old acquaintances. The party was in full swing. Grace drew her daughter aside so they could talk privately. "Honey, I know it's going to be hard to say good-bye when the time comes. But I want you to know that we'll never be apart for long again. You'll visit me in Paris and I'll fly here as often as I can. We can talk on the phone and write letters and—"

"But it's not the same as having you here," Lila burst out.

Grace sighed. "I wish I could stay longer. But my business is in Paris. My *life* is there."

"Is it?" Lila asked tearfully. "What about *me?*"

Grace looked into the mirror of her daughter's eyes. *Lila's right. What do I mean by "my life" anyway?* she thought. *What could be more important than my relationship with the daughter I've rediscovered after all these years?*

"I'm sorry, Mom." Lila brushed away her tears. "I didn't mean to sound like a baby. But it's been so great spending time with you. All our heart-to-heart talks and doing things together like playing tennis and shopping and going to museums and plays . . . I'm back to my old self, but I'm just a little worried that I won't be able to hold it all together when you leave."

"It *has* been great," said Grace, her own eyes damp with emotion. "I promise you, Lila, I'll—"

"*There* you are!" a voice cried shrilly.

Pierre sprang into the room where they'd been talking. Throwing his arms around them, he pulled them both close for a hug. Grace saw her daughter wrinkle her nose in distaste. "Pierre, we were having a private talk," Grace said.

"But the party is languishing without the beautiful hostess and her equally ravishing guest of honor," Pierre declared in his usual exaggerated manner. "Come along, ladies."

He herded them back down the hall. Grace cast an apologetic glance at Lila. "We'll talk more later," she whispered.

"Sure, Mom."

Back at the party, although Grace was immediately drawn into a lighthearted conversation with some of Lila's friends, she continued to mull over the scene with her daughter. *I missed so much in the fourteen years she and I were separated,* Grace thought sadly. *Do I really want to miss any more?*

"It was the best idea to invite Mom to stay here for the rest of her trip," Lila said to her father the next day. "This way she doesn't have to keep driving back and forth. Plus we won't see as much of the revolting Pierre!"

George had to laugh. "Yes, we can consider ourselves fortunate Pierre decided he'd rather stay on in Beverly Hills."

"Where he's close to all the tanning salons and body-sculpting studios," Lila said, rolling her eyes. "Ugh. How does Mom stand him? He drinks too much, he's a flirt, he's . . . gauche. I refuse to even think about him for another second."

They were having breakfast on the terrace. Grace had just stepped inside to take a call from her office in France—she was president of a multi-million-dollar stationery company. Lila looked toward the windows. They could see Grace standing in profile, the phone to her ear. "Doesn't she look so natural here, Daddy?" Lila asked more seriously. "Doesn't this just feel right?"

For weeks Lila had been dropping frequent unsubtle hints. George knew she was hoping against hope that her parents would get back together. *And I'm still hoping too,* he admitted to himself. *Despite Pierre.* But his wife's ridiculous boyfriend wasn't the only obstacle. There was the past. Could they really put it behind them? He and Grace still hadn't talked about what he'd done to her fourteen years ago, and why he'd done it. George wasn't sure he understood it himself, even after all these years.

"It could never happen," he told Lila with a morose sigh. "She made it clear from the start this was just a visit. She has her business in Paris, and there's Pierre, and . . . oh, a whole lot of things."

"Nothing matters but the fact that you two are still madly in love with each other," Lila declared, dismissing the rest with a wave of her hand.

George raised his eyebrows. "Pardon me?"

Lila laughed. "Don't you see it, Daddy? The way she looks at you. And you're so different when she's around! Not that you're not always a great guy, but with Mom you're so relaxed and warm and funny. You seem . . . happy."

George looked at his daughter in amazement. How could a sixteen-year-old be so perceptive?

"Take my word for it—Pierre's not a factor. Just go for it with Grace," Lila urged.

George chuckled. "I wish it were that simple."

"It is!" Lila argued. "I'm sure she's just waiting for you to—"

Lila cut off her sentence. Grace was walking across the terrace. "Sorry that took so long," Grace apologized. "Hope I didn't miss anything interesting."

Lila and George exchanged a glance. Lila winked at her father. "No, Mom."

　　❖　　　❖　　　❖

Grace stood at the guest-bedroom window. *How strange,* she thought, pushing aside the curtain so she could see the starry night sky. *I'm a guest in the house that used to be my home.* Below, the Fowler Crest gardens looked enchanted in the moonlight. Grace had planned to do some paperwork, but she felt herself drawn outside. Grabbing a sweater, she left the house by the back stairs.

The night air was cool and fresh. Grace strolled through the gardens, stopping in front of an antique rosebush. *Could it be?* she wondered, bending to sniff the delicate blossoms. When she and George married, she'd brought with her to Fowler Crest a cutting of an old rosebush her grandmother Isabelle swore she'd carried across the ocean from France. According to family legend, that bush had been descended from one first cultivated by Isabelle's great-grandmother Celeste de Bocage, in honor of Isabelle's mother, Rose.

Grace snipped a bloom and tucked it in her pocket. *It's as if they're all still here in spirit,* she mused fancifully. *All the women who came before me.* Just then she heard a footstep on the flagstone path behind her. When she saw who it was, her heart leaped. "George! You startled me."

"Sorry about that," he said. "I felt restless tonight for some reason. Needed a walk."

"Me too," she confessed. They stood facing each other. It was the first time they'd been alone,

339

really alone, Grace realized. The darkness wrapped around them like a blanket, creating an atmosphere of intimacy and expectation.

George must have felt it too. He stepped closer. "Grace, I have to say something," he declared suddenly. "I have to be sure you know how sorry I am for destroying our marriage and tearing Lila away from you. I don't know why I reacted so violently—I guess I was still insecure about my humble roots. I thought you regretted our marriage. I thought . . . I don't know what I thought," he admitted. "I didn't have my priorities straight, that's for sure. I've always regretted how things ended between us."

Grace let out a long sigh. "Me too."

"After we were married, I took you for granted," he acknowledged. "I didn't give you the attention you deserved. What a fool I was. Will you ever be able to forgive me?"

"Of course I forgive you," she said. "We were young when we fell in love—the whole marriage thing happened pretty quickly. Maybe we didn't know each other as well as we needed to. We both made mistakes."

She placed a consoling hand on his arm. Swiftly George took both her hands in his and looked straight into her eyes. "Grace," he said with quiet intensity. "Do you believe in third chances?"

"What do you mean?"

"We had a second chance when I came after you the night of your engagement party at the country club. We ran away together. And now . . . here we are."

"Here we are," she agreed.

The attraction between them was electric. George pulled Grace closer. "I just don't want to make the same mistake my grandfather did," he whispered, "and wait until I'm old and gray to reconcile with the woman I love."

Their mouths met in a passionate kiss. When they parted a moment later, Grace clung to George, laughing breathlessly. "I feel like a teenager again," she confessed. "Sneaking into the garden for a secret kiss."

George glanced over his shoulder, grinning. "Only this time we're hiding from our teenage daughter instead of your parents."

They kissed again, then stood for a long moment in a pool of moonlight, not wanting to let each other go. Finally Grace stepped back. "I should go inside," she said reluctantly. "I told Pierre I'd phone before I went to bed."

George cupped her face gently in his hands. "We both have a lot to think about. But I know what *I* want."

"Pierre and I are supposed to fly back to France the day after tomorrow," she reminded him.

"He can go without you. Stay here with me and Lila in Sweet Valley, Grace," he pleaded. "Where you belong."

George's proposal was breathtaking. Grace felt herself falling for him just as passionately as she had eighteen years before. *Stay here in Sweet Valley,* she thought, dazzled. Could it really be that easy?

"You don't have to say anything now," he added. "Tomorrow night at dinner at the Cote d'Or, I'll ask you properly." He kissed her hand. "I want to do it right this time, Grace, from start to finish."

They kissed good night, and Grace hurried off through the shadowy garden. Her heart soared as bright and high as the moon above. There were obstacles to deal with—namely, Pierre. But she had a feeling she already knew, when George asked her "properly," what her answer would be.

Two weeks later, at sunset, Grace and George met again in the garden of Fowler Crest. A diamond ring glittered on the fourth finger of Grace's left hand, the same engagement ring George had given her the first time he proposed. And she wore a long white gown, the wedding dress he'd had made for her in Paris after they eloped.

It was their wedding day.

The mansion's backyard had been transformed. White lights twinkled in the boughs of the trees. Water lilies and oil lamps floated in the swimming pool. An enormous tent with a white canopy sheltered dozens of tables draped in white cloths and glittering with silver and crystal. There were fresh flowers everywhere.

The wedding guests were all seated, and the orchestra had played the processional march. The moment was hushed, expectant. George and Grace stood in the gazebo, which had been turned into a chapel. Before they turned to face the minister, George squeezed Grace's hand. "Are you ready?" he asked.

Grace glanced at her daughter . . . her maid of honor. Wearing a mauve silk gown and holding a bouquet of tea roses, Lila was beaming, a smile of pure happiness on her young face. *We've come full circle*, Grace thought. *We struggled for so long alone, but now we're together as we should be. And we'll never be apart again.*

She looked back at George, her eyes bright with love. "Yes," she whispered. "I'm ready."

They stepped up to the altar. "Dearly beloved . . ." the minister began.

Bantam Books in the Sweet Valley High series
Ask your bookseller for the books you have missed

SIGN UP FOR THE SWEET VALLEY HIGH® FAN CLUB!

Hey, girls! Get all the gossip on Sweet Valley High's® most popular teenagers when you join our fantastic Fan Club! As a member, you'll get all of this really cool stuff:

- Membership Card with your own personal Fan Club ID number
- A Sweet Valley High® Secret Treasure Box
- Sweet Valley High® Stationery
- Official Fan Club Pencil (for secret note writing!)
- Three Bookmarks
- A "Members Only" Door Hanger
- Two Skeins of J. & P. Coats® Embroidery Floss with flower barrette instruction leaflet
- Two editions of *The Oracle* newsletter
- Plus exclusive Sweet Valley High® product offers, special savings, contests, and much more!

Be the first to find out what Jessica & Elizabeth Wakefield are up to by joining the Sweet Valley High® Fan Club for the one-year membership fee of only $6.25 each for U.S. residents, $8.25 for Canadian residents (U.S. currency). Includes shipping & handling.

Send a check or money order (do not send cash) made payable to "Sweet Valley High® Fan Club" along with this form to:

SWEET VALLEY HIGH® FAN CLUB, BOX 3919-B, SCHAUMBURG, IL 60168-3919

NAME _____
(Please print clearly)

ADDRESS _____

CITY_____ STATE _____ ZIP_____
(Required)

AGE_____ BIRTHDAY_____ /_____ /_____

Offer good while supplies last. Allow 6-8 weeks after check clearance for delivery. Addresses without ZIP codes cannot be honored. Offer good in USA & Canada only. Void where prohibited by law.
©1993 by Francine Pascal   LCI-1383-123